# RUNAWAY GIRL

## EMILY ORGAN

## Books in the Runaway Girl Series

BY EMILY ORGAN

❧

***Runaway Girl***
***Forgotten Child***
***Sins of the Father***

❧

# Also by Emily Organ

# RUNAWAY GIRL

*'Men have had every advantage of us in telling their own story. Education has been theirs in so much higher a degree; the pen has been in their hands.'*

- Jane Austen, *Persuasion*, 1818

Get a free short story to accompany this book.
Details can be found at the end of *Runaway Girl*.

# Prologue

She was supposed to be dead.

Pain jolted through her body with every lurch of the cart. She fought the urge to cry out, knowing that any noise she made would attract attention. She had to stay silent or they would realise she was still alive.

The girl next to her lay motionless. She reached out and touched the girl's arm; her skin was cool. The musty sacking cloth thrown over them offered no protection from the cold night, but it hid her movement.

*Where were they being taken?*

She could hear the murmur of men's voices above the creak of the cart and the thud of a horse's feet in the mud. Her ears continued to ring with the laughter, the shouting and the screams. She could still smell the sour stench of wine on breath, stale sweat on flesh. The memories churned her stomach, making her want to vomit. Her throat was sore from where her neck had been squeezed and she felt sharp pains in her head and shoulder.

*Had she fallen or been beaten?* She couldn't remember.

*Was the other girl really dead?* It felt cruel to pinch her arm, but she did it to make sure.

There was no response.

Her fingers travelled up to the girl's neck to feel for a pulse. Again, there was nothing; all she could feel was a chain of rosary beads, which had done little to protect the girl wearing them.

Rage bubbled in her stomach. She wanted to stop the cart, grab the men's knives and slit their throats. They had murdered this girl without a thought, and now they were going to dispose of her body to cover up their dirty deed.

It was possible the men realised she was still alive, but they threw her into the river anyway, hoping she would drown if there was any doubt.

The cold water felt like a dagger of ice striking her chest. She immediately sank and opened her mouth in panic, taking in a gulp of foul water. Kicking and flailing, she managed to come up for air. Out of her mouth came a gasping noise she was unable to control.

Moonlight danced on the surface of the oily black water. Although it looked beautiful, the river stank like a latrine and there was a revolting taste on her tongue that made her gag. She splashed to keep afloat but again felt herself sinking, her dress dragging her down. She kicked as hard and fast as her legs would allow, flapping her arms and managing to keep her face clear. The cold was freezing her limbs, and with each stroke it was becoming harder to move. A dark, rectangular object came into view. *Was it a boat? Or the riverbank?*

Her left hand brushed against a slimy wall. Her instinct was to recoil, but she realised that she might be able to cling on to whatever it was. She reached out again and discovered something else there in the slime; something that was also slippery but felt like metal. She gripped on to it and took a deep breath before her face sank under again. It took all her strength to wrench her head back up. She choked as putrid water sloshed up her nose and pooled at the back of her throat. Under she went again and the fight to survive started to leave her.

*She couldn't give in; she had found something to hold on to. Surely she could drag her way out of the river.*

She managed to steal another breath of air at the surface and pulled herself closer to the piece of metal she was grasping. It felt like an iron ring, and attached to it was a greasy chain. With renewed hope, she grabbed the chain with both hands and pulled herself along it. The wall lowered down into the water, and with one desperate fling of her arm she managed to grasp the top of it. She felt timber and dug her fingers in as she reached for it with her other hand. She was clinging to the edge of a wooden jetty.

*She had found a way to get out of the water.*

Her body was heavy, tired and shuddering with the cold. She felt her nails break as she dug them into the timber of the jetty. She pushed her right foot against the slimy section under the water and managed to raise herself up slightly. The water absorbed in her dress weighed her down, but she pulled herself up and out of the river with a strength that could only come with the desperation of fleeing death.

She slowly clambered up the wooden steps. The cold had permeated every part of her body and she shivered violently as she curled up on the jetty, panting and retching.

'She's made it to shore!' came a shout.

She looked up and saw the shadowy silhouette of the horse and cart further along the bank. In the moonlight, she could see two figures running towards her.

*She wasn't safe yet.*

Her limbs moaned and ached as she uncurled herself and

shakily got to her feet. Her wet dress clung to her legs and her body shook so much with the cold that it felt impossible to move. But the men were gaining on her and she had to get away.

She had lost her slippers, but her feet were so numb she barely felt the stony ground as she ran. To her right was the river and to her left were several tall, dark warehouses. She looked desperately for a light or any sign of someone who could help her, but the darkness was deepening and she could see the moon was about to be covered by cloud.

The footsteps behind her grew closer.

'Just cut her throat this time and be done with it!'

Between the dark warehouses she spotted an even darker gap and ran towards it just as the cloud blocked the moonlight. Plunged into darkness, she knocked into a wall before finding the gap she was looking for: a narrow, stinking alleyway.

She heard the men run past.

'It's blacker than the devil's bum hole!'

'Where is she?'

She staggered further back into the passageway, her heart pounding in her ears and her body shaking so violently it was difficult to remain on her feet.

❧

Snow fell thickly the following evening. The waterman looked up at the darkening grey sky and decided to make this the final crossing of the day.

His passenger was a well-dressed young man with a cloak pulled across his nose and mouth to keep the stench of the river out. It was a smell the waterman no longer noticed, having lived and breathed the river for more years than he could remember.

One of the oars struck something soft in the water. The waterman grunted and pushed it away. Anything broken, rotten or unwanted was dumped into the Thames, and each day the tide heaved itself in and out of London, depositing the river's grim contents onto its mud and gravel banks. Whatever the waterman had pushed away would come to rest somewhere for the rats to find.

'Wait!'

Surprised by the outburst, the waterman saw his passenger pointing at something in the water. Peering over the edge of his boat, he saw a piece of muddied cloth floating near the surface.

*More rubbish.*

But then he saw the hand.

'There's someone in there!' shrieked the passenger.

The waterman remained calm. This wasn't the first time he had pulled a body out of the river. Carefully, he steered the boat towards the floating bundle, and as he drew nearer he could see strands of long, red hair floating like seaweed, then a leg and a foot, still with its slipper on.

*A woman. Perhaps even a girl.*

He handed his oar to the passenger. 'Keep it steady while I pull 'er out.'

The little wooden boat started to rock as he stood up.

'But I don't know how!' panicked the young man.

'Paddle, steady-like, with the oar to keep 'er still,' snapped the waterman. 'The eddies will drag us away, else. And move yerself over to that side of the boat; far as yer can to stop it tipping when I leans over.'

The passenger did as he was told. He sat on the edge of the boat and paddled frantically as the waterman reached into the river and grabbed hold of a leg. The girl floated towards him, and he caught a glimpse of her serene, white face. He leant in further and hooked his sinewy arm under her waist before hauling her out of the river. The limpness of her body and the water absorbed in her dress made her heavier than he had expected.

The boat rocked as the girl's body slid onto its floor in a pool of muddy water. Large flakes of snow were beginning to settle on her.

'She's young,' muttered the waterman. *Younger than my own daughters*, he thought to himself.

She had not been in the water long enough for her flesh to soften and swell. Her dress was cream-coloured and well-tailored, and she wore a set of expensive looking rosary beads around her neck.

'Is she dead?' asked the young man, his voice wobbling.

The waterman glared at him and grabbed the oar back. 'We'll 'ave to raise the hue and cry when we gets to the other side,' he said. 'By the look o' that bruising on 'er neck, I'd say she's been murdered.'

'Do I have to be part of it?' asked the passenger. 'I have an appointment.'

'Of course yer have to be part of it!' growled the waterman, 'You saw 'er first. You'll 'ang if you neglect yer duty. The coroner 'as to be told and we'll need ter find the man what did this.'

The waterman rowed on in silence, the snow whirling around the boat as if it were the only vessel on the river. He watched the young man's face as he leant in closer to look at the girl, his curled lip softening. Tenderly, he moved her hair from her face and made sure her eyes were firmly closed. Then he removed his cloak and laid it over her body, the stench of the river long forgotten.

# Chapter One

The late winter sun streamed through the narrow windows of the children's dormitory and cast golden arches across their beds. Alice unfolded a cream woollen blanket, laid it on the stone floor and called the children to her. They became a jumble of little heads as they arranged themselves on the blanket, some sitting properly while others pushed and jostled. A dozen children between the ages of two and twelve were to ready take part in songs with Sister Emma. Among them, Alice thought she saw a familiar head of brown curls. It took a moment to remind herself that he could not be there and the yearning inside hit her with a sharp pang.

She distracted herself by carrying Nicholas – a sickly five-year-old who struggled to walk – over to the blanket and seating herself next to him. She tucked her legs in next to her and arranged her tunic neatly over them. Matilda and Peter, the youngest children, dropped into her lap and she put her arms around them, giving each a gentle squeeze. Her legs would be numb by the time Sister Emma finished her songs, but this was Alice's favourite time of day when Constance and the children – everyone who mattered to her – were around her.

This was to be the last time they were together.

Constance sat on the opposite side of the blanket, her fair hair hanging in two long plaits. Like Alice, she wore a brown hospital tunic, which was shapeless, ankle-length and tied at the waist with a rope belt. The dourness of her clothes contrasted with her milk-and-honey complexion, almond-shaped eyes and delicate, upturned nose. She caught Alice's eye and tried to suppress a giggle as Sister Emma dragged a stool over from the fireside and perched her large bottom on it. With her teeth protruding beyond her lips, Sister Emma looked like a fat rabbit dressed in black robes.

At just fourteen, Constance found the peculiarities of the nuns amusing. She had lived at St Hugh's Monastery since she was born; an illegitimate baby conceived at a brothel in Southwark. Now she was older, she helped look after the foundlings and assisted with the cooking, cleaning and washing at the monastery hospital. Alice smiled fondly at Constance and rolled her eyes as Sister Emma's shrill voice filled the room, but they both knew the children enjoyed the songs and many of them performed actions to accompany the words. Well fed, clean and educated by the nuns, the children were more privileged than many others of their age who lived in the cramped sprawl of London. But missing from the foundlings' lives was the love of a parent. Alice tried to be a mother to each of them but never felt she was an adequate replacement.

Alice was twenty-five and short, with dark hair and violet eyes. Her long plaits were rolled and pinned to either side of her head and covered with a cream veil. Along with the brown tunic, this was how she dressed every day. Satin dresses and silken veils belonged to her previous life. Alice wasn't a nun or even a lay sister; she was a widow who had started helping at St Hugh's after the plague. Here she could distract herself by helping others, happy in the knowledge that she was doing something meaningful. The whitewashed walls of St Hugh's were thick enough to make London seem a world away, and the scent of incense created an air of serenity and calm. St Hugh's was a refuge for Alice and she offered her help in return for the sanctuary the monastery provided. After two years of looking after the children of St Hugh's she couldn't imagine any other life. It gave her great joy to see the children grow and learn, and this helped her forget her own pain.

St Hugh's was an ornate stone building, distinctly more solid than the crooked timber structures around it, which were prone to falling down. The monastery was run by a small order founded by Abbot Beroldus, a crippled monk who had lived in Norfolk two hundred years previously. St Hugh's was home to a number of monks and nuns. Prior Edmund was in charge, as the senior abbot was conducting a tour of monasteries in East Anglia and had not been seen for some years. The hospital at St Hugh's was as old as the monastery; some patients only needed quick medical treatment while others were long-term residents.

''E's out there now! I've just seen 'im!'

The rough voice startled everyone and Sister Emma paused mid-song. Alice glanced over to the doorway where Hilda, one of the hospital's oldest patients, stood brandishing a piece of shiny metal.

Lifting Matilda and Peter from her lap and onto the blanket, Alice got to her feet and limped over to Hilda as the blood flow gradually returned to her legs.

'Can I have that please, Hilda?'

'No!' The metal object was raised up in defence, but Alice

relaxed when she saw that it wasn't a knife but the silver Communion spoon from the chapel. Hilda's eyes stared wide and unblinking from her creased face. One eye was blind and milky white, and her dirty grey hair stuck out in greasy clumps around her head.

Alice held out her hand. 'Please give me the spoon, Hilda. It belongs in the chapel. Shall we put it back there?'

'But 'e's out there!' Hilda turned away and ran. Her movements were surprisingly swift for an elderly lady.

Alice followed her as she ran between the beds and screens in the infirmary hall, heading towards the main door.

'Hilda! Stop!'

The patients who were awake watched the chase as they lay in their beds. Hilda reached the large oak door, which opened out onto the busy street. Alice was close behind, but Hilda lashed out at her with the spoon before turning to face the door and pulling the large iron bolt open. The door swung inwards with a creak and Hilda darted through the gap.

'There 'e is!' Hilda screeched.

Alice followed in time to see the old lady launch herself at a large pig, which was chewing something in the mud by the monastery steps. It ducked out of her way and scampered across the street with a squeal as Hilda lay sprawled in a filthy puddle. Alice made her way down the steps as a chill wind blew up the street and whipped at her tunic.

'Come on, Hilda.' Alice placed her feet either side of the puddle, bent down and hooked her hands under Hilda's arms. She felt her back complaining as she tried to pull Hilda up and the old lady scrabbled awkwardly back onto her feet. She was covered in wet mud, which stank of excrement.

'It's cold out here and I can feel snow in the air,' said Alice. 'We need to go back inside and clean you up.'

As they walked towards the arched stone doorway, Alice heard a shout from further up the street.

'Is this the hospital?' A dishevelled man rode towards them. His black horse was limping and he held the reins of another horse, which was walking by his side. Strapped across the saddle of the second horse was the body of a man.

'What *happened?*' Alice asked, pushing the spoon under her belt. She ushered Hilda through the doorway of St Hugh's and scrambled across the mud to where the man and the horses had stopped.

'We were attacked on the road,' he replied. His cloak was dirty and torn, and he pulled down his hood to reveal a swollen eye and an angry red cheekbone. He handed Alice the reins of the second horse and she moved towards the man slumped across the saddle. He was lying on his stomach, tied into position by a rope. A green hood covered his head and one arm hung limply beside it. She lifted the hood and pushed his dark, wavy hair to one side. He was younger than the first traveller and his face was puffy as a result of dangling upside down from the saddle. His eyes were closed and his lips were pale. Alice held her hand under his nose and was relieved to feel his breath on her fingers.

'When did this happen?' she asked the first man.

'Shortly after dinner time. We stopped on the road. It was a foolish idea, but we needed to stop to go for a... well, you know what I mean,' he said with a cough. 'Thieves leapt out from the trees and threatened us with knives and axes. We fought back, but Valerian was struck in the chest.'

Alice lifted Valerian's cloak and saw a pool of half-dried blood on the saddle.

'I'll get him some help. Are you injured?'

'Just a punch in the face, I'll be fine. It is Valerian I'm worried about.'

Alice ran back to the doorway of the hospital and shouted

for help. Sister Katherine, a thin stick of a woman, arrived quickly and glanced questioningly at the Communion spoon tucked under Alice's belt. Fortunately, there was no time to explain what it was doing there.

Within moments, the nuns had helped the travellers into the hospital and the monks had taken the horses to the stables for food and rest. Valerian was carried to a bed in the infirmary hall. His cloak and tunic were ripped and soaked with blood, and his eyes flickered open and closed.

Alice brought bowls of water and fresh linen to the nuns, who removed Valerian's shirt to reveal a bloody wound on the right side of his chest. Brother Ralph, a small, round monk, knowledgeable in medicine, started to clean the wound.

'Ugh!' Alice felt a hand on her arm and turned to see Constance standing next to her, her eyes wide as she stared at the blood.

'It is not as bad as it looks. These men have been attacked but we can treat them.' Valerian groaned with pain, which Alice took to be a positive sign.

'Who attacked them?' asked Constance. Alice rested her hand on her shoulder and tried to guide her away, concerned that the injured men were worrying her unnecessarily. But Constance refused to move and remained rooted to the spot, fascinated and appalled at the same time.

'Some bandits on the road,' Alice replied.

'Bandits? Will they come here?' Constance's large eyes now stared at Alice.

'No they won't, we are quite safe here.' She patted Constance's shoulder reassuringly despite sharing the same fear. The streets of London were dangerous. Only a few years previously death had stalked the city as plague took grip, fed by the filth in the streets. Alice had learnt that it was safer to stay indoors.

Valerian's companion talked animatedly about their

journey and the attack. His name was Roger Granville, and he and Valerian were employed by the Earl of Wykeham. They had been travelling on the earl's instructions from St Albans to London when the thieves ambushed them and made away with coins and jewellery. Roger appeared to be enjoying the audience around his bed as he re-enacted the fight, waving his arms about wildly. The travellers had leapt back onto their horses and ridden hastily from their attackers, but as they were galloping away Valerian had fallen from his horse. It wasn't until Roger had tried to help him up that he had noticed how badly injured his friend was.

Brother Ralph smeared a thick, greasy ointment onto the wound on Valerian's chest. 'Does it hurt?' he asked his patient.

'Not as much as my head,' mumbled Valerian. 'Can someone please quieten that man?' He pointed weakly at Roger and there was laughter. Valerian screwed his eyes shut and groaned again. 'My wound is probably best left alone, it will heal quite well I am sure.'

'Some poppy syrup will help you,' replied Ralph. 'I will bring you some shortly.' He began to bandage a strip of linen around Valerian's chest.

'I have no need for poppy syrup.'

Alice hoped Valerian hadn't lost too much blood and would recover quickly. Unexpectedly, he opened his deep, brown eyes and looked at her. He was handsome, with angular cheekbones and a strong jaw. Alice reddened as he grinned at her.

The bell chimed for prayers and Alice broke away from Valerian's gaze.

'Come, Constance, it is time to prepare the children's supper.'

There was a lively blaze in the kitchen fireplace, which flickered shadows onto the white walls. Alice hung a cauldron of pottage from a hook above the hearth.

'There was a lot of blood,' said Constance as she began to slice bread at the long wooden table in the centre of the room.

'It often looks worse than it is, the men will be fine.'

'The man said the bandits came from nowhere and attacked them. Does that happen often?'

'No it doesn't,' Alice smiled, hoping Constance wouldn't dwell on what she had seen. 'It is unusual.' It had also bothered her to see Roger's battered face and the wound on Valerian's chest; reminders that the world was not safe. She noticed the Communion spoon still in her belt and pulled it out, placing it on the table. 'I caught Hilda trying to attack a pig with this.'

Constance laughed. 'Old Sister Eleanor won't be happy. She told Hilda that if she took the Communion spoon again she would be stricken with the falling down sickness. Sister Eleanor says a patient once picked it up and was discovered on the floor of the chapel in a sleep as still as death and stayed that way for three days.'

'I'm worried it will happen to me as well now.'

'I'll pick you up if you suddenly fall down with the sickness.'

Alice laughed. 'That would be very kind of you, Constance. Sister Katherine also saw me with the Communion spoon. I'll be in trouble once she has finished with the new patients.' She walked over to the fire, dipped a reed into the flame and used it to light the candles on the table.

'I wish I had known that it is unusual to be attacked by bandits. I have no idea about these things; I have seen nothing of the world,' said Constance with a sigh.

'There is plenty of time for that.'

'How old were you when you left your home?'

'Sixteen, when my parents decided I should be apprenticed to a leather merchant.'

'And then you were married?'

'When I was eighteen.'

'So I'm almost there.'

'No, you are not,' laughed Alice, reaching over to tickle Constance's waist. Constance ducked out of the way, giggling.

Alice stirred the pottage with a large wooden spoon, releasing an aroma of oats and peas. 'Do you remember me saying I would speak to my friend Yvette de Beauchamp, the silk merchant? She will be looking for a new apprentice soon and you are doing so well with your embroidery that I think there's a good chance she would take you on.'

'And escape this place!'

'There is nothing wrong with St Hugh's.'

'I'm worried if I stay much longer I'll end up a nun.'

'There are worse things that could happen in life.'

'Such as?'

Alice didn't answer. She pulled the spoon out of the pottage and wiped it on a piece of linen. She did not wish to frighten Constance with a list of things that were worse than being a nun. Alice knew from her own experience that life was a fragile existence and often a game of chance. Constance was young and Alice wanted her to stay within the safe confines of St Hugh's for a while longer.

'Yvette has invited me to dinner next week. I'll ask her then about your apprenticeship.'

At least if Constance was staying with a trusted friend, Alice would feel better about her leaving St Hugh's. She knew she had to let her go eventually, and she could see a great deal of potential in Constance. She was a bright, happy girl; well educated by the nuns and a skilled embroiderer. There was no need for her lowly birth status to hold her back. Alice liked to picture Constance as a beautiful young woman in a colourful dress and jewels in place of the brown tunic she wore each day at St Hugh's. It made sense that she would leave one day.

*Just not yet.*

'An apprenticeship with Yvette could take a long time to arrange. I would like to do something soon. Really soon. Can I visit your house? I have never seen it and you have told me so much about it and the shop you once had. I want to see more of your embroidery! You are lucky, you did lots of things before you came here. You were married and you had your son. You have done so much and I have done nothing!'

'Constance!' Alice's voice was louder than she had anticipated and the girl stared at her, stunned by the outburst. Alice couldn't help herself, there had been something in Constance's words that had stirred her and she wasn't sure if it was anger or distress.

She took a deep breath. 'Constance, I'm sorry I shouted. All I wanted to say was that your time will come. Quicker than you think, I promise you. Just please wait a little longer. I will show you my home, but please do not be in a hurry to leave St Hugh's. Trust me, this is a good place to be.'

Matilda toddled into the room and was drawn to the shiny Communion spoon on the table. She snatched it up in her chubby little hand and grinned up at Alice with a toothy smile. Alice smoothed Matilda's curls and gently prised the spoon from the toddler's hand, replacing it with a wooden one. Matilda pushed her bottom lip out and threw the wooden spoon to the floor as she began to cry. Alice picked her up and sat her on her hip, managing to distract her with a small chunk of bread. As Matilda pushed the bread hungrily into her mouth, Alice rested her cheek against the little girl's soft hair just as she had done with her son so many times.

# Chapter Two

❧

Alice still lived in the home she had once shared with her husband, Thomas. It was a three-storey, timbered townhouse on a busy street just a short walk from St Hugh's. On the ground floor was a shop with a shutter that opened out onto the street, and this was where Alice and Thomas had sold the leather gloves they had made. These days she used just one room in the house. She was at St Hugh's so much of her time that she only returned home to sleep. In the other rooms sat dressers filled with colourful Italian pottery and pewter drinking cups; carved wooden chests filled with clothes; bed linen and vellum-bound books. Most of these items were now unused but were kept free of dust by an old servant called Griselda, who would have become homeless if Alice had ever asked her to leave.

There was a small chest in Alice's bedroom that was plain except for two ornate iron hinges, but it was so important to her that she kept the key to it on a chain around her neck. The conversation from earlier that day with Constance prompted Alice to open the chest when she returned home. The thought of Constance growing up and making a new life for herself was difficult to accept. Opening the chest was something Alice did at times like this when she felt worried; when she yearned for familiarity and the happy days she had known before her husband and son had died.

The candle on the table flickered as she pulled a rolled woollen blanket from the chest and opened it out onto the floorboards. Inside were six small figures carved from wood: a horse, a sheep, a cow, a dog, a duck and a man. Each figure bore the dents of small teeth marks and had suffered other knocks from being banged against the floor, dropped, thrown and placed in and out of copper pans. Her son had loved these little toys. They felt warm and smooth in her hands as she gathered them up. She held them against her face and was sure she could smell her son again, hearing his laugh and feeling the way his body fitted against hers as if he were a part of her. Once more she felt her heart crack and an ache surge through her body.

She wiped away her tears and reached into the chest for the other items that were important to her: a cotton baby tunic; a little woollen hood; her husband's belt with a brass buckle; a prayer book bound in wood and leather; her mother's gold brooch; and a small casket, which held two locks of brown hair intertwined. One was baby soft and the other coarser. Also in the chest was a small linen bag, which she had filled with dried lavender. Its scent was starting to fade and Alice knew she would need to refresh it with recently dried flowers. She placed everything on the woollen blanket and picked each item up in turn, shifting them around in her hands to see if there was anything she hadn't noticed about them before. The cotton tunic felt soft and fragile in her hands. It no longer smelt of her son, but of the fading lavender scent of the chest. The belt had retained its scent: musty sweet leather coupled with the metallic buckle. She often held and examined these items, thinking about the people they had belonged to.

Her husband and son now lay deep in the ground at the edge of the city, where improvised grave markers stood crooked among tufts of grass. Each wooden cross was intended to mark a resting place, but the bodies had been buried together: crammed in side by side and piled on top of each other. There had been no time for proper graves, there hadn't been enough people to dig them.

Even the priest was gone by then.

There was a streak of red in the east as Alice walked to St Hugh's the following morning. The January air numbed her face as she threaded her way between people, horses and carts, skipping over the worst of the mud. A group of dirty-faced children teased a dog with a stick, their laughter echoing painfully in Alice's head. She had slept badly the previous night; worry had kept her awake, although she wasn't sure why.

The ornate bell tower of St Hugh's rose above the rooftops, and as Alice neared the monastery she saw the main door standing open. It was usually closed and her first thought was of the patients shivering in their beds. She walked up the steps as the bell chimed eight and heard loud voices in the infirmary hall. Stepping inside, she saw the place was crowded with monks, nuns, lay sisters and lay brothers, and even the large bulk of Prior Edmund in his voluminous black-and-white robes.

'What has happened?' she asked, but no one heard.

Sister Emma was red-eyed and gesticulating wildly. Sister Katherine's face was more morose than usual and Brother Rufus was standing with his hands together in impromptu prayer.

Walking around the edge of the crowd, Alice saw a red puddle on the floor. She was used to seeing blood, but this was a large amount and appeared to be connected to the hysteria taking place around her. Some of the blood had been mopped up with linen sheets, which were lying in a pink-tinged pile. Nearby there was another blood-stained sheet covering what appeared to be a body.

A chill ran through Alice's bones.

She knelt down next to the covered body. *Was it someone she knew?* She had seen enough of death for it not to frighten her, but from the amount of blood on the floor she could see this person had experienced a violent end.

Holding her breath, Alice reached for the corner of the sheet and slowly lifted it. A man lay underneath, dressed in hospital robes. His eyes were closed, his mouth hung open and his hair was matted with blood.

It was Roger Granville, the traveller who had arrived the previous day.

Alice replaced the sheet, stood up and looked around for someone who could tell her what had happened. *Constance would know what was going on.*

Sister Katherine caught her eye and walked over to her. 'Terrible things have happened, Alice.' Her eye sockets were arched and hollow.

'I can see that. What happened to Roger?'

'Murdered. And Constance has run off with the other one.'

# Chapter Three

'*Run off?*' The conversation she and Constance had had the previous evening about her wanting to leave St Hugh's ran through Alice's mind. 'With whom? Do you mean Valerian? The man with the injury?'

'Yes. He has murdered Roger and eloped with Constance. We can only assume that the two men argued about Constance and Roger was killed in the fight. Or perhaps Roger tried to stop them running away.'

Sister Katherine looked sadly at Roger's body lying under the sheet. 'The hue and cry has been raised, and the bailiff and coroner have been informed. They will be with us shortly.'

'No, this cannot be right,' said Alice, her eyes fixed on the bloody sheets on the floor. 'Surely Valerian would not have killed his friend? Or taken Constance? And even if he had tried to take her she would have refused to go with him. She doesn't know him; she has no interest in him. She's just a girl.'

She turned back to Sister Katherine, 'Are you sure she's not here?'

'We have searched every corner of St Hugh's.'

'I'm going to look for her.'

As if a spirit had possessed her, Alice ran as fast as she could up the winding stairs to the dormitory Constance shared with three of the lay sisters. *Had Constance slept in this room the previous night?* The sheets and blanket were pulled neatly over her small, wooden bed and it was difficult to tell whether she had neatened the covers that morning or the morning before.

A simple wooden cupboard housed the lay sisters' clothes. Alice opened it and saw four woollen cloaks hanging inside. One was small enough to fit a child and Alice recognised it as Constance's, which meant that if she were outside she would be suffering in the cold by this time.

Alice ran off to look in the nuns' dormitory, frightening one of the monastery cats as she did so. Then she checked the latrines and ran back down the stairs to the day room before running around each side of the cloister calling Constance's name and disregarding the silence that was usually imposed there. She dashed through the labyrinth of dingy corridors and looked in the kitchen, library, refectory and then the infirmary kitchen, where she and Constance had prepared supper together the previous evening. She stopped there for a moment, her breath quick and shallow as she took in the scene. The room was stark and cold that morning and no one had found time to rekindle the fire. A shaft of weak morning sunlight filtered through the arched window.

'Constance!' she called, her voice echoing around the walls, panic rising in her chest. There weren't many places left to check. She was forbidden to enter the lay brothers' and monks' dormitories, but Alice knew she would not be able to rest until she had looked.

The dormitories were empty apart from Brother Jarvis, a tall, lean monk with a large nose, who was standing next to a bed adjusting his tunic. He was surprised to see Alice but smiled as if she were a welcome intrusion.

'Have you seen Constance?' she asked.

Jarvis' expression quickly changed. 'No, we've already searched every room. It seems she has run away.'

'She can't have!' Alice left and ran along the corridor to Prior Edmund's apartments. She was not allowed to enter without the prior's permission, but she guessed he was still with everyone else in the hospital. The heavy oak door was ajar and she stepped into a set of rooms that were more comfortable and plushly furnished than the rest of St Hugh's. The walls were brightened with colourful wall hangings, and the chairs and benches were festooned with cushions. Gold and silver treasures lined the mantelpiece, and the place felt warm. It smelt of the sickly scented oils with which the prior anointed himself.

Alice checked around the furniture, knowing there was little chance Constance would be hiding behind the prior's chair. She realised there had been no need for her to run around St Hugh's when everyone else had already searched each room for Constance. Perhaps she had needed to do it so she could begin to accept the dreadful fact that Constance was no longer there. It was impossible to believe she was gone but Alice was determined to do everything she could to find her again.

She walked back down the spiral stairs and into the chapel, where the brothers and sisters were gathering. She glanced through the doors and watched them take their seats among the long pews that ran along the length of the walls, facing each other. The monks sat on one side, the nuns on the other, while the prior stood in the presbytery preparing for prayer. Alice knew she would be needed in the children's dormitory, but there was somewhere else she had to visit first.

A small door at the chapel entrance would take her to a

steep flight of steps that led down to the crypt. There was a narrow passageway to walk through to reach it and Alice could just about see where she was going as she walked towards the glowing light in the crypt. The light came from four oil lamps that were kept alight night and day in the stone wall niches of the vaulted chamber. At the far end of the crypt was an elaborate shrine to Saint William, a former abbot. His remains were contained within a reliquary of gold filigree, which was well polished and gleamed in the lamplight.

Standing in the crypt, it was obvious to Alice that Constance was not there, but it had still been worth a look. This shrine was popular with pilgrims and people visited it when they were in need of guidance. It was possible Constance had witnessed Roger's murder and sought refuge there. Alice said a short prayer at the shrine, praying that Constance would be found.

'Why did no one protect her?' Alice couldn't prevent her outburst once she reached the children's dormitory.

Sister Emma shrugged her shoulders. 'I agree. Someone should have been there to stop it happening,' she said. 'The brothers drink every night in the refectory with no thought to what else could be happening within the building. Their larking and boisterousness would have drowned out any sound of a struggle. And to think a man was murdered! While patients slept and others drank! God help us!'

'They left a young girl responsible for covering the fires at night. She was on her own and someone took advantage of her without anybody else knowing about it.'

'Apart from the man who is dead. If only the dead could speak.'

'If only.'

The children were playing with three rabbits that belonged to Sister Emma. Their favourite was the pure white one, which was being passed from child to child. Unfortunately, two children wanted the rabbit at the same time and a squeal rose up.

'Careful!' shouted Sister Emma. 'Don't pull Baynard's ears like that!' She went over to sort out which child should be cuddling which rabbit and then returned to Alice.

'These are difficult times,' she whispered so the children couldn't hear. 'The plague may have left us, but Sister Eleanor says there is talk in the countryside of a new sickness awakening from deep within the forests and woodlands. Some say it is carried by unearthly beasts, fiercer than a wolf and slyer than a fox. The lands of great manors are being emptied just as they were during the plague, and there is word that a lord in the far north was driven mad by fear of the sickness and set fire to his house and the homes of all those who worked his land. He burned the animals and the crops, his wife and children, and finally himself. He was seen running up a hilltop screaming and covered in flame. Evil spreads until it is barred by a power superior to it. We must pray to keep the sickness beyond London's walls. I hope it doesn't reach Constance. I feel so bereaved today I am unable to sing to the children.'

Alice, Sister Emma and the children joined the monks and nuns in their prayers. Alice was squashed between Emma and Sister Margaret, with her arms around Matilda. The prior was surrounded by a cloud of incense and spoke in flowing Latin. Above his bald head the sunlight streamed through the brightly coloured window, depicting the Virgin Mary and her mother, Saint Anne. Sister Margaret constantly scratched her arms and legs, and Alice hoped the fleas wouldn't hop onto her or Matilda.

Everyone prayed for Roger's soul and for the safe return of Constance and Valerian, but the prayers did nothing to soothe Alice. The day felt surreal and fear curled in her stomach.

Matilda sucked her thumb and played with Alice's veil. She looked up at her and grinned, pulling her thumb out of her mouth and leaving a trail of dribble on Alice's sleeve. Alice smiled, hoping the little girl wouldn't sense her anxiety.

Thoughts of Constance spun and whirled in Alice's head. She pictured her raking the cold ashes over the hot embers and covering them with the large clay bell to ensure that the fire smouldered until it was relit in the morning.

She remembered Constance smiling as she said good night.

*See you in the morning.*

It made no sense that she could disappear without a trace.

Everyone had accepted the story that the two travellers had fought over Constance and that Valerian had won and taken her away. Alice did not understand how they could be so sure this was what had happened.

*Valerian had been lying injured in bed. How could he have recovered quickly enough to kill a man, snatch a girl and disappear? Everyone was praying and waiting for the bailiff and coroner to arrive, but surely there was something else they could do? The search for Constance hadn't extended beyond St Hugh's. She was out there somewhere and no one was looking for her.*

Alice was desperate to get outside and search. Every moment she sat listening to the prayers felt like a wasted moment. Constance could be travelling further and further away from her and she was helpless to do anything about it. She glanced around at the sombre faces: nuns on one side of the chapel and monks on the other. She wondered why they had no desire to look for Constance. *Did they think God would somehow return her to them while they sat praying?*

An image of Constance leapt into her mind again. With her fine-boned features and delicate build she was like a little bird. *She would be cold out on the streets. She would freeze to death if they didn't find her soon.*

Brother Wilmot had been the first to find Roger's body in the infirmary shortly before Prime, the prayers they said at daylight. He said there had been a lot of blood on the floor and that Roger appeared to have been hit on the head with something heavy. The main door had been open and the two travellers' beds were empty, with the blankets thrown back as if they had risen in a hurry. Brother Wilmot said he thought Roger had been dead for a few hours when he found him because his skin was cool, and his neck and face were starting to stiffen.

Brother Wilmot had woken the other monks and patients, and soon everyone had been up and looking for the missing traveller. There had been no sign of the murder weapon and no horses were missing from the stables, so he believed Valerian must have taken the weapon with him and escaped on foot. He would have been wearing the simple patient's tunic because his and Roger's clothes were still being washed. It had taken a while for anyone to notice that Constance was also missing. She appeared to have left in a hurry with no time to pick up her belongings.

Alice looked down at Matilda's happy face and hoped she didn't start asking for Constance. *What would she say to her?* Peter, who was just three, pushed his way along the pew towards Alice and started to climb onto her lap. Not wanting to share her space, Matilda shouted and pushed him away. Peter cried out, so Alice told Matilda in a hushed voice that she must share her lap with Peter. She pulled Peter onto her knee and buried her face in their little heads as a tear rolled down her cheek. The prior continued his prayers while Alice hugged the children and waited.

*But she couldn't wait.*

Her stomach felt knotted and there were flames of anger in her chest. They were rising and pushing to escape.

*She couldn't fight this feeling. She couldn't stay where she was and do nothing.*

*She had to find Constance.*

It felt as though something was pulling her up from the bench. She suddenly found herself standing with Matilda and Peter in her arms, every face in the chapel turned towards her. She started to speak before she had thought about what she wanted to say. Prior Edmund paused mid-sentence and stood motionless with his hand in the air. He stared at Alice out of the corner of one eye and waited for her to sit down again.

But she didn't.

Despite the glares of disapproval, she was determined to speak. It felt like the right thing to do.

'Father, we need to find Constance!' Alice heard her voice ringing loud and clear up into the arched stone ceiling. Her head was spinning and she felt as though she was watching herself acting a part that was beyond her control.

There was silence.

Sister Katherine rose from her place in the pew in front of Alice, her gaze icy. 'Please sit down, Alice.'

'But we need to look for her!' The words escaped from her mouth again. 'It needn't be all of us. Perhaps some of us could look for Constance while the others stay here and pray.'

Sister Isabella stood up and turned to Alice. 'If we pray, God will guide us to her.'

'Please sit down, Sister Isabella,' said Sister Katherine. 'And I should not need to ask you again to return to your seat, Alice. The Lord does not look favourably upon those who disturb prayers.'

'Absolutely not,' added Prior Edmund, his jowls wobbling

as he spoke. Alice knew he disliked her; he preferred quiet women – preferably nuns – who obeyed the rules. A woman who thought for herself was abhorrent to him.

'Please let me look for her, Father,' Alice begged. 'I want to try and find her. I cannot sit here and do nothing.'

'Do *nothing?*' elderly Sister Eleanor shouted out in a croaky voice. 'We are asking the Lord for guidance and you call this *doing nothing?* I say let the meddlesome widow go and look for Constance.' She waved her hand dismissively. 'She has no hope of finding her among the crowds in this city. They could have left by one of the gates and be on their way to France by now.'

'And perhaps Constance does not wish to be found?' added the prior. 'Valerian may have poured enough seduction into her ear to convince her to leave us.'

'She would have taken her cloak,' replied Alice. 'If she had planned to leave she would have prepared herself. And I know she would not have left willingly.'

'Alice Wescott, you are a widow,' said the prior with a leering look. 'You have been married. More than anyone else here, you understand the powers of seduction.'

Alice felt her cheeks grow hot and she bit her lip.

'It is wrong that our communion with God has been halted by this woman who is not one of us,' croaked Sister Eleanor again. 'Allow the widow to satisfy her curiosity by looking for the girl so we can continue with our work. Remember that we are also praying for the soul of a dead man. Idle chat during such a time is wickedness.'

The prior looked questioningly at Sister Katherine, who twitched her mouth slightly in subtle acquiescence. Matilda and Peter felt heavy in Alice's arms as she waited for a response.

'So be it,' said Prior Edmund. 'I do not know what the bailiff and the coroner will make of this flightiness before they have had the opportunity to pass judgement on this unfortunate incident, but you may go and look for Constance if you wish to. I understand that as a lay person you choose impulse rather than prayer to soothe your soul. It is a common weakness.'

Alice clenched her jaw and glared at the prior as he continued. 'Someone will need to accompany you and I suggest it is one of the brothers.'

She did not want anyone to go with her, but it was preferable to not being allowed to search at all. She bent down to place Matilda and Peter on Sister Emma's lap. Matilda started to cry and clung on to Alice's arm.

'Don't worry, I'll come back very soon,' she whispered to the little girl. But Matilda's wails grew louder and a rush of guilt swept over Alice as she looked down at her crumpled red face. Peter was also becoming teary-eyed. She wanted to stay with them, but she had to search for Constance.

'Sssshhh,' she whispered, trying to soothe Matilda and giving her a hug. 'Sister Emma will look after you.'

Sister Emma disentangled Matilda from Alice's tunic and hugged the little girl to her large bosom. Matilda's cries pierced the silence and Alice could feel disapproving eyes on her as she deserted the children to find the runaway girl. It would have been easier to keep quiet; now she looked foolhardy and cold-hearted at the same time.

Matilda's sobs subsided as the prior waited for one of the monks to volunteer to accompany Alice.

'I will go, Father.' A tall, broad monk with a wide forehead and craggy features stood up. Brother Jon. Alice had never spoken to him before but he always looked miserable to her. He was about twenty-five and she knew he spent much of his time outdoors looking after the gardens. His build looked better suited to physical work than being bent over manuscripts. She was not looking forward to having this morose man as her companion.

'May God give you his blessing on your search,' said the prior, 'and you must ensure that you return by sundown.'

The nuns in Alice's pew moved their knees to allow her to pass.

Only Sister Emma smiled at her.

# Chapter Four

The bell of St Hugh's chimed eleven as Alice and Brother Jon stepped out into the street. Grey clouds rolled low overhead and small flakes of snow settled on their cloaks. Jon had replaced his sandals with heavy-duty leather boots. Alice pulled her cloak around her and shivered as she looked up and down the busy street where houses, inns and shops jostled for space, their upper storeys overhanging the muddy street below.

'So what do we do now, Mistress Wescott?' asked Jon. It was the first time he had addressed her. Alice wondered if there might be an opportunity for them to separate and carry out their own searches so she wouldn't be trapped with him all day.

'Please call me Alice. And I am wondering the same thing.' She looked up at him and noticed his eyes were as green as her husband's had been. She quickly glanced away to the jagged outline of the roofs and chimneys above her and then down at the well-trodden mud as if she somehow expected to see Constance's footprints there.

'To the gatehouse,' she said assertively, pretending that

she had a plan. 'We must ask the gatekeepers if they saw anyone trying to leave the city last night.'

They walked towards the gate, against the flow of the crowd arriving for market day. Brother Jon's stride was long and Alice found herself scampering to keep up with him. Filth had been trodden into the mud by the relentless crowds of people, horses and carts. Animal offal, rotten food, urine and excrement mixed into a foul-smelling, muddy pulp that stained their feet and clothes. Feral dogs and pigs scavenged whatever they could and the rats ate anything that was left over.

A noblewoman passed them wearing a red silk dress trimmed with gold brocade, an intricately embroidered purse hanging from her gold belt. A servant helped keep the lady's skirts out of the mud while another carried her hawk. The lady reminded Alice of her friend Yvette, a wealthy woman who was also widowed but had continued to run her husband's silk merchant business after his death. Alice and Yvette's lives had taken different paths since their husbands had died.

Jon was quiet and Alice felt the need to break the silence. 'How long have you been at St Hugh's?' she asked.

'Twenty years,' he replied. 'My parents sent me there when I was seven.'

'And your family?'

'My father is Sir Robyn de Grey and my mother was Lady Mary de Grey. She died eight years ago. I have three older brothers – all knights – and a younger sister.'

'But you did not choose to become a knight?'

'No,' he replied curtly.

Alice was about to ask why when he continued.

'The reason, I believe, is atonement. My father has fought in many battles and seen many terrible things. Sometimes his work may have conflicted with the laws of God. With three sons training to be knights, he was able to spare one to serve in the Church. It is a way to purge the sins of my family, and it means my brothers have someone to pray for them when they go away to fight.'

The street narrowed until the crooked buildings on either side were almost touching above their heads.

'I am not sure my prayers have been sufficient to purge my family's sins, however.'

'A farthin' fer a poor old woman!'

The rasping voice interrupted Jon and a gnarled hand with long, yellow fingernails clung to Alice's arm.

She tried to shake free. 'Get off!' she shouted.

The old lady's crumpled face snarled. 'The devil will seek you in yer bed tonight!'

'Leave her alone!' shouted Jon, pushing the beggar woman away and putting his arm around Alice's shoulders. They walked on a few steps before he pulled his arm away, and Alice felt herself blushing from the physical contact.

'At St Hugh's they call you the widow,' said Jon.

'Yes,' Alice replied, still wondering what Jon had intended to say about his family's sin. 'It is a sensible description. I am not a nun or a lay sister, and I am the only widow at St Hugh's.'

Alice wondered what Jon already knew of her; about how her husband had been a successful leather merchant and had died two years earlier, just as the plague was reaching its end. She hoped he wouldn't mention her son. Although she wanted to talk about him, she found it too upsetting.

'Why do you work at St Hugh's?' asked Jon.

'I heard many sisters at the hospital had died during the Great Mortality and I thought I should do something to help. I was lost at the time.'

This was how she described the days and nights she had

lain feverishly in her bed, praying that she could join her son in his grave.

'I was spared and I felt it was my duty to give something back. Now I feel I'm doing something helpful. It gives me a sense of purpose.'

'But you could have continued with your husband's trade as some widows have done. He was a glove maker?'

'Yes, we both were and we had several apprentices and a shop. We made gloves for noble men and women, and royalty occasionally. But I did not have the skill to continue my husband's trade without him.' Alice also knew she had lacked the strength to continue alone.

'You must have been to school, then?'

'Yes.'

'Well, what else is there to learn? I think you could have been a successful merchant in your own right.'

'Thank you,' said Alice, 'but I disagree.'

*What did Jon know?*

She thought of Yvette de Beauchamp with her fine house and beautiful dresses, and how she had seemed happier than ever after her husband died. Alice was no Yvette. 'I feel I have made the right decision. And the children at St Hugh's mean a lot to me.'

They reached the tall stone gatehouse. Crowds of people filled its archway and the gatekeepers were busy checking who was coming into the city. Alice avoided looking upwards to the top of the towers, where the shrivelled heads and limbs of traitors were impaled on spikes. Pushing her way through the archway, she tugged on the sleeve of a gatekeeper, hoping to attract his attention. He was too busy to talk, but a fellow gatekeeper came to speak to them. Alice could tell he was impatient and she was impressed when Brother Jon stepped in to do the talking, despite the fact that there had been no reports of a man and a girl trying to leave the city during the night.

Alice looked at the crowds around her and realised they could have slipped through this gate unseen during the day when everyone was too busy to notice. *Perhaps Valerian had hidden Constance somewhere and waited until daylight to leave?* Alice sighed and a heavy feeling shifted down to her feet. The search already felt futile given that there were five other gates they could have escaped through. The task ahead felt over-whelming.

The busy crowd knocked and jostled Alice and the smell from the mud beneath her feet turned her stomach. She hated these streets and she hated the disease that had lurked there and taken her family from her. She hated this city because now it had also taken Constance from her. She didn't want to be out here in the cold and the filth. She wanted to be back in the children's dormitory at St Hugh's cuddling the children by the bright fire. But she had to be out here now. She had to find Constance.

*We are quite safe here.* Her misplaced words to Constance the previous day echoed in her mind. She had been a fool to reassure her of something that hadn't been true. St Hugh's was no longer safe; the dream of sitting by the fire with the children was nothing but a dream. Everything had changed within a few hours and this was her reality now. Her heart pounded and she could taste something metallic in her mouth, like blood.

They left the gatehouse and walked back down the street.

'Why did you offer to help me?' she asked Jon as they wove their way along Gracechurch Street through the crowds of people. Conversation was the only way she could keep herself calm, even if it was with a monk who had little to say for himself.

'To find Constance,' he replied. There was a pause before he spoke again. 'I think you were brave to stand up to Prior Edmund the way you did and I wanted to help.'

Alice was starting to think better of him now.

'Constance is too young to be out here on her own,' he continued. 'I fear what could happen to her. And as for that man who took her... I want to get hold of him myself.'

Alice wondered why Jon had not spoken out in support of her at the chapel. Then she thought of Sister Emma's secret smile and wondered if many of them had stayed quiet out of fear. Alice didn't think of herself as brave; she had only done what she felt was right.

'I think we should knock on the doors near the hospital and find out if anyone saw or heard anything last night,' she said.

Jon nodded in agreement.

They called in at the tavern next to the hospital, then at the blacksmith's and a couple of shops. They knocked on the doors of a few private houses and tried the inn. The innkeeper's wife told them she had heard dogs barking the previous night but had seen nothing out of the ordinary near the monastery.

'We need to find out what the patients saw,' said Alice. 'I find it hard to believe that no one was awoken by a struggle during which a man died and a girl was snatched.'

'We should speak to the patients later,' replied Jon, 'after the bailiff and coroner have done their work. We do not want to be seen to be taking charge.'

'But Constance is my friend!' exclaimed Alice, angry at the idea of having to wait for these disinterested noblemen to have their say.

'I realise that. But I also know that these people get upset when their authority is undermined. They want to decide what should be done about a missing girl. You will not help yourself by trying to take control of the situation.'

'I have to do something!'

'I know,' said Jon patiently, 'but you need to do it carefully. You have to pretend you're listening to these people and allowing them to be in charge. If you upset them you will not be offered the opportunity to look for Constance further. You're lucky I volunteered to come with you to give you some credibility after you stood up and interrupted prayers.'

Something within her snapped. '*Lucky*, am I?' she shouted. 'My friend is missing and it's supposed to be a privilege to wander the streets with your help trying to find her, is it?'

'There's no need to get angry,' replied Jon, reddening at the stares they were attracting as Alice raised her voice.

'I'm not angry! And I don't need you to help me,' said Alice. 'I didn't ask for anyone to come with me when I stood up during prayers. It was the prior who forced you on me. I am quite capable of looking for Constance on my own.'

She pushed past Jon and marched down the street as quickly as the crowd would allow. Hot tears pricked the backs of her eyes and she felt increasingly angry at every bump and jolt she received from the people around her.

The street broadened at the crossroads and the crowd thinned. Small, icy snowflakes blew horizontally in the wind and Alice pulled her cloak tighter around her as she scoured faces, hoping to catch a glimpse of Constance. Occasionally, a girl with long, fair hair made her heart leap, but it sank again when she realised it was not her friend. *Where should she search for Constance next?*

She didn't like the look of the bedraggled man limping

towards her. His clothes were ragged and he leered at her with a toothless grin.

'What 'ave we 'ere, then?' His voice was low and gravelly, and he had an unclean, sour smell.

A dirty hand reached out and grabbed her cloak. She tried to prise his fingers off but his hand clung on like a claw.

'Get off me!' she yelled.

'I've got a penny for a kiss from them sweet lips.'

He leaned into her, his odour overpowering. She recoiled, but her back was up against the wall. *Would no one help her? This would never have happened if she had stayed with Jon.*

Alice told herself she had no need for Jon; she could manage on her own. With a swift movement she turned to one side and shoved her elbow into the man's chest. It wasn't a strong blow, but it was enough to topple someone who was already unsteady on his feet.

The man fell backwards into the mud as she pulled her cloak out of his hand and ran. She chose Bridge Street, which led downhill towards the river, and once she was certain she had run far enough she paused next to a fruit stall to catch her breath. She looked down at her hands and saw that they were shaking. He had only been a lecherous old man and had been easy to deal with, but she felt nauseous from the smell of him. The purse that hung from her belt contained sprigs of lavender. Alice pulled them out and held them under her nose. The scent helped drive his smell away and reminded her of the precious items she kept in the chest in her room.

A familiar tall figure strode down the street, his brown cloak pulled across a black-and-white monk's habit. He wore his hood over his head, but she recognised the line of his jaw. He did not notice her until she called his name.

'There you are.' Jon was being decidedly cool with her.

'Where are you going?' she asked.

'Down to the river.' His short reply and the way he stonily fixed her eye told her he was angry.

'Why there?'

'They find people in the river.'

Alice shuddered. 'You mean *dead* people?'

'Sadly, yes. It happens,' he continued, 'and I do not like the thought any more than you do, but hopefully she's gone nowhere near the river and we will find her safe and well. I'll see you back at St Hugh's.' He started to walk away.

'Can I come with you?'

Jon stopped and turned. 'I thought you were happy looking for Constance on your own?'

'I am, but as you are going down to the river to search it makes sense that I come with you.' Alice felt awkward trying to make peace with Jon, but she was beginning to realise she needed him.

'Does it?'

'Yes.'

'I'm not sure I want to be shouted at again. I prefer my own company.'

'Now you're sulking.'

'I am not.'

Alice realised how petty their conversation was becoming. It was time to clear the air and start afresh.

'Jon, I'm sorry I shouted. I should not have said what I did. I'm grateful you offered to help me look for Constance and I think I need your help after all. We have a better chance of finding her if we work together.'

'I hope so.'

'May I come with you, then?'

'Yes.' Jon strode off ahead and Alice, feeling relieved, ran to catch up with him.

A herd of pigs was being driven up the hill, so Alice and

Jon took shelter beneath the awnings of an alehouse until they had passed.

'The guards at the bridge will know if anyone has been pulled out of the river,' said Jon.

A one-legged soldier fell out of the doorway behind them and into the mud, where he lay drunkenly laughing. Two friends picked him up and carried him back into the alehouse.

'I am certain Constance has been nowhere near there. It's just something we need to check.'

Alice nodded, hoping the guards would have no news.

They continued downhill towards the bridge and Jon stopped to buy a meat pie from a street trader. He offered to share it with Alice but she declined. Despite not having eaten all day, she had no appetite.

Crowds of people jostled around the entrance to London Bridge. The crooked, timber-framed buildings that lined it left space for only a narrow, congested passageway across the river. Alice and Jon found a guard to speak to: a large, red-faced, talkative man with boils on his neck. He wanted to know what a monk and a widow were doing walking around together. He said he had heard stories of what the monks got up to in their free time, especially south of the river in the brothels by Winchester Palace. He winked at Alice as he said this, but Jon ignored him and asked whether anyone had been pulled out of the river.

'We've not 'ad no one in the river fer a few days,' said the guard.

Alice sighed with relief.

'Last we 'ad were three or four nights back. A cripple threw himself in off the bridge, 'e had no arms. We gets a few who've been damaged in the war. They can't fight no more and they can't work. Their wives throw 'em out the 'ouse and they drinks and ends up in the river. We gets girls, too, ones who've got themselves in trouble, you know.' He winked more solemnly this time.

'Is anyone ever pulled out of the river alive?' asked Alice.

'Out o' *that?*' asked the guard, gesturing towards the brown expanse of water flowing beneath them.

Alice could feel a sharp, dank taste at the back of her throat.

'It's full o' shit. And it's tidal here, so if you falls in you gets dragged down one way or the other, dependin' on what the tide's doin'. Most likely yer 'ead gets smashed against the arches o' the bridge. Or yer get pulled under by the strength o' the tide. We gets animals in there all the time: dogs, cats, pigs, sheep, cows, 'orses, deers, chickens. The river gets everything 'cep' the rats. If they fall in they always gets out again. And they eats most of the stuff in the river, too. If yer carcass gets washed up on the bank down there it'll be eaten by the rats 'fore anyone sees it.'

Alice felt her mouth locked into a grimace.

'Who you looking fer?' asked the guard.

'A girl called Constance. She's small with fair hair tied in long plaits. She was wearing a brown tunic when she went missing. She's a lay sister. She didn't have her cloak with her.'

'And were she last seen by the river?'

'No, she went missing from the hospital at St Hugh's. We think she was taken. We thought we would come and make sure she hadn't been found in the river. And it is good that she hasn't.'

'She wouldn't stand a chance in it,' confirmed the guard. 'She'd be dead and drowned in an instant. Sounds like she'll catch 'er death o' cold, too, if she wen' out without a cloak. If she dint die last night it'll proberly be tonight.'

Alice didn't want to hear any more from the guard.

'Good luck finding 'er,' he added, gesturing to the crush of people in the gateway of the bridge. 'There's a lot of people in this 'ere city, so I hope you find 'er. How old did you say she war?'

'Fourteen.'

'God bless 'er. I'll keep 'er in me prayers and you keep on prayin' too, young man, like the good monk yer are.' The guard slapped Jon on the shoulder. 'Shall we let yer know at the 'ospital if we finds 'er?'

'Yes, thank you,' said Alice.

It was a cold walk back to St Hugh's and Alice felt a sense of hopelessness sinking in. She prayed Constance would be waiting for them when they got back to the hospital so their search could come to an end. *I'm sorry I ran away*, Alice pictured her saying. *It won't happen again.*

The snow fell more heavily and began to settle on the mud, the frostiness at the edge of the puddles crunched under Alice's feet. The guard was right; Constance would freeze to death if she stayed out in this weather another night. The image of a little body, frozen stiff where it had curled up in defence against the cold, flashed into Alice's mind, but she brushed it away.

'I feel like we're not going to find her.'

'I know,' agreed Jon, his brow crumpled. 'You feel so helpless when you're looking for someone.'

'That makes it sound like you've done this before.'

'I have,' he looked at her. 'Did you not know?'

A memory from the previous summer came back to Alice. 'Your sister. I remember now. She ran away?'

'That's what everyone said. I don't believe Elizabeth ran away, she would not have done something like that. She was happy and was soon to be married.'

'What happened?'

'She went missing, just like Constance. She went out with one of the servants on market day. They needed to buy a few things, I forget what. It was busy and the servant girl, Eloise, lost her in the crowd. Elizabeth never returned home. All we could do was walk the streets as we have done today, and call on her friends and anyone else who knew her. No one knew what had happened to her.'

'Do you think she is...?' Alice couldn't bring herself to say the word.

'Dead? No. I would know if she were dead. I pray every day for her safe return. I have to believe that one day my prayers will be answered.'

They walked on in silence. It made sense to Alice now. *This was why Jon wanted to help look for Constance. It was because he had been through this before. Maybe by helping with the search he was hoping he would find his sister or stumble upon a clue as to what had happened to her. There was little chance the disappearances were linked, but how could two girls vanish like this? How often did it happen in a city the size of London?*

The light in the street was starting to fade and there were fewer people milling about now as they shut themselves indoors away from the cold to huddle around fires. Dim orange light shone through the gaps between shutters and doorways.

And that was when Alice saw Valerian.

# Chapter Five

I t was the pale hospital tunic that caught Alice's attention. The man wearing it was walking away from them down a narrow side street.

Alice grabbed Jon's arm. 'Valerian! He's down there!' She pulled Jon after her into the almost dark alleyway. 'Come on!' She lifted her skirts and ran along the street, her feet slipping in the muddy snow. She stumbled into a woman carrying a bundle of laundry, prompting the woman to swear at her. Alice apologised breathlessly and ran on.

'Alice!' she heard Jon call after her. 'What are you doing?'

'Come on!' She turned round and beckoned to him. 'I saw him!' She carried on, treading in filth that raised a stench so foul she had to cover her mouth and nose with one hand. She crashed into a barrel, which slopped something onto her cloak as she struggled to see Valerian among the shadowy figures ahead of her. A barking dog emerged from the gloaming and blocked her way.

'Move!' she yelled. The dog growled and bared its teeth.

Jon caught up with her, panting. 'This is not a good idea.'

'He's just ahead of us!'

'Are you *sure* it's him?'

The dog barked at them and Alice looked around on the ground for something to throw at it. Everything was covered in a dusting of snow, but she could see some broken pieces of wood that looked as though they had once been part of a bucket. She picked up a piece, threw it at the dog and missed. The dog continued to bark.

'It was definitely Valerian?' asked Jon.

'Yes! He was wearing the tunic patients wear, no cloak or hood.' Her heart was pounding loudly in her ears. 'He looked just like him, I swear it was him.'

The barking continued.

'Can we move?' asked Jon. 'I don't like that dog.'

'But that means going back the way we came and Valerian went that way!' Alice pointed towards the end of the alleyway, which was lost in darkness.

'We need to get back,' said Jon.

Alice remained where she was and a new flurry of snowflakes began to fall.

'Quiet!' she yelled at the dog.

'Come on,' said Jon, resting his hand on her forearm. His touch felt reassuring.

Reluctantly, she turned and walked with him back down the alleyway. 'Maybe you thought you saw him because you wanted to,' said Jon. 'We're both tired, we have been walking all day.'

'I *did* see him.' Alice wasn't about to be talked round. 'It was him!' She tried to wipe away whatever it was that had slopped onto her cloak. It felt cold and slimy.

'We need to get back,' said Jon. 'The prior instructed us to return before sundown.'

It was dark by the time they reached St Hugh's and the snow

had settled on the steps of the hospital. Alice's hands and feet were numb with cold and she was relieved to reach the warmth of the infirmary hall, where a large fire crackled in the grate.

Sister Katherine wore a haughty expression and asked how their search had gone. Brother Jon said he would update the prior, leaving Alice reluctantly alone with Sister Katherine. She showed little surprise when Alice told her they had found no trace of Constance. Alice wanted to tell her that she had seen Valerian, but she could not be sure that the memory was real and she felt stupid mentioning it. Perhaps Jon was right and it had been something she had just wanted to see.

'The bailiff has sent some men out to look for Constance and Valerian,' said Sister Katherine. 'Everyone is agreed that Valerian has abducted her, although many people think she went willingly.'

'I don't believe them,' replied Alice.

'Constance is a young woman of shameful birth,' said Sister Katherine. 'To elope with a man working for the Earl of Wykeham is an ambitious strategy. When they marry she will have elevated her status. I think she would have made a good nun, but I understand her motives.'

'Constance would never have left with him! And she certainly wouldn't want to marry him!' Alice fumed. *How could Sister Katherine pass judgement when she hardly knew Constance?* 'She wanted to do more with her life. We discussed a possible apprenticeship with Yvette de Beauchamp. She was a sensible girl and she showed no interest in marriage. There were other things she wanted to do first.'

'But she wanted to leave St Hugh's?' asked Sister Katherine.

'She wanted to see more of the world,' replied Alice, 'and that is to be expected. She has spent her entire life here.'

'You have just provided a motive for her running away,'

said Sister Katherine. 'She wanted to see the world and an opportunity to elope with one of the earl's men presented itself.'

'She would never have run off with a man she didn't know! He took her and I believe she is in danger. It looks as though he killed Roger, too, presumably because Roger tried to stop him.'

'Either that or the men fought over who would have her,' replied Sister Katherine.

'Can I speak to the patients about what they saw last night?'

'It has already been done. They did not see anything; they were asleep, as you would expect.'

'But how? Someone was murdered!'

'It obviously happened quickly. Roger was killed by a blow to the head, which could have been administered swiftly without waking anyone who was sleeping nearby.'

'Perhaps Roger was angry that Valerian was planning to leave him. Or maybe he tried to stop Valerian taking Constance.'

'Alice, this is conjecture. None of us truly knows what happened last night and I suspect we will never find out. There are no witnesses...'

'She was taken!' interrupted Hilda, swaggering up to them. 'Just like them other ones! They was all taken!'

'Who was taken, Hilda?' asked Alice.

'The woman is suffering from lunacy. She talks nonsense,' said Sister Katherine.

'Hilda?' Alice stared at her and the old lady stared back, her milk white eye seemingly fixed on Alice's face. But Hilda spoke no more. She licked her lips and walked away.

'Are you sure no one saw anything?' Alice asked again.

'The patients were all asleep, Alice.' Sister Katherine rolled her eyes.

'She should not have been left alone.'

'Who?'

'Constance! She was alone and Valerian took the opportunity to snatch her. If one of the brothers had been with her, it would never have happened. I hear they were drinking together in the refectory again last night. Surely one of them should have been watching over her?'

'It is not for me to say how St Hugh's is managed, but let me say that I agree with you,' replied Sister Katherine. 'Whatever happened, the events of last night were beyond our control.'

'And there's something else I don't understand,' continued Alice. 'Although there is no doubt he did it, I cannot imagine Valerian taking Constance and killing his friend. He seemed like a good man.'

'I am not sure how you determine that. You only met him briefly.'

'He didn't seem like someone who would snatch a girl.'

'Does anyone? Often the most charming ones are the most trouble. Men are unpredictable creatures.'

Alice wondered what knowledge Sister Katherine had of charming men.

The nun lowered her voice and continued: 'Sadly, it was inevitable that sin would be visited upon us here at St Hugh's. Things have changed a great deal since we lost Prior Harold and many others in the plague. There is no longer the level of discipline we once had; silence, routines and prayers are not properly observed. We have a prior who occupies his time with drinking, money, a pet monkey and a wife in all but name. Our duty to God has been neglected and this is how he is punishing us.'

'We have to do whatever we can, Sister Katherine.'

'Of course. And I, for one, will do my best to maintain the standards to which we once adhered. Please do not allow this tragedy to distract you from your good work. You are a mother here to the children at St Hugh's, and your time is better spent with them than chasing after a girl who wanted to leave anyway.'

Alice was about to argue when an urgent knock at the door interrupted them.

Sister Katherine answered the door and, after a few words were exchanged, an official-looking man with a humped back wearing a knee-length scarlet jacket and a large blue velvet hat marched in. He paused to brush the snow off his arms and shoulders before summoning two guards, who came in holding a man between them. The man's wrists were shackled together and he wore a simple wool tunic.

It was Valerian.

He was in a sorry state, with his eyes sunken and his dark, wavy hair falling into his face. Alice suspected the wound to his chest would also be giving him pain.

*So she had seen him in the dark passageway. She would find Brother Jon shortly and tell him.*

'Someone fetch Prior Edmund,' ordered Sister Katherine, glaring at Valerian. 'What have you done with the poor girl?' she spat.

'All in good time, Sister,' said the man in charge, who Alice guessed was the bailiff. He had a hooked nose and wore a sneer that suggested he felt superior to everyone around him. 'We will allow the criminal to speak once the prior is here.'

Alice stared at Valerian, trying to gauge from his expression what had happened. He looked frightened and not at all like someone who had abducted a girl and murdered his friend.

'Where is Roger?' Valerian asked.

'In the chapel,' replied Sister Katherine sternly.

'How is he?'

'He is dead, you foolish man!'

Valerian's shoulders slumped and his mouth dropped open.

*If he had attacked Roger he hadn't intended to kill him,* Alice thought to herself. She continued to watch him as he leant against one of the guards for support. He was given a shove for his trouble and forced to stand upright. His eyes were fixed to a point on the floor in front of him. He looked lost.

Prior Edmund swept into the hall with a small, grey monkey sitting on his shoulder, its long tail hanging down his back. He raised an eyebrow when he saw Valerian.

'Let's discuss this in my apartments,' he said.

The prior led the way and everyone trooped after him. Too distracted to notice that Alice was following, it was only when they reached the door of the prior's apartments that he looked at her quizzically.

'I have been searching for Constance all day, Father,' she explained. 'Please let me hear what the bailiff and Valerian have to say. I am desperate to hear news.'

Prior Edmund scowled, but he didn't argue. Instead, he turned and led the group into the warm room, which was well lit with candles.

They all remained standing as the bailiff spoke: 'Father, this man was found wandering the streets after curfew. He told us he was trying to prevent a girl from being snatched, but as the watchmen could not find any sign of the girl he was held in detention. I visited him this evening after my meeting with you here at St Hugh's and have brought him here so you may confirm that this is the same man who went missing at the same time as Constance Brooker.'

'It is,' replied Sister Katherine.

'There, you have your answer,' said the prior. 'I didn't see the two men – Valerian or the one he murdered – when they were here yesterday, but I trust Sister Katherine's word and I believe Mistress Wescott also recognises this man?'

Alice nodded, feeling uneasy about how unhappy Valerian looked.

The bailiff smiled smugly. 'Then it pleases me greatly that we now have the man responsible for the horrifying murder of Roger Granville and the abduction of Constance Brooker.'

'That's not true!' shouted Valerian.

The bailiff sneered again and held up a hand to silence him, but Valerian ignored him.

'Roger and I tried to stop the men taking her!'

'There was no sign of any other men last night,' said the bailiff to the prior.

'They escaped!' said Valerian. 'They got away! I was trying to follow them but I had no lamp, so it was hard to see. I followed them for as long as I could!'

He glanced at Alice as he spoke, and as their eyes met she believed him. There was something earnest about him, and the way he spoke sounded genuine.

'I did not hurt Constance or Roger. He fought the men to stop them taking Constance and they clubbed him across the back of the head. I tried to fight but I was still struggling with this wound,' he pointed at his chest with a shackled hand. 'I have told this story over and over, but no one believes me.' His eyes were wide as he looked around at everyone in the room.

Alice wanted to say that she believed him, but she kept quiet as she looked at the disdainful expressions on the faces of the prior, the bailiff, Sister Katherine and the guards.

*Perhaps Valerian was simply good at lying.*

'Tell us what you did with the girl!' demanded the bailiff. 'Has she met the same sorry end as your friend Roger?'

'No!' said Valerian, 'They took her! I've told everyone this many times.'

'Who did?' asked the bailiff, half-smiling and half-sneering.

'The three men!'

'It is very convenient that these men suddenly vanished along with Constance, do you not agree, Prior Edmund?' said the bailiff.

The prior nodded. 'It seems the mystery has been solved,' he said, handing the monkey on his shoulder a walnut. 'And there was no need for you to spend the day wandering the streets of London after all,' he said, turning to Alice. 'I told you the bailiff would sort this out.'

'But what about Constance?' asked Alice, angry that the prior considered the incident resolved.

'Ask this man,' said the prior, gesturing at Valerian.

'They have taken her and you need to find them,' said Valerian.

'Which direction did they take? Where did you last see them?' asked Alice.

'We were near St Paul's, as I remember.'

The prior snorted. 'That helps little. Many places in London are near St Paul's.'

The bailiff smirked. 'There was no sign of three men and a girl on the streets, and this man claims he does not know where he last saw them. He cannot even create a convincing story to cover his tracks.'

'What happens now?' asked Alice.

'Valerian will be detained and I will speak to his employer, the Earl of Wykeham. If proven guilty he will be executed without delay.'

'He works for the Earl of Wykeham?' asked the prior, raising his eyebrows. 'The earl is an influential man.'

'And a good man,' interrupted Valerian. 'He will know I

did not do this. He will believe me when I say I tried to help the girl and that all I feel is anger that they killed my friend and took her away. I hope she is safe.' He looked down at the floor.

'Let's find out what the Earl of Wykeham thinks tomorrow, shall we?' said the bailiff. 'I shall not keep you any longer, Prior Edmund. Thank you for confirming that this is the man who is responsible for these terrible crimes.'

'Thank you for bringing him here,' said the prior. 'Before you leave, may I suggest you take him to the chapel, where he can spend some time repenting of his sins before the Lord?'

'A fine idea,' replied the bailiff. 'Good night.'

Alice left the prior's apartments and looked for Brother Jon so she could tell him about Valerian. As the sound of plainchant echoed throughout the monastery, Alice realised he was probably in the chapel. Rethinking her strategy, she went to the lay sisters' dormitory. The three women Constance had shared a room with were getting ready for bed.

'I wish I'd waited up 'til she came to bed last night,' said Agnes, a middle-aged, frizzy-haired woman who stood in the middle of the room in her chemise. 'I could've raised the hue and cry once I realised something was wrong. Instead, I went to sleep and when I woke this morning I just thought she'd got up early. Thinking about it, that was unusual for Constance because she was always the last to get up. But I didn't think anything of it; not last night and not this morning. And now she's gone and here are all her things, and I don't know how I'm going to sleep tonight knowing she's not here.'

'Or me,' said Alice, opening the cupboard once again and feeling the rough wool of Constance's cloak between her fingers.

'She wasn't the type to go running away like that. I always thought she was happy, and that was a good thing given that she was a foundling and her mother was a whore and she never knew what a proper family was like. Sometimes in those instances girls go looking for love, don't they? They disappear with the first man to give them a sideways glance. But she wasn't like that.'

Alice's head felt heavy. She left Agnes talking as she opened the wooden drawer that belonged to Constance and carefully looked through her things. Constance didn't have much, but the pieces of linen she used to practise her embroidery stitches caught Alice's eye. She picked each piece up and ran her finger over the raised stitching of flowers and birds. Much of the work was done in a simple, plain yarn, but there was a detailed woven design worked in red and gold thread that Yvette de Beauchamp had lent Constance to practise with. Alice picked this piece up and held it near the candle, the golden threads twinkling in the light. Then she found a piece embroidered with a simple songbird in blue.

'I would like to keep this with me,' she said to Agnes, 'until we find Constance again. I want you to know I have this in case anyone wonders what's happened to it. I'll keep it safe until we have her back with us.'

Agnes nodded and Alice looked again at the stitches so recently threaded by Constance's hand. She folded the piece of linen and put it in her purse, feeling a tug of happiness that she had something to remind her of Constance.

Alice lay awake long after the candle burnt itself out that night. Her mind was spinning. Unanswered questions and flickers of memory scattered around her head like leaves in the wind. Mixed in with these was a sense of guilt. *She should have been able to protect Constance. Why hadn't she been there?*

Panic surged through her body and she felt as though she was being washed away by it, unable to grasp on to anything. Her breath was shallow and she couldn't get enough air into her chest. She sat up, gasping, a cold sweat on her forehead.

She wanted it to all stop.

*Someone needed to make this stop.*

There was a thump on her front door. *Could it be Constance?* It sounded too heavy for a girl's hand. Alice pulled her cloak on over her chemise, climbed down the wooden stairs and ran across the cold stone floor to the doorway. The light of a lamp outside shone through the gap beneath the door. She grabbed the large iron key from its hook on the wall and her fingers fumbled as she turned it in the lock.

'Who is it?' she called out.

'Brother Jon.'

The door swung open with a creak and she saw that he was standing with another man, who held the lantern. The second man looked like a guard, but it was difficult to tell in the gloom.

'Has she been found?'

'No.'

'What then?' She pulled her cloak around her, embarrassed to be seen in her nightwear.

'They found a girl in the river.'

'Oh.' Alice shivered. *Please don't let it be Constance.*

'We should go and see...'

'Yes, we should,' she interrupted. She didn't want to hear him explain. 'I need to get dressed. Would you like to come in?'

'We will wait out here.'

# Chapter Six

Alice's head felt thick with tiredness and her face stung with the cold as they walked through the dark streets. The man accompanying them was a guard from the bridge and he led the way, his lantern throwing a weak light onto the snowy ground. Alice lost track of where they were, but the guard seemed to know a shortcut to the bridge through the narrow passageways. Alice could have stretched out both hands and easily touched the dingy walls either side of her.

'Thank you for calling on me,' she said to Jon.

He formed a dark, hooded figure next to her, but occasionally she caught a glimpse of his pale face.

'Does the prior know you're out here?' she asked.

'No, we were not able to wake him. He's sleeping off the wine. Sister Katherine suggested I come and find you. If it is Constance, we will need you to confirm it. You knew her best.'

Alice prayed that the girl wasn't Constance, but realised if it wasn't her it would be another girl who was probably missed every bit as much. It was awful that someone had been pulled out of the river at all.

'I heard they have Valerian now,' said Jon, 'excellent news. I heard they plan to execute him. I hope he confesses what he did with her before he dies.'

'But we don't know for sure that he took Constance,' said Alice. 'He says he tried to save her and that Roger tried too, and that's why they killed him.'

'Who did?'

'The men he said took Constance.'

'It sounds a little too convenient. And you believe him?'

'I saw how he was; he was in a bad way. He didn't know Roger was dead and he didn't seem to be lying.'

'He has had ample time to come up with a believable story.'

'Did you see him?'

'No, I heard about him from the prior.'

'Prior Edmund and the bailiff are convinced he murdered Roger and took Constance. They have captured someone they can execute for the crime, and then they will be able to forget all about it. They don't seem to care about where Constance is now. I don't think she is of any matter to the prior.'

'She was a foundling,' replied Jon. 'She had no status and no one to stand up for her.'

'Apart from me! And why do you speak of her as if she is no longer alive? This girl they pulled from the river may not be her.'

'Sorry. It may not be her, you are right. But I'm certain Valerian is responsible and that sadly he may have done to her what he did to Roger. I'm surprised you are able to defend him when you were so close to Constance.'

'I saw him, and I believe him. There was something about his face that made me believe he was telling the truth.'

'You decide a man's guilt or innocence by the look on his face?' Jon laughed. 'If you were a man you would make a worthy judge! Do you not know that murderers always profess their innocence?' Alice jabbed him in the arm with her elbow.

'Ow!'

The guard stopped and swung his flickering lantern in their direction. 'What's goin' on? Is it thieves?'

'No,' replied Jon, 'I bumped my head on that sign hanging down back there.'

The guard grunted and they continued on their way. Soon the stench of the river lay heavy in their nostrils.

The small, dismal room was cold and smelt of damp earth, and shadows flickered as a single candle spluttered in the corner. Alice decided to avert her eyes from the ominous bundle of sackcloth that lay on a wooden bench in the centre of the room until the moment she had to look. The guard told them the girl had been discovered by a waterman and pulled out of the river earlier that evening. Water had pooled on the table and was dripping steadily onto the stone floor.

'She ain't been in long,' he said, his voice gravelly and devoid of emotion. 'Usually they're bloated and 'ave the flesh hanging off 'em. Oftentimes they've lost limbs or even their 'eads. I'm still amazed at the colours human flesh can turn.'

Alice gulped and placed a hand over her nose and mouth.

'But this one,' he walked over to the bundle, 'she's alrigh'. Not smellin' yet.'

His relaxed attitude sickened Alice and she fought the urge to turn and run out of the cell-like room. Jon stood close by; she felt his body tense as the waterman spoke. *What if the girl turned out to be his sister, Elizabeth?*

Alice gripped his warm hand and wrapped her fingers

tightly around his. He looked down at her, his green eyes dark and serious.

The guard flung back the sackcloth in one swift movement, exposing the body.

*It wasn't Constance.*

*But was it Elizabeth?*

Alice looked up at Jon's face and saw a glimmer of recognition. 'Is it...?'

'No,' he replied quickly, 'it is not my sister.'

Relieved, she gave his hand a squeeze.

'And it is not Constance,' she said to the guard.

'But the rosary beads around her neck...' Jon's voice faltered, and then he recovered himself. 'I think they belong to Elizabeth.'

Alice took a moment to comprehend what he had said. 'Those rosary beads belong to *Elizabeth*? How do you know?'

'They were made especially for her. They're just like mine.' He felt around his neck and pulled out a loop of rosary beads from under his cloak. 'Twenty-four beads: eight of amber, eight of jet and eight of coral, threaded into green silk and this.' He showed Alice the pendant, an intricate silver lion. 'We each have a different pendant. I have a lion and Elizabeth has a fleur-de-lis.'

Alice glanced back at the girl and saw the silver, three-leafed lily resting on her white chest. It was glinting in the candlelight.

'So do you know this girl? Is she a friend of Elizabeth's?'

He shook his head. 'I do not recognise her.'

'But these beads were made especially for the two of you. Is there a chance the same beads could have been made for someone else?'

'My father asked a paternosterer to make each of us a set of rosary beads shortly after our mother died. The paternosterer could have made an identical set of beads for someone else, but I cannot imagine he would have done so.'

Jon was pale now and grinding his teeth. 'Something terrible happened to this girl. Look, you can see the marks around her neck.'

Alice didn't want to look but she allowed herself a glance at the angry bruising on the girl's throat.

'Someone must have strangled her and somehow my sister has met this girl. Maybe the same person took them both. How are we going to find out? I don't know what to think.'

He scratched the back of his head. 'This makes me afraid that Elizabeth has also been harmed. There is a link between them and we need to find out what it is. I need to find my sister, and we need to find Constance. Who is doing this?'

He turned to look at Alice, his face wretched with tears running down his cheeks. Alice wanted to wipe them away, but instead she gave his hand another squeeze, which she hoped was comforting.

'We *will* find them. I'm sure whoever did this must have Constance. There are too many coincidences here. Do you recognise this girl at all? Have you ever seen her at St Hugh's?'

'I told you, no.'

'Maybe she's a thief what stole yer sister's beads?' the guard conjectured.

Reluctantly, Alice looked at the girl's face again. She appeared to be about the same age as Constance. Her skin was porcelain white and her hair was red and hung loose. Watery mud trickled from her nose and mouth.

'She didn't drown,' she heard herself mutter. *What had the girl's last moments been like? What sort of monster would do such a thing to her?*

'What happens now?' Alice asked the guard.

'Coroner deals with 'er now. The family 'ave probably reported she's missin' and he'll pay 'em a visit. Sometimes they go unclaimed. If she's a thief and 'as no home to speak of then no one will be lookin' for 'er.'

'Whoever she is, she needs dignity and a burial,' said Alice, walking over to the girl and pulling the cloth back over her cold body. She felt better having given her some privacy again. 'Her soul needs to be put to rest. I pray her family will be found soon so they can be reunited with her.'

'Do yer want them rosary beads?' the guard asked Brother Jon. 'They's yer sister's, ain't they?'

'No, she must keep them,' said Jon. 'We don't know how she came by them, but they should stay with her now.'

# Chapter Seven

J on was in the garden by sunrise the following morning. Digging wasn't possible in the frozen earth, so while he waited for the dusting of snow to melt he positioned himself in front of a small apple tree, his breath clouding in the cold air. In his right hand he held a hoe. Its handle was three feet long and the perfect weight for practice. He held it upright in front of him and started practising small cuts in the air; back and forth, and then to the left and right. This kept his wrist and forearm strong and was an exercise he remembered his brother showing him when he was a boy.

Still focusing on the apple tree, he began to make larger swings in the air with his pretend sword and once he had finished the exercise with his right hand, he switched to his left. Some days he had someone to practise his sword work with. Brother Ralph was occasionally willing and would spar with him using an old shovel handle. Jon knew this was absurd and that practising strokes with a hoe in the monastery garden was hardly a training schedule a squire would receive, but he did what he could to maintain some semblance of sword skills.

Years previously he had watched his father, Sir Robyn, preparing to go away and fight. He had tried to hold his father's coat of chainmail but it had slipped through his hands onto the floor because it was so heavy. Jon had longed for the day he would be strong enough to wear that chainmail with the de Grey family's blue and gold surcoat over the top. He wanted plates of shiny armour on his shoulders and arms, and a sword to hang from his belt. He pictured himself resting his hand on the hilt of his sword, ready to attack or defend whenever he was needed.

The tree in front of Jon became the faceless man who had murdered the girl pulled from the river. He closed his eyes and saw her pale face and sodden dress dripping with water. But in his mind she became his sister, Elizabeth, lying dead with her eyes open and unseeing. With an angry lunge he jabbed the hoe into the heart of the tree's branches and then pulled back before striking again. A few thrusts like this would easily be enough to kill the man. Jon stood back and surveyed the tree. Should he cut the man's head off now or slice him from groin to throat? He went for the slice and accidentally knocked a branch off the tree. The mistake flipped his mind back to gardening work and his anger subsided. Cursing, he picked up the branch from the ground and examined the point where he had removed it from the tree. There was a jagged stump left on the trunk that would need trimming back to a neat cut.

Jon sighed and stepped back from the tree. He dropped his hoe and stretched out his arms. Glancing over to the windows of the children's dormitory he saw Alice holding one of the children. They both smiled at him and waved. He smiled awkwardly and returned the wave, embarrassed to see they had been watching. He knew the gardens were overlooked and that anyone could see him practising sword work instead of gardening, but he hadn't expected anyone to take the time to watch him.

He waved at them again and then bent down and occupied himself with a wooden trug filled with garlic bulbs for planting. As he separated out the cloves of garlic he thought again about the girl in the river and how she could have known his sister.

*It was several months since Elizabeth had vanished, why should her rosary beads appear now? Was she still alive?*

He felt his throat tighten. *Elizabeth would never have chosen to run away, someone must have taken her. Just as Valerian had taken Constance.* He gripped the cloves of garlic tightly in his fist. *Would Elizabeth and Constance ever be found? The men who took them needed to be hunted down and dealt with.*

*If only he had the chance to do it himself.*


Footsteps on the gravel path told him someone was approaching. Jon looked up and saw Alice. He got to his feet and smiled at her. Her appearance was demure and he wondered how she would look without her veil, with her dark hair worn loose around her shoulders. He liked the deep blue of her eyes and in them he noticed a flicker of understanding; something shared after their ordeal in that mournful room by the river the previous night.

Alice looked at the cloves of garlic in his hand. 'Will those grow at this time of year?'

'I'm not sure.' He peeled off a thin layer of skin from one of the cloves. It was too delicate to feel with his cold fingertips. 'But I'll plant them anyway. I always try to occupy myself out here; it's better than being trapped inside.' He nodded towards the main building, where each of the gargoyles wore a cap of snow.

'At least there are fires in there.' Alice shivered. 'I saw you doing your sword work this morning. With the apple tree.'

Jon grimaced. 'I am not much good at it really, but I have a feeling I might need to use a sword one day soon.'

'You think so? But you don't have a sword to use.'

'Oh, but I have,' Jon lowered his voice and looked around him to check no one was around to overhear. He had a secret and he felt he could trust Alice with it. 'It is wrapped up in old vestments and hidden at the back of the press in the day room. No one ever looks in there, and the only use the vestments have had in recent years is as a home for the moths.'

A smile played on Alice's lips. 'But what if someone finds it there?' she whispered.

'So far no one has. And if they do, how will they know it belongs to me?'

'Because you're the only sword-fighting monk at St Hugh's!' Alice grinned.

Jon shook his head. 'They will not think it is mine. The sword could have lain there for a hundred years and belonged to the Knights Templar for all they know.'

'Why do you think you might need your sword again?'

'I don't want to tempt fate,' he crossed himself, 'but with Constance being taken and the girl found in the river, I have a feeling something terrible is happening. It was difficult when Elizabeth disappeared, but now I feel there is real evil at work. I want to be able to protect us all. Let me show you something that gives me hope.'

Jon led Alice to a silver birch tree, which stood in the corner of the garden close to a small door in the garden wall. Carved neatly into the tree's pale bark was a series of little notches, one above the other. The notches at the bottom were fresher than those at the top.

'Each day Elizabeth is missing, I carve another mark.'

Jon had never shown anyone the marks he had made on

this tree before. Perhaps people had noticed them and wondered what they were, but Jon had never discussed them. He had a feeling Alice would understand why he had cut them. She squinted at the notches, trying to work out how many there were.

'I've carved about two hundred now,' he said to save her counting. 'I stop by here each day and pray for her, even though my prayers are not heard. I will keep doing it until one day they are.'

'They will be, I feel sure of it,' said Alice. He noticed dark shadows under her eyes.

'You look tired this morning.'

'I didn't sleep much.'

'Would you like me to get you some milk of the poppy from Brother Ralph?'

'No, thank you. I'll sleep better tonight, I am sure.' Alice blew on her hands and rubbed them together to keep them warm. 'I can't stop thinking about the girl they found in the river yesterday.'

'Nor me. How can we find out who did that to her?'

'I don't know. And who *is* she? Someone must be missing her.'

'They may have been reunited with her now. Word will have travelled.'

An image of Elizabeth's body lying dead and sodden on a trestle table flashed into Jon's mind. He shuddered. Alice was gazing across the garden as if she were thinking the same about Constance.

'I hope they find the person who killed that girl,' she said. 'I cannot understand how someone could do that. Why?'

'Who knows?'

'We need to work out what's happening,' said Alice, 'because something sinister is going on. These are not normal events and we need to think about what we know so far. Elizabeth went missing last summer. And she was about to get married. To whom?'

'Geoffrey Edington. Some people said she left because she didn't want to marry him. He is not the husband I would have chosen for my sister, had I had a say in the matter. He is dour and serious. He is a small man and Elizabeth is tall. They would not have looked right together. Would you like to borrow my gloves? I'm not using them and you look cold.'

'No, thank you, I'll be fine.' Alice pushed her hands into the sleeves of her cloak.

Jon continued: 'However, Elizabeth seemed happy about marrying Geoffrey. She had grown up knowing she would have to marry the man our father chose for her and the Edingtons are wealthy. Like many women of her status, Elizabeth believed she would learn to love him after they were married. She was never opposed to marrying him and would never have run away from doing her duty. She would not have done that to her family.'

Jon felt something release in his chest as he spoke, as if he had been keeping thoughts of Elizabeth locked away there. He had not had the opportunity to talk about her for a long time.

'And Geoffrey Edington has no idea what happened to her?'

'None.'

'What do you know about him?'

'Not much. Only that he is dour, serious and small, and that he works in the household of Sir Walter Rokeby.'

'Sir Walter who visited St Hugh's last week?'

'Yes.'

'So the last person to see Elizabeth was the servant girl.'

Jon nodded. 'Yes, Eloise.'

'And which market were they visiting?'

'It was near Broad Street. And no one saw how Elizabeth

vanished. There were some wild ideas at the time about Eloise colluding with bandits and arranging for Elizabeth to be taken in exchange for money. Poor Eloise suffered much of the blame to start with, but eventually people realised she would not have done such a thing. Eloise said it was too busy to see what had happened to Elizabeth and eventually they believed her. It was a terrible day when I found out.'

Jon paused and examined the garlic cloves in his hand. 'I remember my father coming here to tell me, and I knew it had to be something serious because otherwise he would have sent one of his men. I think he still believes she ran away because, although it is painful, it hurts less to believe that she made a choice rather than being abducted. If she ran away there is more chance of her being alive.' He blinked quickly to disperse the tears that were starting to form.

'When did you last see her?' Alice's voice was soft and steady, as if she was worried about upsetting him.

'Two or three weeks before she went missing. She came to St Hugh's with Geoffrey and a small group attached to Sir Walter on one of his visits. If she had married Geoffrey she would probably be carrying out a role in Sir Walter's household by now. He does charitable work, helping the sick and the poor. It was something she would have enjoyed doing.'

The bell rang for prayers.

'You need to go,' said Alice.

Jon shook his head. 'They will not notice my absence.'

'You'll get into trouble,' scolded Alice with a smile.

Jon shrugged his shoulders and smiled back at her.

'This is what we know so far,' said Alice. 'Elizabeth vanished last summer, Constance went missing two days ago, and at some point the girl in the river was taken from her family. Or I suppose she could have run away. I wonder whether she was reported missing and if anyone is looking for her.'

'I do hope someone has been looking for her.'

'If she has family we need to find out who they are. We could ask them if they know Elizabeth. Perhaps the two girls were friends. Or maybe we could find a connection between how the girl went missing and how Constance and Elizabeth vanished.'

'Valerian took Constance,' said Jon, 'but I find it hard to believe he was in that marketplace last summer when Elizabeth vanished. I cannot see a link between Constance and Elizabeth. But the girl in the river had Elizabeth's rosary beads, so I feel that something awful is happening. I am terrified the next girl to be pulled out of the river will be my sister.'

'I pray it will not be.' Alice removed her hand from her sleeve and rested it on Jon's arm. Her touch felt light and warm through the sleeve of his tunic. 'I think if we find the girl's family we will find out how she knew your sister.'

'Unless she was a thief, as the guard suggested, and stole those rosary beads.'

'She did not look like one.'

'Oh yes, I remember that you judge everyone's character on how they look,' Jon said, smiling.

He noticed Alice chose to ignore his comment. 'Whatever the circumstances, somehow your sister and the girl in the river met,' she said. 'We don't know whether it was before or after they went missing. Do you think the coroner would know who the girl's family is?'

He hadn't thought about asking the coroner. Jon liked the way Alice's mind worked. Most of the people around him were told what to think, so speaking to someone with an independent mind was refreshing.

'I can visit him and find out,' said Jon. 'I will tell him I have an interest because the girl has my sister's rosary beads. I might be able to persuade my father to come along, though he rarely leaves the house these days.' He thought for a moment. 'We are making a commitment, aren't we?'

Alice raised her eyebrows. 'Are we?'

'Yes, we are committing ourselves to finding out what has happened to these girls.'

'You're right.' She stood a little taller, as if trying to match his height. 'We are going to find out what happened to them! Because no one else is doing it are they?'

'They don't seem to be.'

'They are not interested. But we can find out what how Elizabeth and the girl in the river knew each other and we can listen to what Valerian has to say.'

Jon was doubtful about this second line of enquiry. He felt certain Valerian was guilty, but it made sense to work with Alice to find out as much as they could. He would do anything to find his sister again and he wanted to find the men who had harmed the girl in the river and taken Constance.

'We can do it,' Alice said confidently.

The thin, dark figure of Sister Katherine emerged from a doorway and walked towards them.

'The children are asking where you are,' she said to Alice.

'I am sorry, Sister. I will go to them now.'

'But that is not why I came to find you,' said Sister Katherine. 'I looked for you in the children's dormitory, and of course you were not there. I was not expecting to find you here in the garden with Brother Jon.'

She cast him a disapproving look and he scowled back.

'I came to find you because the prior asked for you. He has a visitor, Valerian Baladi. It seems the Earl of Wykeham has ensured his man receives a stay of execution. Valerian is offering to help you find Constance and is waiting for you in the prior's apartments.'

'Thank you, Sister.'

'Now you have your chance to speak to him,' said Jon. He was not happy about the smile on Alice's face. Valerian was likely to tell her a series of lies to cover his tracks.

*How could Alice be so trusting?*

'I would not be too excited by the prospect of speaking to him,' Sister Katherine added with a sniff. 'The man will do his utmost to try to prove his innocence. Everything he says is likely to be a falsehood.'

'I agree,' said Jon. It was the only time he had ever agreed with Sister Katherine.

'Surely Valerian wouldn't return to St Hugh's if he were a guilty man?' asked Alice.

Jon shrugged and began planting the garlic.

# Chapter Eight

A lice struggled to recognise Valerian in his smart green jacket, blue hose and orange hood. He gave Alice a broad grin when she entered Prior Edmund's room and she returned his smile. The prior was sitting behind his table glaring at Valerian. His monkey was seated on the table eating an apple.

'Hello, Mistress Wescott. I am sure you are as unhappy as myself and the bailiff that this man,' he gestured at Valerian, 'is currently a *free man*. His innocence has not yet been proven. But as his guilt has not been proven either, his employer, the Earl of Wykeham, has insisted he be released from the gaol while the bailiff continues his enquiries. He has also furnished his man with a fine set of clothes, as you have no doubt observed. This man has returned here to give us his version of events. Whether we are to believe him or not is another matter. But he asked for you, Alice Wescott, which is why I summoned you. Perhaps you can listen to this finely dressed man and discern whether he has anything worthy to say. I suspect he is wasting our time and will be on his way to the gallows before the week is out.'

Valerian tutted.

The prior continued: 'And ask yourself, Alice, what you think he has done with the girl. He elopes with her and yet she is not here. I suspect he has killed her.'

Alice breathed in sharply.

'I doubt that any of what he has to say to us is the truth. However, I have great respect for the Earl of Wykeham, so I will permit you one more conversation with this man.'

'Thank you, Father,' replied Alice.

She turned to Valerian. 'How is your injury?' she enquired.

'Still bandaged, but healing well. It looked worse than it was, I believe. Thank you for your concern, Mistress Wescott.'

A lock of curly hair had fallen over one of his dark eyes and Alice felt herself flush. She had felt sorry for him when he had been flanked by guards and wearing a hospital tunic, but now he was looking so well she was unsure whether she could trust him after all. Whatever his motives were, she was determined to get the truth from him.

'Perhaps you could explain what you saw the evening Constance went missing?'

'Of course. I think it would be better if we went down to the infirmary hall so I can demonstrate what happened?'

'Are you happy with that, Father?' Alice asked the prior. He shrugged resignedly.

'Mistress Wescott will be safe with me, Prior Edmund,' Valerian said with a bow.

'I am not convinced she will be,' the prior scowled, 'but if she also goes missing you will be a dead man long before you can choose yourself another fancy outfit.'

Alice led the way to the infirmary hall, where Valerian and

Roger had been treated during their stay. Valerian focused his attention on the doorway.

'There was a loud knock at the door here, as if it were something really important,' he said. 'It woke me up and I saw Constance come out of that door there with a lantern.' He gestured towards the infirmary kitchen. 'I saw her open the hatch.'

He pointed to the little shuttered window in the door. 'I couldn't hear what the men said, but it sounded official because Constance immediately pulled at these bolts and fetched the key for the lock. They pushed open the door as soon as she unlocked it and instantly took hold of her. There were three of them. By this time I knew something wasn't right and I tried to get out of bed, but I felt dizzy and fell to the floor. It was dark, and the only light came from Constance's candle and a lantern one of the men was carrying. She let out a shriek, but they must have quickly placed their hands over her mouth because I heard nothing more from her, and that was when I woke Roger.'

'What did the men look like?'

'It's difficult to say. It was dark and they wore cloaks and hoods. But they were well built, perhaps even trained to fight. They did not strike me as common thieves or ruffians. They appeared organised.'

'Do you think they knew Constance was here?' Alice felt a chill in her stomach.

'They seemed to know what they wanted.'

Alice knew she had to suspect that Valerian was lying. He had had plenty of time to come up with a story to cover up whatever he might have done.

'They had weapons under their cloaks,' continued Valerian. 'Roger put up a strong fight and I suppose they knew they had to put an end to it quickly before anyone was roused. I'm not sure what they hit him with, but I would guess that it was a staff of some kind. He crumpled to the floor.'

'Where did he fall?'

'Somewhere near this doorway, just over on the left there.'

'Where you're standing now?'

'Almost. He was about there.' Valerian pointed to the spot where Roger's body had been discovered.

'And what did you do after they hit him?'

'I backed away. I was frightened I would be next. I felt that if I stayed quiet I would be able to follow them without them knowing I was there.'

'At what time did all this happen?'

'I heard the town bells strike ten shortly after I started following them.'

'And if we walk out of the hospital now, do you think you would remember the route they took?'

'I can try.'


After they had put on their cloaks, Alice and Valerian stepped out into the street, where the mud and snow had mixed into an icy brown slush. Water dripped from crooked rooftops as the snow melted. Brother Ralph stepped out of the door behind them, carrying a leather bag. Jon was with him.

Alice greeted them both. 'This is Valerian,' she said. 'He saw Constance being taken and has agreed to show me where the men took her.'

Jon frowned. 'Is that right?'

Alice smiled awkwardly, annoyed that Jon was being so sceptical.

'Valerian, meet Brother Jon. He has been helping me look for Constance. And this is Brother Ralph.'

'Very pleased to meet you.' Valerian grinned, but the monks remained unsmiling.

'I do not wish to be rude,' said Jon, 'but we must hurry. St Benedict's have a monk with the pox and they have called on Brother Ralph for help.'

Without a goodbye, he and Ralph hurried down the street, the tall, broad monk towering over his smaller, rounder companion.

Alice was disappointed that Jon had shown no inclination to hear what Valerian had to say. She was the only one giving Valerian a chance to explain himself.

'Did you notice the looks on their faces?' asked Valerian. 'Everyone thinks I took Constance.'

'I don't think you took her,' said Alice, pulling up the hood of her cloak. 'Now tell me where the men went.'

'They turned right here and I followed them this way.'

Alice walked with him up Gracechurch Street, which looked different from how Valerian had seen it that night. It was unlikely he would remember the route the men had followed, and Alice had not walked far before Valerian began to forget which turn he had taken next.

'I think it was right into this next passageway... No, not that one. A bit further on... Yes, this one. We went down here and then we turned left, I think.'

They paused by the junction with Cornhill as Valerian tried to recall where he had walked that night. A leper limped past them, a bell hanging from his disfigured hand. Alice felt revulsion and pity as she glanced quickly at his blistered face. She stepped away from him and waited impatiently for Valerian to decide where Constance had been taken.

Valerian finally admitted he had lost track of the journey. 'It was so dark,' he said, 'and I had to hang back so they wouldn't discover me. I remember seeing the spire of St Paul's, so I assumed we were near there, but now I cannot recall the details.'

*Was he telling the truth?* Alice looked into his dark eyes and felt there was something genuine about them. *If he were trying to cover his own tracks, surely he would have come up with a more credible lie?* He simply looked embarrassed that he couldn't remember any more than he had.

'I am very sorry,' he said to Alice, his brow furrowed. 'I tried to do everything I could. I wanted to fight, but I held back when I saw what they did to my friend. Then I tried to follow them, but I lost them and that's when the night watch got hold of me. They refused to believe a word I said. I am fortunate to have the Earl of Wykeham behind me; otherwise I would have been hung for this.'

He took a coin from his purse and dropped it into the leper's begging bowl. Alice admired the gesture.

The prior appeared to be waiting for Alice outside the children's dormitory when she returned. She guessed he was not there to be convivial.

'Was Valerian Baladi any help?' he asked with a sneer.

'Yes, but he was unable to remember where the men took Constance. It was dark and he lost sight of them, which is a great shame. He did his best.'

'You believe him, do you?'

'I feel he is telling the truth, yes.'

The prior dismissed this with a wave of his hand, the rings on his fingers twinkling. 'Whether it is a half-concocted truth or a half-concocted lie, it will not help him prove his innocence. I shall speak to the Earl of Wykeham and make sure he sees sense. The man needs to be locked up. And there is to be no more of this, do you hear?'

'No more of what?'

'This wandering about trying to find Constance. The matter is in the hands of the bailiff now; it should no longer concern you. You must stay here and do your job.'

The prior's small, pale eyes fixed hers and he lowered his voice. 'I must say that it is unfortunate you no longer have a husband to keep you under control. He would not let you walk the streets of London with other men. In his absence, I must assume responsibility and I have allowed you enough time to search for your friend. What we must do now is keep Constance in our prayers.'

Alice gritted her teeth. 'Prayers alone do not work, Father. I believe scripture says faith by itself, if it is not accompanied by action, is dead.'

The prior drew nearer to her, his breath a sickly mix of wine and honey. 'There is no need to exhibit your intelligence by quoting the words of the book of James at me. Let me tell you that the prayers of doubters are not answered. And that doubting God's power makes you a sinner. You have worked in a house of God for two years and have resisted taking the vows even of a lay sister. That suggests a predisposition to sin. There must be some work of the devil within you.' He curled his lip.

Alice stared back at him, trying not to blink. 'I work here for the sake of the children, Father.'

'Yes, for the children.' He backed away slightly. 'That is the only reason I allow you to stay. No one else under this roof has the affection for them you do. And the foundlings love you as if you were their own poor, unfortunate mother.'

The prior wagged a jewelled finger in her face. 'But if I hear you speak any of these doubting words of the devil to those young ones you will leave this place immediately and never return. And if you continue to distract yourself from your work with this vain search for your foundling friend, I shall ensure that you *never* see those children again.'

# Chapter Nine

T he sound of pipes, drums and celebration rose
from the colourful band of pilgrims on the frozen,
windswept road. Winchester Cathedral was within
sight and this meant their journey was almost over. Behind
them walked a young woman, the gap between her and them
ever-growing as she struggled to find her footing on the
uneven road. Her shoes were held together with strips of
muddy linen and she was grateful to the cold for numbing her
feet so the sores that covered them gave her less pain. Her
cloak and dress were wet and muddy. She was struggling to
walk any further; her knees buckling with fatigue and her
head spiking with fever.

As the pilgrims cheered and sang, Elizabeth stopped and
sank to the ground by the foot of a tree. She had hoped to
reach Winchester to benefit from the safety and warmth of
the shelter it offered, but it seemed unlikely now. The
cacophony of pilgrims' voices died away and two horsemen
passed, flashing her a cursory glance.

If she had been able to speak she would have asked them
to help her, but the life within her was fading fast. She had

fought for too long; her mind and body had given up. Perspiration made her cloak itchy against her chest. She pulled it away from her body and allowed the chill wind to hit her skin. All she could manage was sleep. She could feel herself gently drifting away.

After climbing out of the river and running from her captors five days previously, Elizabeth had found shelter in a warehouse next to the Thames. Shaking uncontrollably from the cold, she had pulled off her sodden dress and wrapped herself in the sacking cloth used to store grain. Thankfully, no one had discovered Elizabeth in the warehouse; nor had she been spotted the following day stealing clothes that had been hung out to dry in a narrow lane of houses near London Stone.

Elizabeth had had no doubt that she would have to run away. The risk of being found by the men who had taken her was high, and this time they would certainly kill her. She couldn't rest until London was far behind her, but before she left she had needed money. There was only one way a homeless woman could earn money, and Elizabeth had heard from her brothers about the warren of streets near the river and the reputation of the women found there. Nervously, she had walked these streets, hiding from voices and shadows as she prepared to separate her mind from her body again.

As twilight fell, she had reached a street in which the buildings were crammed together and the smell of burning rose from the blackened aftermath of fire. She had hidden in the ruins as a woman staggered past her. Then she had heard a man's voice and her attention was drawn to the dim outline of two figures. A man and woman were discussing a price and Elizabeth had listened carefully so she could negotiate with a customer of her own.

It hadn't been long before a swaying figure stumbled

towards her, singing to himself. Elizabeth had moved out into the middle of the street and lifted her skirts.

'In need of some company?' she had asked, affecting a brash, confident voice despite her terror.

The dark figure had given a guttural murmur of glee and lurched towards her. His hand had grabbed the back of her naked thigh and he had pushed himself against her, chuckling happily. He stank of wine, but she could tell that his cloak was made from good-quality wool. She had deduced that he was a man of reasonable status, hopefully with some money on his person. His odour and the feel of his hand on her leg had been sickeningly familiar. She had desperately fought the urge to pull away. It was clear what he wanted; Elizabeth had simply prayed that he wouldn't harm her.

'It'll be twopence,' she had ordered.

She had felt a swell of relief as he let go of her to fumble with a leather purse at his belt, cursing as he tried to untie it with his drunken fingers. Keeping her skirts lifted, Elizabeth had assessed his size and build in the murkiness. Although stronger and slightly taller than her, he was inhibited by drink. She had decided there was no need to suffer; that she could manage this situation an easier way.

'Would you like me to help you, Sir?'

He had swayed against her and mumbled something about the money. He had removed the purse from his belt and at this point Elizabeth saw her opportunity. As he held the leather purse in his hands, she swiftly kicked him in the shin. He yelped and she snatched the purse from his hands, running as fast as she could up the dark street.

'Stop her! That whore took my money!' he had yelled.

Elizabeth had prayed no one would help him. She passed a couple of shadowy figures and then heard a boy's voice.

'Get her!'

A group had gathered, and from the look of them she

deduced they were more interested in taking the money for themselves than in wanting to stop a thief. A surge of energy had found its way to her legs and she ran faster, her feet sliding in the mud. The gang of boys would have happily cut her throat for the money. To them she was a cheap whore no one would miss.

She could hear the thud of feet behind her, but she ran on, half-blind, in the dark. Up ahead was a dim light, which she had run towards. *Was it a building or a person with a lantern?* she asked herself. As she got closer she was reassured to see a cloak, staff and hat illuminated in the dim glow. It was a man from the watch.

'They're after me!' she had panted.

Elizabeth had caught a glimpse of his dark eyes under the brim of his hat. He glanced at her with distaste and then looked past her at the gang giving chase. Thankfully, he had stepped to one side and let her pass, ready to tackle the street gang. Elizabeth had kept running as she heard a grunt and a yell behind her, but she didn't look back. The alleyway had led to a wider, more respectable, street. Out of breath, she had slowed to a walk and listened to the silence around her. All she heard was a shop sign squeaking on its hinges.

It wasn't safe on the streets and the long winter night meant it would be many hours before the sun rose again. Elizabeth had walked along the road in the shadows, hoping to find shelter. Eventually, the smell of fresh horse manure had led her to the warmth of a stable. Once inside, she placed her fingers inside the purse to determine the value of her stolen coins.

The money bought her a new dress, cloak and pair of shoes the following day, and she had enough money left over for food and accommodation for the journey she was planning. Fortunately, she had chosen a rich man the previous night.

Elizabeth had decided on Winchester because that was where the pilgrims were going. She had first encountered them at an inn near Merton Priory and had overheard a conversation about their pilgrimage to the shrine of St Swithun at Winchester Cathedral. Their laughter, stories and songs provided welcome relief from the grim life she had led for so long. Guiding the group was a minstrel dressed in red and green, who wore a hat covered in badges from the many pilgrimages he had undertaken. He constantly sang, sipped ale from a leather flagon, played his lute and irritated his companions, but Elizabeth found his liveliness refreshing. She felt it was wise to stay close to the pilgrims on her journey because it was dangerous to travel alone.

The minstrel asked Elizabeth to join their pilgrimage every day of the journey, but she declined time and time again. She was wary of becoming too close to anyone in case she accidentally revealed who she was. Instead, she called herself Gwendolyn and explained that she was travelling to stay with an aunt in Winchester.

Having lived in London all her life, this broad expanse of countryside was a new experience for Elizabeth. She enjoyed the peace and space around her, but the scarcity of buildings worried her. There were inns and villages along the road, but between these lay tracts of lonely open space and woodland, which provided convenient hiding places for thieves.

Elizabeth felt nervous. *She might have escaped the men in London, but was there new danger out here?* She had never walked great distances before and her feet soon became sore. Each evening she bathed them and wrapped them up in the bandages an innkeeper's wife had given her, but the blisters remained inflamed.

The inns along the way varied in quality and she never felt

completely safe. Some of the men who stayed at the inns reminded her of the men from whom she had run: loud, arrogant and often drunk. The smell of sweat and stale ale left her nauseous and trembling; her mind associating these odours with the terrible events she had recently endured.

Sleep came only when her mind was exhausted and burnt out, and even when she slept she awoke convinced that something was pressing down on her chest. Gasping for air made the sensation worse, sending a flood of paralysing panic through her limbs. A cold sweat broke out on her face and a sense of dread churned in her bowels. When she recovered from these attacks she would lie awake in the dark listening to the breathing of her fellow travellers, convinced she was the only person awake in the world.

Some nights brought with them the urge to throw herself from a window or the gallery of an inn; it felt like the only way to stop the anguish. She wanted to scream out the anger that blazed insider her: anger at the men who had taken everything from her; the men who had killed the girl and thrown her into the river. *Where was God's justice? Why were they allowed to abuse and degrade without punishment?*

The light that came with morning made Elizabeth feel she could start afresh each day. She still had some strength within her to find refuge; a place where she would feel safe and could shut out the sadness and the shame.

The pilgrims were frustratingly slow in their progress, stopping often to eat, drink and sing. Sometimes Elizabeth went up ahead on the road. She wanted to travel faster than them, but she needed someone nearby in case she was attacked again.

She began to feel unwell on the fourth day and found herself struggling to keep up with the pilgrims. The cold was slowing her down and she stumbled over rocks and puddles in the road. Her mind became muddled, and she struggled to remember when she had last eaten or how long she had been walking. Aware that she wasn't thinking clearly, Elizabeth blamed tiredness to begin with, but as a cough developed she realised she was falling ill.

She was no better after a night at another inn and the following morning she decided she would ask the pilgrims for help. But she was too late. Excited by the prospect of it being the last day of their journey, they had marched on ahead and she could no longer keep up. Her body was stiff and aching, and she felt hot and drowsy. Having refused the pilgrims' help for several days, Elizabeth realised too late that she needed them.

For days she had done her best to keep going. She had escaped her prison and survived a strangling attempt. She had stolen clothes and money, endured the cold and walked until her feet bled. As she stopped at the side of the road just outside Winchester she thought about her family, who she hadn't seen for so long. They would always wonder what had happened to her. If only she could have had the chance to explain it to them.

Perhaps she could explain it to her mother as, eight years after her death, they were soon likely to be reunited.

Elizabeth closed her eyes and slept.

# Chapter Ten

She woke to an overpowering smell, which scalded the inside of her nose and forehead. It was pungent and medicinal, and smelt reassuringly clean. Elizabeth opened her eyes and saw an elderly woman leaning over her, wiping her face with a cloth. A dark hood covered the woman's head, and her eyes and lips were almost lost in the heavy lines of her face. Elizabeth could taste the smell now; it was bitter and she wanted to spit it out. She realised her body was warm and there was no longer any pain. She hadn't felt so comfortable in months. She tried to sit up but the woman nudged her head back onto the pillow again. She seemed to be muttering or chanting words that Elizabeth didn't recognise.

Elizabeth closed her eyes again. She didn't know what was happening but it felt like a good thing.

She felt safe.

When she woke again, the old lady was holding out a bowl of greenish brown liquid, urging her to sit up and drink. It tasted disgusting but she drank it because she believed it would help her. *Who was this woman in whom she was placing so much trust?*

Elizabeth was finally conscious enough to take in her surroundings. She lay on a straw mattress on the floor of a one-roomed home. She still wore the dress she had travelled in, but her feet had been re-bandaged and two blankets were keeping her warm: one woollen and the other sheepskin. In the centre of the room was a fire, its grate set into a hole in the earth floor. The only ventilation was a narrow flue at the top of the timbered ceiling, and occasional billows of smoke stung Elizabeth's eyes.

The floor was strewn with rushes, and bunches of dried herbs hung from the rafters. Amulets on long chains and pieces of parchment adorned with elegant writing were strung from the ceiling. On the walls hung shelves cluttered with pottery jars, copper bowls, small wooden caskets and all manner of trinkets, which glinted and shone in the firelight. There were highly polished stones and shells, glass beads, old coins, brooches and simple crosses fashioned from gold or bronze.

Elizabeth could see the skull of a small animal. She guessed from its teeth and the roundness of its skull that it had been a cat, and on the shelf next to it was a pile of small white bones. There were rows of little bottles, some made of glass and others of a dull metallic colour, possibly lead. She felt she was surrounded by a lifetime of someone's gathering and collecting.

'How yer feeling?' asked the woman.

'I feel better than I did, thank you. How did I get here?' It was the first time she had spoken in a while and her voice croaked.

She cleared her throat and continued. 'I was on the road and my feet were so sore. I think I had a fever.' Elizabeth tried to recall her most recent memory, but it was hazy. 'I'm well enough to travel again now. Thank you for looking after me. Can I ask your name?'

'Millicent,' replied the lady. 'My daughter was the one who found you on the road. Almost dead, you were. She brought you 'ere. She don't 'ave the time to look after you, she got nine bairns to take care of.'

'It was very kind of her to help me, she has saved my life. And so have you, it seems. I don't know what you made me drink, but it has helped. I am very grateful to both of you. I have some coins somewhere.'

Elizabeth scrabbled about with the purse in her belt. 'I will pay both of you well and then be on my way.' She was grateful to have met such kind people. If Millicent's daughter hadn't found her, robbers might have done. It was unlikely she would have remained alive.

The old lady held up a crooked hand to stop her. 'No you won't. I don't take payment, I never does. And you ain't going nowhere; you ain't better yet.'

'But I feel better.'

'No you ain't. Now lie down again.'

Elizabeth sighed and did as she was told. 'How long have I been here?'

'Three nights and three days.' The old woman got to her feet, picked up a scruffy broom and started sweeping up the rushes. She moved quickly for someone so old and bent.

'That long?'

'You almost died, remember? It takes a long time to get better when you've been almost dead.'

It was frustrating, but Elizabeth knew she would have to do what Millicent said while she was under her roof. Perhaps the following day she would be able to leave and continue her journey.

'You ain't told me yer name yet,' said Millicent, as if Elizabeth had been rude to omit the information.

'Gwendolyn.'

'And where yer travelling to, Gwendolyn?'

'Winchester, to see my aunt.'

'You ain't very well organised to be travelling. What you got with you? A cloak, some feeble shoes and a purse. You should've 'ad food and drink with you, and other people to travel along with. And an 'orse. From the way you speak I'd say you was highborn enough to have a carriage all of yer own.'

Millicent gathered up the rushes she had swept from the floor, opened a small, rickety door and put them outside. She collected fresh rushes from a basket in the corner of the room. 'You ain't a runaway, are yer?'

'No.'

'Because everything about you suggests you's a runaway.' Millicent started scattering the fresh rushes on the floor.

Elizabeth couldn't tell Millicent the truth. She knew people often found themselves in trouble with the authorities for harbouring runaways. Everyone belonged somewhere and women were the property of their fathers when they were single and their husbands after they were married.

'I left in a hurry. Something happened, but I cannot say what because...' Elizabeth's voice trailed off and Millicent paused from her work to turn and watch her. The silence felt awkward. 'Because it is too upsetting.'

'Your aunt's expecting yer, is she?'

Elizabeth nodded. She hated lying, but she suspected Millicent doubted her story in any case. She decided she would keep up the lie for the next day or two and then give the old lady as many coins as she could spare and leave for Winchester.

# Chapter Eleven

❧❧❧

I t was a short stumble from The Swan to Heward Lovell's front door. He drank at the tavern every evening, and whenever he had coins left over he took a lady home with him. Tonight he had money for company and, as he staggered through the door with his lantern and a girl, he was too preoccupied with his giggling companion to notice the two men waiting for him in the dark. They hit him over the head before he had time to react, and as he slumped to the floor the woman was ordered to leave without making a sound.

Both men wore dark tunics. They had pulled down their hoods but Heward could see that one was bald and hatchet-faced with wide shoulders, while the other was small and wiry with narrow eyes and puckered skin on one cheek.

This second man picked up the lantern and held it in Heward's face. 'Tell us what 'appened to the girls.'

Heward looked up at them with a bewildered expression on his face. 'What girls?'

The men hauled him to his feet and threw him against a table, sending bowls and candlesticks clattering to the floor.

Heward's hands and feet were shackled together with chains. He was hauled onto the table and the large, bald man held a knife to his throat.

'Tell us what 'appened to the *girls*,' repeated the small man.

'I don't know what you mean.'

The small man walked to the end of the table and started to unlace the boot on Heward's left foot.

'Get off!' he shouted, kicking out.

The bald man pressed the knife blade against his throat and he stopped kicking.

'You know I don't need to go explaining who the girls are,' said the small man, who was holding up a stubby knife that glinted in the light of the lantern. 'Care to tell me more now?'

Heward glanced down nervously at his foot, unable to move his head with the knife at his throat.

'Let me get off this table and I'll tell you.'

'It don't work like that,' grinned the bald man, displaying a few rotten pegs for teeth.

The small man removed Heward's boot and placed the blade of his knife beneath the nail of his little toe.

'Care to tell us now?'

'We took them down to the river,' spluttered Heward.

The bald man nodded to encourage Heward to say more, but Heward remained silent. The small man pushed his blade under the toenail and Heward screamed in pain.

'Quiet,' said the small man, 'you'll wake yer neighbours. And we don't want none of them round here poking their noses in, else we'll have to kill both you and them, won't we? Now, tell me, were the girls dead or alive when you took 'em down to the river?'

'Dead.'

'And how did they die?'

'Well, one of them was fighting too much and we had to

calm her down. I had hold of her and she bit me, so I put my hands round her neck. I kept my hands there too long. It was never my intention to kill her, it was an accident. We took her down to the river and threw her in.'

'And the other one?'

'We had to get rid of her because she'd seen me strangle her friend and would have told everyone what had happened otherwise. So I did the same thing to her and she fell down quickly.'

'Did you weigh their bodies down with rocks so they wouldn't be discovered?'

'Yes.'

'Liar!' The blade was pushed under another toenail.

Heward let out an unearthly scream as blood trickled down his foot and dripped onto the floor.

'I once tortured a man by forcing him to eat his own toes,' said the small man. 'Now let's see if you can tell us the truth this time and you might be spared.'

'No, we didn't weigh them down with rocks,' said Heward through gritted teeth.

'Anything else you wanna tell us?'

'No.'

There was another push from the blade, which lingered a little longer this time. Heward screamed again and his body bucked with the pain.

'Let's try again. I know when you ain't telling the truth. One more lie and you die.'

There was a long pause as Heward lay on the table, trembling. The knife remained at his throat and both men stared at him, waiting.

'She got out.'

'Who did?'

'One of the girls. She got out of the river.'

'So she weren't dead?'

'No. We thought she was. She climbed out of the river and ran off.'

'And you caught 'er?'

'No. She got away.'

'Thank you, Heward Lovell.'

The small man nodded at the bald man. In one swift movement, Heward's throat was cut. His head slumped to one side as his blood flowed onto the table.

# Chapter Twelve

❦

'Sir, these streets are the filthiest in the city. I do not think it wise to visit this family.'

Sir Walter did not welcome advice from others. He glared at his assistant, Theobald FitzAlan, a lean man with hair the colour of a fox and a forked ginger beard.

'Nonsense, I will not hear of it. They need my help.' He marched on ahead of Theobald, sidestepping the worst of the sewage in the alleyway and ducking his head to avoid the laundry that had been strung out to dry.

'These clothes will be dirtier now than before they were washed,' snickered Theobald.

Sir Walter strode on, proud to be helping in whichever way he could. People ducked out of his way and stopped to doff their hats as he passed. He greeted everyone he came across, aware that his flamboyant clothing made him an unusual spectacle in this part of London. His jacket was brocaded with gold, but only its sleeves were visible beneath his squirrel fur tabard. Over this he wore a bright blue velvet cloak. A curtain of red fabric swung down one side of his hat, looped under his chin and was pinned to the other side with a gem-studded brooch.

Few members of the nobility visited this part of London, but Sir Walter made an effort to support the local people. He had visited them during the plague, his men bringing food, ale and blankets to those who were suffering. Despite spending time in the diseased streets, Sir Walter had never fallen ill himself. Seeing as he seemed destined to be untouched by the disease, he felt it was his duty to help people less fortunate than himself.

The miserable homes around him were single-storey wooden shacks, their walls rotten and slimy with damp. He stopped at the house they were visiting and laughed at Theobald, who was holding a silver pomander under his nose. Everything around them stank, but Sir Walter did not require the clean smell of herbs and spices; he had endured the horrors of battle without such frivolous items.

The family was expecting him. A woman in a grey tunic stepped out from a doorway, which was covered with a dirty rag in place of a door. She curtseyed as soon as she saw Sir Walter and held her hands together in prayer.

'Sir Walter! We are blessed! Thank you for comin' to see us again.'

'How is he?'

'Very bad, Sir.'

Sir Walter stepped into the house and was met with the unmistakeable stench of death. He recoiled slightly, but recovered himself sufficiently to crouch next to the man who was lying on a dirty blanket laid over a bed of straw. The man was the woman's husband and father to the many children Sir Walter could see watching him as his eyes adjusted to the gloom. The man had no weight on him and his bones protruded through his yellow, waxy skin, his face reduced almost to a skull.

Sir Walter called to Theobald, who was waiting outside in the street. Theobald brought in a bag containing blankets and food, gagging at the stench in the room. Sir Walter dismissed him again and spoke softly to the man, reassuring him that his wife and daughters would be well looked after once he was gone.

After spending ten minutes with the man, Sir Walter stepped back into the street where Theobald was waiting. The man's wife followed him out.

'Your husband's health is much deteriorated, I see,' said Sir Walter.

The poor woman nodded, her face creased with worry.

'I am sorry my physician could not help him. I will ask Father Adam to come and visit him as soon as he is able.'

'Thank you, Sir Walter.'

'The young woman inside, is she one of your daughters?'

'My eldest? That's Cecily. She's quite a woman now,' she said proudly.

'Please could you ask her to step outside and talk to me? I have a large household, as you know, and I need more staff.'

'You would think to employ my Cecily, Sir Walter?' The woman gasped and a smile broke out across her face.

'I need to speak with her first.'

'Of course, Sir Walter, of course. I shall fetch 'er at once.'

The girl was prettier when she stepped out into the daylight than he had first thought. She had taken care to plait her red hair neatly, although she wore a shabby tunic. She smiled meekly at Sir Walter as he took a step back to admire her.

'My, my. So you are Cecily.' He stroked his beard, guessing that she was about thirteen. 'A budding flower indeed.' He was pleased to see that she returned his smile.

'You must be cold in that thin tunic. Why not try my cloak on for size?'

He pulled off his blue velvet cloak and rested it around her shoulders, causing her to stagger slightly under the weight of it. 'Now that's better. You look quite the noblewoman now. Would you not agree, Theobald?'

'Indeed, Sir Walter.'

'I'm worried it's gettin' muddy, Sir.' Cecily looked down at the hem of the cloak, which was trailing in a filthy puddle.

Sir Walter laughed. 'There is no need for you to worry yourself on that account. Let me help you adjust it a little.'

He put his hands on her shoulders and pulled the cloak around her firmly before running his hands across her chest, feeling the softness of her breasts through her thin tunic. He heard her gasp and sensed her freeze as he ran his hands over the lower parts of her body, groping at what he could through the rough material of her clothing.

He enjoyed the moment when a girl became aware of what he was doing but was too terrified to object. He leant into her and sniffed her neck, listening to her short, shallow breath in his ear. She was as still as a statue and he could hear her family moving around inside their filthy home, just an arm's length from where he and Cecily stood. He grinned with satisfaction, nipped at her ear lobe with his teeth and then removed the cloak from her shoulders.

'There. Tell your mother I will contact her again shortly about a position of employment in my household.'

The girl nodded, biting her bottom lip. Her face was red and her eyes were watery. He liked this change in her; the power he had over her was more arousing than the girl herself.

'And God bless your father.'

He put his cloak back on.

'It is time for us to leave, Theobald. I'm having dinner with Yvette de Beauchamp and the woman is fiercer than a scalded cat when I'm late.'

Alice felt uncomfortable in her dress. She looked down at her bosom and remembered how she had filled the gown out when her husband had been alive. Now it hung from her shoulders and sagged around her chest, even though Griselda had laced the back as tightly as she could. The fabric was a beautiful emerald green, which shimmered in the candlelight, and Yvette de Beauchamp had embroidered the low neckline and hems of the sleeves with gold.

Alice fastened a gold chain belt across her hips, twisted her hair into two plaits, and rolled and pinned them to either side of her head. A jewelled headband kept her light silk veil and wimple in place. She wasn't used to dressing like this any more.

As she stroked the smooth fabric of her dress, she was reminded of the drunken, rowdy dinners her husband had hosted for his fellow merchants and guild members in the hall downstairs. During this time Alice and Thomas had been close friends with Simon and Yvette de Beauchamp. They had been happy days, when the business was thriving and there was always a social gathering to attend.

Both Alice and Yvette had been widowed during the plague and these days their friendship was reduced to the occasional dinner invitation. Alice didn't enjoy these events and on this occasion she had no interest in going at all. Her mind was still spinning in the aftermath of Constance's disappearance and she did not feel like socialising. But she knew Yvette would be offended if she did not attend, so she had reluctantly made the effort.

The hall of Yvette de Beauchamp's home was ablaze with candles. They hung on wall brackets and in elegantly wrought iron candlesticks along the length of the dining table. Alice counted sixteen candles in the chandelier that hung above her. The wall hangings were deep red in colour and were embroidered with blue cockerels and golden parrots. On the table, bowls were filled with plaice, eels, herring, venison, rabbit and goose served in sauces fragrant with spices, onions and herbs. Large pies with thick golden pastry crusts were decorated with cherries and bay leaves.

Yvette sat at the centre of the table, her voice already loud as a result of the Burgundy wine. She had finely plucked eyebrows and a receding chin, and she wore a low-cut dress of patterned white and gold. Her neck, fingers and hair glittered with jewellery, and a small white dog sat on her lap.

Alice's mind was elsewhere. It had almost been a week since Constance had vanished and as each day passed Alice could feel her friend slipping away from her. Constance's smile was fading in her mind with the progression of time and Alice had to screw her eyes shut and force herself to picture what she looked like. Sometimes she could remember every detail of her face, but at other times it became a blur. Alice was forgetting the sound of Constance's voice and struggling to recall how her laugh had sounded. She wanted Constance back with a desperation that made her entire body ache, and this evening she had to ignore it in order to sit calmly at Yvette's dinner table and make polite conversation.

'Our final guest is here!' sang Yvette in a high, excitable voice. 'Sir Walter Rokeby!'

A tall, broad man of about sixty walked into the room, sharing a joke with one of Yvette's servants. He had a square face, wavy grey hair, a neat grey beard and piercing blue eyes that creased with smile lines at their corners. He wore a damask red jacket fastened with tiny gold buttons and a gold hat draped with fur.

'The beautiful Mrs de Beauchamp!' he said as he removed

his hat and greeted Yvette warmly. She gestured for him to sit at her side.

'I am sorry I'm late,' he announced to the guests. His voice was resonant and as smooth as honey. 'I have just been visiting a poor man on his death bed.'

There was a sad, collective sigh from around the table, which he acknowledged with a solemn nod. 'Thank you for your sympathy. And as we dine here tonight in splendour, we must remember in our prayers the poverty-stricken and the sick.'

'Noble words, Sir Walter,' said Yvette, backed up by a hum of similar mutterings from the other guests.

Sir Walter's chalice was filled with wine and plates of steaming food were brought to him. Alice watched as he tucked into a joint of lamb, chuckling between mouthfuls at something Yvette was saying, the grease shining on his thick, wide lips. Sir Walter was well known and Alice recognised him from his visit to St Hugh's the previous week. He was renowned as a benevolent and generous man who had fought many battles in Scotland and France. Alice had heard it said that he had been a brave knight, risking his life to defend others and treating the enemy with the perfect balance of contempt and respect. His wife had died many years earlier and Alice had heard that he had been so devoted to her he would never consider loving another.

He lived at Chilham Palace, a home awarded him by the king for services to the nation. His fighting days were over and these days he spent his time helping those who were sick and in need. When the plague had been at its worst, he had visited many of the afflicted's homes and had never caught a cough or sneeze himself. People said his resistance to sickness was a blessing from God in return for his kindness and generosity. He had even bought several acres of land, which he had consecrated as a burying ground for those who died in the plague. Alice's husband and son were interred there.

Alice recalled his recent visit to St Hugh's and how he had paraded around the infirmary halls in his extravagant blue coat and velvet hat. She had found him pompous, but the patients had been overjoyed by his visit and the prior was always happy when Sir Walter visited because he was in the habit of making generous financial donations.

The rich food in front of Alice looked unappetising, and she struggled to chew and swallow it. She wanted to escape from the warm room and the overpowering scent of sandalwood and rose. It took considerable effort to remain calm and smiling in her seat as Yvette addressed her.

'That is a fine gown you're wearing this evening, Alice. I remember it well and I hope you told my guests who did the embroidery work on the neckline,' she said.

'I recognise that as your very own handiwork, Yvette,' replied Sir Walter. He chewed on a piece of meat and looked at Alice thoughtfully, appearing to recognise her from St Hugh's. Alice shifted uncomfortably as all eyes in the room were trained on her chest. 'Most exquisite,' added Sir Walter, raising his chalice in appreciation and then taking a large gulp from it.

'Thank you, Sir Walter,' replied Yvette. 'I love seeing Alice in a beautiful dress. She spends so much of her time in a habit, which does nothing to flatter her figure. Did you know she is a nun?'

There was a murmur of surprise around the table.

'I'm not really a nun,' Alice said, forcing a smile to hide her anger at the provocation. 'I work at a hospital as a nurse.'

'Nurses are usually nuns,' said a round-faced man with pitted skin.

'Yes, they are. And I help them.'

'And you may yet become a bride of Christ?' asked the man.

'No.'

'Which hospital do you work at?' asked a lady in an extravagantly beaded hat with a long veil.

'St Hugh's,' replied Alice.

'Ah! That is where I have seen you before,' said Sir Walter with an exuberant slap on the table. 'I knew I recognised you. I was there only last week.'

'I remember,' said Alice.

His gaze lingered a few seconds too long, making Alice feel increasingly uncomfortable.

'Prior Edmund is a good friend of mine,' Sir Walter explained, raising his drink to his lips once again.

'A place suffering from scandal,' interjected Yvette. 'A young foundling has run off with a stranger who entered the hospital under the pretence of being attacked. And he has murdered his friend in the process!'

'So I heard,' said Sir Walter, prodding the eel on his plate with a knife.

'She was taken,' said Alice. She felt Sir Walter's eyes resting on her again.

Yvette laughed, as if to shake off some embarrassment. 'I know she was a good friend of yours, Alice, and it is difficult to imagine the young thing planning to elope, but she was clearly seduced. That's what the prior has said.'

'The man they believe took her denies it,' Alice replied loudly so everyone could hear. She was reluctant to publicly disagree with her friend, but she felt Constance needed to be defended.

'Of course he would deny it,' muttered Sir Walter. 'Ooh, is that goose?' he asked a servant who was approaching him with yet another plate of food.

'He says some men took her and that he tried to stop them.'

There was laughter around the table, but Alice ignored it and continued. 'He works for the Earl of Wykeham, who has requested a stay of execution until his guilt or innocence has been determined.'

'The Earl of Wykeham?' asked Sir Walter. 'He is also a good friend of mine. What is the name of this man you speak of?'

Alice paused, unsure whether to speak his name or not. She concluded that there could be little harm in divulging it. 'Valerian Baladi.'

'Interesting name,' said Sir Walter.

'He sounds like a criminal just based on his name!' laughed Yvette, feeding the dog on her lap a piece of bread.

'And if it was not this Valerian who took the girl, what do you suppose happened to her?' asked the man with the round face.

'I think she was taken by the men as he says,' replied Alice.

'I heard of another girl running off recently,' said the lady with the beaded hat. 'Her father is a taverner near St Clement Danes. It is thought she ran off with one of the customers.'

'Or perhaps she was also taken by someone,' suggested Alice. She was annoyed by the assumption that all missing girls ran off voluntarily.

'She could have been taken, I suppose,' said the woman in the beaded hat. 'She was last seen helping her mother and father serve the food. It was a busy day in the tavern, and when they searched for her she had vanished.'

'Alas, these things happen so often in a large city,' said Sir Walter. 'They are a sad symptom of these modern times. Often when a girl goes missing it is because she has got herself into trouble and has to escape in order to avoid bringing shame upon her family.'

The venison and its rich sauce sat heavily at the back of Alice's throat. She sipped some wine in an attempt to wash it away, but it merely made the sensation worse. She thought about Jon's sister, Constance and the girl who had been pulled from the river. *Could she be the girl who had disappeared from the tavern, or was she yet another girl?*

Yvette clapped her hands, distracting Alice from her thoughts. 'And now is the time for music!' She flung her hand in the direction of three minstrels, who started to play.

Alice tried to eat more, anxiously aware that Sir Walter was watching her.

# Chapter Thirteen

'Her name is Juliana and she is a taverner's daughter,' whispered Jon.

He and Alice stood by the tree he had chopped down first thing that morning. Gusts of wind from the night before had uprooted it and left it leaning precariously over the vegetable borders. Jon had cut it down before it fell and was planning to chop it up for firewood.

He had deliberately caught Alice's attention as she watched him from the window and she had come outside so he could tell her about his visit to the coroner. As Jon whispered, Alice kept an eye out for anyone who might see them together, the prior's threat fresh in her mind.

'I knew it!' she whispered in reply. She was impressed Jon had managed to uncover this information. 'I'm sure this is the girl they were talking about at Yvette's dinner last night. Has her body been returned to her family?'

'Yes, the coroner told me they held her funeral yesterday.'

Alice swallowed a lump in her throat as she thought about the grief Juliana's family must be suffering. 'Did you tell him she was wearing your sister's rosary beads?'

'I did. I think he was more interested in reuniting her with her family than listening to me. They had reported her missing and were invited in to see her as we did.'

Alice felt choked again. She knew what it was like to see a child dead, but the knowledge that the child had suffered at someone else's hands was unimaginable.

'Do you know who her parents are?'

'The coroner gave me their address so I could speak to them about the rosary beads. They run The Swan on The Strand. I would like to find out if their daughter knew Elizabeth. Stand back.'

Jon brought his axe down on a large branch, separating it from the tree. Alice admired his strength.

'What is the coroner planning to do to find out who murdered the girl?'

Jon shrugged his shoulders. 'There is not a lot more he can do. He has spoken to the waterman and his passenger, who found her in the water, and is satisfied they had nothing to do with her death. But they have no idea where she was put into the river. She could have floated far upstream or downstream from where she was thrown in. He is certain she was strangled.'

Jon swung his axe at another branch, severing it cleanly from the tree trunk with a loud crack. He paused to wipe his brow. 'I find it hard to hold out any hope for Elizabeth. If one girl was murdered and thrown into the river, it is most likely they have done the same with my sister.'

'They might not have.'

'I cannot understand why she was wearing the rosary beads.'

'Neither can I.'

'And I might have caused more trouble by mentioning the fact to the coroner.'

'What do you mean?'

'By telling him my sister's rosary beads were around Juliana's neck, I could have implicated Elizabeth in the murder.'

'Your sister would never have done such a thing!'

'Obviously not, I know that. But my sister is someone Juliana can be linked with, so if you were the coroner and were trying to establish who a person of interest might be, what would that tell you?'

'If you put it that way, you can see why the coroner might be suspicious. But your sister would never have harmed anyone like that. And no one has seen her since last summer.' Alice was trying hard to reassure Jon, but she could not provide any answers. Elizabeth's disappearance was a mystery.

'Perhaps she joined a gang of bandits and has been murdering people ever since.'

'Oh, Jon. You know that can't possibly be true. I think the person who took your sister is the same person who took Juliana. We need to speak to her parents and find out how long Juliana had been missing. Perhaps she was at the same marketplace as your sister when she vanished. Sadly, I am going to be hindered in my search for the girls.'

'Why?'

'Prior Edmund told me that if I continue to be distracted from my work he will ensure that I never see the children again.'

'He said *that*?' Jon scowled and took a swipe at a small branch with his axe.

'I can only presume he thinks the authorities will find Constance and that there is no need for me to do anything further. But we can't leave it to them, can we?'

Jon shook his head.

'We know they have no interest in searching for missing girls,' Alice continued. 'They are happy to show how powerful they are by hanging someone who might be responsible, but actually searching for someone? They have other things to do.'

'So you are no longer able to help me find the girls?' asked Jon.

'Of course I'll help, but I will have to do it secretly.'

'You must be careful.' Jon's brow furrowed and he looked past her as if something had caught his eye. 'Someone has seen us. Who is it?'

A figure in a red cloak walked through the garden towards them.

'No need to hide. It is not the prior, just your friend Valerian,' said Jon.

'My friend? He is *not* my friend!' hissed Alice.

Valerian greeted them both.

'You are a free man, I hear,' said Jon.

'For the time being,' replied Valerian with a shrug, 'but I am still a condemned man unless I can prove that someone else took Constance. I tried to show Alice where the men took her, but I lost my way that night. I am sorry I was not able to be of much help.'

Valerian looked at her sorrowfully with his large, dark eyes and Alice wondered why he had come back to St Hugh's if there was little else he could do to help.

Jon snorted in reply. Without warning, he swung the axe high over his head and chopped a large branch in two. Valerian leapt out of the way.

Alice did not like the change in Jon's mood when Valerian was present; he became uncharacteristically curt and ungracious.

Valerian also appeared to find Jon's manner rude. 'Why did you choose life in a monastery, Brother Jon?' he asked.

'It was my parents' choice.'

Jon began chopping the branch into smaller pieces.

'That is unfortunate. Will you ever be able to leave?'

'No, I have made my vows. Why would I want to leave?'

'Do you never wonder what you might be missing?'

Jon stopped his work and faced Valerian, standing significantly taller than the visitor. 'I come from a family that fights. I know what life is like out there.'

'Are you the only one who became a monk?'

'I am fulfilling a duty my family has to God.'

'Your family is full to the brim with knights and you have to be a monk? That is bad luck, Jon.'

Valerian winked at Alice and chuckled. She returned his smile but her shoulders were heavy. Valerian was not helping himself by antagonising Jon.

'It is a worthier existence than yours,' retorted Jon. 'I would rather be a monk than an earl's errand boy. What status does your family have? Very little, I am sure.'

'He was only joking with you, Jon,' said Alice, keen to diffuse the situation.

'And why are you defending him again?' demanded Jon angrily. 'I would march him to a dungeon, given the chance, and he could rot there for all I care. Hanging would be a mercy. How can you trust this man, Alice?' he pointed the head of his axe at Valerian. 'For all we know, he is a murderer.'

'That is not true,' said Valerian, looking warily at the axe in Jon's hand. 'I would never hurt a girl, or anyone else for that matter. I tried to help Constance. Why does no one believe me?'

'Because you are an insolent pig with no manners.'

The two men stared at each other while Alice gathered up the small pieces of wood Jon had chopped.

'Let's stop this now,' she said. 'Petty arguments will get us nowhere.'

Jon took the firewood from her. 'I have work to do,' he said tersely, striding towards the monastery building.

'I have admiration for anyone who devotes his life to God,' said Valerian as they watched Jon's retreating form.

Alice felt disappointed that Jon had walked away.

'It is something I could never do,' Valerian continued. 'But it is said that many do not respect their vows. I have heard stories about priests and prostitutes. It must be hard to be true to your vows when those around you are disobeying them.'

Alice said nothing. It was no secret that Prior Edmund had fathered children with a woman named Tillie Buckley. The children lived in the hospital as if they were foundlings.

'You have not been foolish enough to become a nun, though?' enquired Valerian. 'I hear you are a widow.'

'Yes.' *Had he been asking about her? With whom had he been discussing her?*

'Would you marry again?'

'I don't know,' she retorted, flustered by the question. 'I have never thought about it.'

'You must have a lot of admirers among all these monks.'

'I hardly think so. They have taken their vows!' Her face flushed red.

'That does nothing to stop their urges, though, does it?'

She glared at him. 'Your talk is utterly inappropriate, Sir! This is the reason Jon walked away. Do you not wish to make any friends here?'

'I am sorry,' said Valerian, holding up his hands in apology. 'I spoke out of turn. Often I mean to joke and people take me seriously. I do not mean to offend. But I still cannot understand how a man becomes a monk.'

'What about yourself?' asked Alice. 'Clearly you are not a monk. Are you married?'

'I almost was,' he grimaced, 'but I got into trouble and the young lady did not wish to marry me after that.'

'Got into trouble doing what?'

'I will not say. I can tell you are easily shocked,' he said with a grin.

'I am not!'

'Yes you are. You are somewhat high-strung and I need to watch what I say.'

Alice realised this was another of Valerian's jokes. She shrugged. 'There is little that can shock me given what I have already heard and seen.'

'Well then,' Valerian chuckled awkwardly. 'I seduced her sister.'

'*What?*'

'I knew you would be shocked.'

'No, I am not.' She found herself smiling. 'I need to get back to the children; I should not be loitering here.'

'You were meeting the monk out here without permission, then?' Valerian said with a smile. 'I didn't realise you were the disobedient type. I shall be quick in that case. I came here to say thank you for believing me; it is of great importance to me. All I wish to do is clear my name and help find Constance. If I can be any assistance to you at any time, you must let me know.'

'I shall.'

'Thank you, Alice.' He rested his hand on her arm.

Alice looked into his dark eyes and thought about him seducing his betrothed's sister. She was unsure why the thought had suddenly entered her head and the flush on her cheeks spread down to her throat.

'I will doubtless see you again soon, Valerian.'


Sister Emma bustled over to Alice as soon as she arrived at

the children's dormitory. She spoke quickly, as if she were out of breath. 'Thank the Lord you are here. It is Nicholas, he is not well.'

Alice hurried over to his bedside. Nicholas' face was pale and his skin was hot and clammy.

'Can you bring me some water and a cloth, please? And fetch Brother Ralph. We need something for this fever.'

Alice crouched by the side of Nicholas' bed and watched his chest rise and fall. His eyes flickered open and closed. She held his hand and squeezed it gently, reminded of the hours she had spent by her son's bedside when all her love and prayers had been spent in vain. She hoped this time would be different.

Matilda toddled over to see her, a fraying rag doll in her hand. She looked quizzically at the tear on Alice's cheek, but Alice smiled and quickly wiped it away.

An argument broke out among the children, who were playing with wooden swords in the middle of the room. One had rapped another on the head and a wailing noise ensued.

With Sister Emma on her way to fetch Brother Ralph, Alice had to leave Nicholas' side to separate the boys. She sent half of them out into the garden to play with their new ball. Then she rushed back to Nicholas. She was reluctant to leave his side when he was so poorly. If she had arrived earlier she could have sent for Brother Ralph sooner. She felt a pang of guilt for failing to reach the dormitory on time.

Nicholas fell asleep after drinking a draught of water boiled with feverfew, his regular, calm breaths reassuring Alice that his fever was fading.

Sister Emma joined Alice at the bedside. 'I pray that he recovers,' she said. 'He never was a strong boy, was he?'

Alice shook her head sadly.

'I wonder how Constance is,' continued Sister Emma. 'I think about her every day. It has been more than a week now since she was taken.'

'Yes,' Alice sighed.

'Have you spoken to Hilda?'

'No, not recently.'

'She says she saw everything that happened when Constance was taken.'

'Really? She rambled to me about Constance being taken like the others were, but I felt she was making little sense.'

'What she saw is too terrible to describe!' whispered Emma.

'What did she see?'

'I cannot say!' Emma's eyes grew wide and Alice felt a stab of frustration.

'You have to tell me! If Hilda saw something it might help us find out who took Constance. The bailiff will also need to be informed. His men are still looking for her.' Alice hoped this final statement was true.

'Fine. And may the Lord forgive me for the evil of which I am about to speak.'

'I am sure he will.'

'And may my soul not be made impure by words the devil himself would use.'

'I'm certain it will not, Sister Emma. What did Hilda see?'

Sister Emma's dark eyes fixed on Alice with an unblinking stare. 'The great door was flung open and a black mist drifted inwards, accompanied by a stench so foul it could only have come from hell itself. From the dark mist, two hands manifested themselves,' she said, demonstrating with her own hands held out, claw-like, in front of her. 'And the three-headed beast stepped out of the mist and into the hall. Its roar was so fearful that Hilda said the heart of a man could have stopped beating upon hearing the dreadful sound. The jaws of the beast dripped with blood and it had the head of a lion, the head of a bear and the head of a...'

'Wolf?' The story was beginning to sound familiar.

'Yes!' said Sister Emma, gripping Alice's arm with excitement.

'I have heard about Hilda's beast before,' replied Alice resignedly. She was annoyed at herself for believing that Hilda had seen something useful, especially after the incident with the pig.

'He has struck before?'

'I am not convinced he has ever struck. As far as I am aware, he has never ventured further than the confines of Hilda's head.'

# Chapter Fourteen

✥

Sitting at his highly polished table, Sir Walter poured himself a goblet of wine and thought of the attractive, sour-faced widow he had seen at dinner the previous night. It was unfortunate that she worked at St Hugh's and knew Constance; he was unhappy about the coincidence. He had watched the small, dark-haired woman as she picked at her food. She would have been beautiful had it not been for a touch of bluntness around the face and the steely look in her eye.

He had noticed the shadows under her eyes and the lines beside her mouth, presumably caused by the strain of losing her husband. He had heard about Thomas Wescott but had never met him. He knew Wescott had been a leather merchant and had become wealthy at a young age. His death had made Alice an eligible widow and it was surprising that no one had coerced her into marriage once again. A second husband would keep her out of harm's way, he was certain of that. Not that he would consider her himself; he preferred his women younger.

*Would the sour-faced widow do anything about Constance's*

*disappearance?* This was the question that most concerned him. Often missing people could be explained away by an act of God or an act of evil they had supposedly brought upon themselves. But he could tell that Alice had an enquiring mind. *Why else would she have worked so long at St Hugh's but not joined the holy order herself?* This made her a sceptic. Believers could easily be fooled, but not those like Alice. He would need to keep a close eye on her, especially at a time when a series of mishaps had threatened the tight control he held over his household. Today he was going to ensure he had full control again. His men had been summoned and he had a plan.

His falconer came into the room. He was a squat man with a hooked nose that was not unlike a beak. 'Here he is, Sir Walter.'

'Magnificent.' Sir Walter rose from his seat to inspect the sparrowhawk perched on the falconer's arm. The bird wore a leather hood over its head to keep it calm, and had straps and a silver bell attached to its feet. Sir Walter stroked the soft feathers on the hawk's back and admired its barred white chest and lead grey wings. It was too young yet to have amber-tinged feathers at its throat.

'I've been taking him everywhere with me,' said the falconer. 'I took him around the market and I'll be taking him out on horseback tomorrow.'

'Wonderful. I want him out catching duck for me,' said Sir Walter. 'And maybe a heron or a crane from time to time.'

'He will certainly do that for you, Sir Walter.'

Theobald and Richard Neville appeared in the doorway. Sir Walter dismissed the falconer and invited them to take a seat.

Theobald carried several rolled parchments, which he placed

on the table. He sat down and Richard took the seat next to him. Richard was large and chubby compared to Theobald, with dark, curly hair and eyes as hard as granite. The two men clearly disliked each other.

Sir Walter commanded his servant to bring more wine and unrolled one of the parchments.

'I understand there has been some carelessness,' he said, his eyes trained on the document in front of him.

Unsure which of his guests he was addressing, neither spoke.

'Anyone care to enlighten me?' Sir Walter asked, looking up at them.

Theobald glared at Richard.

'I am not sure what you are alluding to, Sir Walter,' said Richard, picking at his thumbnail.

'We have lost *two* whores,' said Sir Walter, dropping the parchment onto the table, where it rolled back up neatly. 'Your men were responsible, Richard.'

'I can only offer you my sincere apologies, Sir Walter. The men have been dealt with. I spoke to them firmly.'

Sir Walter suspected the conversation had not been firm enough, which was why he had sent two other men to visit Heward Lovell.

'I cannot understand how this happened,' said Sir Walter, stroking the fur on the right-hand sleeve of his bright green jacket. 'The wenches were fine when I was with them. In fact, one of them put up quite a fight.' His face broke into a lecherous grin. 'She was young. The older ones are more passive, I find. They seem to accept their fate with more dignity.'

He chuckled to himself, before switching to a stern expression. 'Are you aware one of the whores escaped after your idiot men threw her into the river?'

He could see that his question had unnerved Richard.

'No. I think that must be a mistake. It is highly regrettable that the girls died, but I can assure you that they did indeed die.'

Sir Walter stood up and paced around the room. He was pleased to see Richard's hands trembling.

'Let us pretend they did both die,' said Walter as he walked behind Richard's chair. 'Was throwing them into the river a suitable course of action? A place where they could easily be found?'

'No, Sir Walter.' Richard examined his hands once again.

'Then why did you allow your men to dispose of them in this fashion?'

'I do not always know what my men are...'

'Doing? That is most unfortunate. Especially when it transpires that one of the harlots did not die. She was alive when your pig-brained men threw her into the river. Not only did she climb out again, but she ran off. And *your men*,' Sir Walter stood behind Richard and grabbed him by the throat with a thick hand, '*couldn't catch her.*'

Theobald stifled a snigger.

'I was not aware...'

'No, of course you weren't,' Sir Walter tightened the grip on Richard's throat. 'You have no control over your men whatsoever. You are too busy fornicating with any whore who has breath in her body to pay attention to them. I take it you were ignorant of the facts I have just furnished you with?'

Richard struggled to speak, his voice panting and rasping. 'I knew most of it, but I did not realise one had made her escape. They assured me she was dead.' He began to choke.

Sir Walter gave Richard's throat a final squeeze, causing the man's face to turn scarlet, then released his grip.

Richard coughed and tried to recover his breath as Sir Walter walked calmly back to his seat. 'Presumably you also have no idea that the coroner was informed and the dead wench's family have been reunited with her corpse. The funeral took place earlier this week. People of consequence in London are now aware of her death. Is this a helpful development for us?'

'No,' the word came out as a croak.

Sir Walter leaned forward. 'I want you to find the missing girl before she talks to anyone else. If you fail me once more, the next death will be yours. Have I made myself understood?'

Richard nodded and Sir Walter dismissed him.

Sir Walter sat back in his chair and sighed. He was cursing the day he had decided to have Elizabeth de Grey for himself. He had enjoyed the challenge of choosing someone so well-known: the daughter of his rival, Sir Robyn de Grey. She was eighteen years old, pure and beautiful.

When he had heard she was to be married to his own vintner, Geoffrey Edington, the challenge of having her had presented itself. It had been a risky move, but Sir Walter was aroused by risk. Whores no longer held any interest for him; all he had to do was pay them and they did whatever he wanted. They were so eager to please they presented no challenge and he hungered for more.

He still invited prostitutes to his palace, but they were fodder for his men at the parties he hosted. He liked girls who were difficult to obtain: the younger, fresher ones; innocent and unsullied. He wanted to show them what he could do to them, regardless of their background or status. No one was above him. He could reduce them to nothing; he had power over them all.

The thrill of snatching his first girl had been tremendous. He remembered seeing her at work at an alehouse on Three-needle Street. He had ordered two of his men to return to the alehouse later that evening and encourage her to step outside with them. When they had brought her to him that night it had been like receiving a gift. It proved that he could have any girl he wanted. All he had to do was look around him during the day, give one of his men the nod and the girl would surely be his. The girls he took rarely put up much resistance; their instinct was to comply with official-looking men. And if there was a struggle, the men could easily overpower the girl. Sir Walter enjoyed fear. It fired his loins more than anything else.

Sir Walter had started helping himself to girls while the city was being ravaged by the plague. Londoners had been too busy nursing their sick and burying their dead to notice a few girls disappearing. Buoyed by escaping the plague himself, Sir Walter had spent a good deal of time helping those who were suffering. It improved his public standing and gave him access to more girls.

He loved the duplicity of his work. He was so charitable and generous that no one would ever suspect he was stealing girls from their homes, keeping them prisoner and molesting them. As soon as he lost interest in a girl he would put her to work in one of the brothels, and there she would live under a new identity, too frightened to contact the family she had left behind. None of the girls had ever died or escaped previously as his men had never shown incompetence before now.

The more he thought about the widow, the more she bothered him. If she had been younger he would have been tempted to add her to his household. But she looked at least twenty-five and was old meat as far as he was concerned. In any case, people of import such as the prior and Yvette de Beauchamp would notice if the widow mysteriously disappeared. He would have to make sure she was contained for the time being rather than taking drastic action. St Hugh's was still reeling from the disappearance of the young girl.

Perhaps when the fuss died down he would be able to find a more permanent solution for the widow.

Sir Walter addressed Theobald. 'You can stop smiling about your friend finding himself in trouble. You are here because I need some records updated, but there is something else I need you to do, which I do not trust that clumsy Richard Neville to deal with. I want you to speak to the Earl of Wykeham and ask if we can borrow his man, Valerian Baladi. I have invited the earl to my party this evening, so it will be no trouble for you to approach him. Offer him some whores, the young ones. That will make your job easier.'

Theobald nodded in reply. 'Of course. May I ask why we want his man?'

'You do not need to know why. Just make sure he hands Valerian over to us and bring him to me as soon as you have him. Now, on to business.' Sir Walter unrolled another piece of parchment.

Theobald was responsible for managing Sir Walter's affairs with Brother Rufus at St Hugh's. A talented and discreet scribe, Brother Rufus was well versed in history and blessed with an excellent imagination. His creative writing had earned the Rokeby family a prestigious pedigree with close connections to long-dead kings and saints, and thanks to Brother Rufus Sir Walter now had plenty of documents to prove it. Brother Rufus had also ensured that Sir Walter owned vast tracts of land and property in Kent and Middlesex by forging Royal Charters. Although people were suspicious about how Sir Walter had expanded his empire, few could dispute the authentic wax seals on the charters Brother Rufus carefully cut from legitimate documents and skilfully remoulded and attached to the forged manuscripts.

'We need to clarify that the farmstead at Walsam and its

associated lands are under my ownership. The Abbot of Walsam Priory seems to think it is his land.' Sir Walter rolled up the parchment.

'And who actually owns the land?' asked Theobald.

'I do, of course!' Sir Walter replied, his face reddening.

'Of course. I shall see to it that the correct charter is drawn up to clarify the matter immediately.'

'Please do,' said Sir Walter. He sat back and fixed Theobald with an unblinking stare. 'And when you meet with the prior, there is something else you must tell him.'

'And what is that, Sir Walter?' asked Theobald, smiling obsequiously.

'Tell Prior Edmund to keep that woman under control.'

'Tillie Buckley?'

'No! Not the woman he fathers bastards with; she is nothing but a toothless harlot. The lay woman; that widow, who, for some indeterminable reason, devotes her time to the hospital. She works there and looks after the children, including Prior Edmund's bastards. She is trouble.'

Sir Walter pointed a finger at Theobald to emphasise his point. 'Her name is Alice Wescott. Her dead husband was a successful leather merchant and I would like to know where she is storing all his money.'

'Is that what you would like me to ask the prior?' stuttered Theobald. 'Where she stores her husband's money?'

'No!' Sir Walter slammed the palm of his hand on the table and Theobald jumped in his seat. 'The widow's money is a matter for another time. I want you to tell Prior Edmund to keep the nosey, goat-faced trollop within the confines of that building. I do not want her wandering about asking questions about issues that do not concern her.'

'And what issues might those be?'

'They do not concern you, either!' roared Sir Walter. 'Just see to it that she is kept under control, is that clear? And with that in mind, there is another document I would like Brother Rufus to draw up.'

That evening, Theobald made his way up a winding staircase towards the sound of laughter and music. His head was pleasantly swimming with wine. At the top of the stairs a guard stood in front of a red velvet curtain. He nodded at Theobald and pushed the curtain to one side, allowing him to enter the room freely.

The minstrels were playing loudly and the room was hot. In the centre, a group of naked women danced and poured wine over their bodies from silver jugs. Men scrambled about them, licking at the wine wherever they found it. Sir Walter stood at the side of the room, clapping and laughing at the display. Around the edges of the room, men and women lay entangled on velvet cushions, a mass of heaving, naked bodies. These women from the brothels were always in attendance at Sir Walter's parties.

Noticing Theobald standing alone at the side of the room, one of them walked over to him and told him to open his mouth. He did as he was told and she poured red wine down his throat from the silver jug. He gulped back a mouthful and the rest sloshed out of his mouth and down his chin. She laughed and started to lick the wine off his face. He pushed her to one side as he caught sight of the Earl of Wykeham at the far end of the room.

The earl was a tall, thin man with bushy eyebrows and a bulbous nose. He was deep in conversation with Richard Neville. Theobald introduced himself and asked after Valerian Baladi.

'An innocent man,' replied the earl. 'I am relieved to have saved him from the gallows this week.'

'Fine work,' said Theobald. 'Sir Walter is also convinced of

Valerian's innocence and he has asked that Valerian attend to some work in his household. He is willing to pay both you and Valerian handsomely as he is rather short of good men at present. If you are happy to acquiesce, you will have your pick of any of our best girls this evening.' Theobald gestured to the nearest corner of the room, where a group of young girls sat on a bench in silence.

'They look scared,' said the earl.

'They are in need of a man's company to lift their spirits,' grinned Theobald. 'The whores are for everyone; Sir Walter only shares his girls with a select few.'

Theobald received a warm welcome at St Hugh's the following morning. Prior Edmund urged his guest to make himself comfortable in his finest chair and poured him a goblet of strong wine.

'Would you like some cake to accompany it?' asked the prior.

Theobald declined.

'I do love a piece of cake soaked in wine,' said the prior, helping himself to a thick slice and using it to mop up the wine that had spilt down his chin.

Theobald knew Sir Walter's money made the prior happy. They drank and chatted about the details of the charter Brother Rufus was to draw up.

'I have asked Brother Rufus to join us,' said the prior. 'He will be here shortly.'

Prior Edmund squeezed his large frame into his chair and made a kissing noise. His monkey jumped onto his shoulder and fixed Theobald with its large brown eyes. The monkey's stare made him uncomfortable.

'Have you met Gilbert before?'

Theobald shook his head.

'I bought him in Egypt, on the return voyage of my last pilgrimage to Jerusalem. Hello there, Rufus. Do come and take a seat.'

A short, plump monk entered the room. With his soft features and small eyes he reminded Theobald of a mole. He sat next to Theobald and declined the prior's offer of wine.

'Brother Rufus does not say much, but you will not find a finer scribe in London,' boasted the prior. 'Did I tell you I stole him from the Cistercians?'

Prior Edmund laughed loudly and Theobald smiled, pretending he had never heard the story before.

'I found him at Alfham Priory, a cold, miserable place by the River Ouse in Yorkshire. He was working on some beautiful illuminations that caught my eye. I knew immediately that I could put him to good use.' He winked at Theobald. 'So I suggested to his abbot that the monk spend a year with me in London to see some of the great manuscripts we hold here and to develop his skill. Well, that was ten years ago and there has never been any talk of him returning.'

He chuckled. 'He is practically a recluse, but an excellent forger nonetheless. Sorry, I slipped up there,' he winked again. 'An excellent *scribe,* I should say.'

They discussed the document Brother Rufus would need to produce in order for Sir Walter to acquire the farmstead at Walsam. Once that conversation reached its conclusion, Theobald asked if he could speak to the prior alone. The prior nodded and Brother Rufus was dismissed.

'After we are finished here, you must remind me to introduce you to Brother Henry,' said the prior. 'He is another skilled brother we have here at St Hugh's. He oversees the pilgrim badges and is responsible for the relics we sell to the pilgrims who visit the shrine of Saint William.'

'Which Saint William is that?'

'Just one of the former abbots. There are so many Saint Williams, are there not? Have you seen our relics?'

Theobald shook his head.

The prior continued: 'A piece of the holy shroud, a nail from the cross, an ampulla of milk from the Virgin Mary, the bones of Saint Peter... these are just some of the relics we offer, all of which are blessed by Rome, of course. Brother Henry is always working to ensure that there is a generous supply. I should add that the money is not important; instead, it is the knowledge that these relics protect and heal our pilgrims that rewards us the most. I carry this myself,' the prior said as he pulled a gold chain from under his robes, an intricate gold pendant hanging from it. 'This holds a piece of the true cross.'

The prior held it out for Theobald to examine. Sir Walter's man could see that it was finely engraved.

'I have worn this since I was a boy. In fact, it belonged to my mother. I have worn it on all of my pilgrimages to the Holy Land and I owe the safety of my travels to it.'

'It is a beautiful amulet, Prior Edmund. I carry a tooth of Saint Thomas in my purse. Here, let me show you while I present another request from Sir Walter.'

'Anything,' said Prior Edmund, spreading his palms in a wide gesture. He examined Saint Thomas' tooth before picking out a walnut from a bowl on the table, cracking it open with a nutcracker and handing it to his monkey.

'It concerns the lay sister you have here. I believe her name is Alice.'

'Alice Wescott, the widow. She is not a lay sister, she is merely a volunteer. But go on,' the prior said, his face darkening.

'I understand she has been asking questions about matters that do not concern her.'

'She has been worried about a friend of hers who went missing a few days ago. We are all concerned.'

'I see.' Theobald was pleased to be enlightened about what Alice was doing to upset Sir Walter, but with no further details he had to think creatively. 'When someone goes missing it is, of course, a matter for the authorities.'

'I could not agree more,' the prior nodded.

'And it would be untoward for a widow who works in a hospital to be asking questions when the relevant authorities already have the matter in hand.'

'Exactly.'

'Sir Walter has asked me to tell you this as a member of London's respected peerage. It is important that people, and especially women, know their place and do not involve themselves in such a way that they impinge upon the work of others.' Theobald was prevaricating, but he was encouraged by the prior's serious and agreeable expression. 'Please understand that this is a piece of advice rather than a direct order. Sir Walter is not in the habit of intimidating anyone.'

'Absolutely, absolutely. I understand,' replied the prior, resting his hand on his heart. 'And please do tell Sir Walter that I am most saddened and embarrassed that the widow has behaved in this manner. I have already reminded her of her duties to St Hugh's and I am confident she will cause no further problems. She does very good work here at the hospital.'

'I am certain she does, Prior Edmund. You always choose the very best people to carry out your good work.'

'Thank you,' the prior said, bowing his head graciously. 'I shall ensure that she remains here at the hospital, concentrating on her good work and serving God rather than the needs of a girl who eloped with one of the hospital patients.'

'Is that what happened to her?'

'Of course. How else could she have gone missing?'

Theobald was relieved to hear that Prior Edmund had no idea what had happened to the girl.

'You may need some assistance keeping the widow under control, and therefore Sir Walter has a further piece of work for your scribe to ensure that everything is laid out clearly.'

'Excellent,' said the prior with a relieved smile.

'And he will pay handsomely for this extra piece of work.'

'Even better!' the prior chuckled. He raised his goblet in celebration and drank.

# Chapter Fifteen

'No, no. Now you've broke it,' said Millicent crossly. She retrieved the drop spindle from the floor and twisted a piece of the wool fleece between her fingers, binding it onto the small strand of wool Elizabeth had managed to spin. 'A girl who can't spin wool; I never saw the like. What was you doin' up in London?'

'I went to school.'

'Did you now?' The heavy lines on Millicent's forehead were exposed as her eyebrows arched.

'It was a convent school,' continued Elizabeth. 'The nuns taught me to read and write.'

'Bein' high born I expect you're good at sewin'.'

'I never cared for it. I didn't care for anything that involved sitting around and gossiping. I preferred to help in the stables. I was there most of the time ruining my clothes. My father despaired.'

'But you ain't never worked?'

'I spent some time in service in the household of my father's friend so I could learn how a household was run. I was to be the lady of my own household after I was married.'

'But you ain't married?'

'No.' Elizabeth gritted her teeth. She was telling Millicent too much. It was obvious she came from a wealthy family because she was unable to carry out practical tasks, such as looking after pigs and spinning wool. Whenever Millicent asked about her background, she found herself telling the truth. *How could she invent something and sound convincing?*

Elizabeth finally felt fully recovered from her fever. Her legs were almost back to full strength and she was helping as best she could with the jobs Millicent had to do each day. She needed to get back on the road and continue her journey. She knew that the longer she stayed in one place the more danger there was of being found out, but for some reason Millicent wasn't keen to let her go. Elizabeth wondered if the old lady was lonely and wanted company. If that were true, she would feel guilty for trying to leave.

She was also sleeping better. Each night, Millicent made her patient drink a variety of disgusting draughts and rubbed a range of strange-smelling salves onto her hands, feet and forehead. Elizabeth thought these might be helping to calm her mind, but felt that this could also be down to the charm Millicent had told her to wear around her neck. It was a piece of triangular parchment with words on it that Elizabeth did not understand. She could read Latin and French, but this was a language she was unable to fathom.

'It's the language of the old people of this land,' Millicent had said. 'Long before me or me ma were even born the old people came in their ships from a land of darkness. They lived on these lands and buried treasures, which only the gifted was supposed to find. That's where these coins and jewellery on my shelves comes from. I found them in a field when I were a girl. The villagers said I were gifted like my ma because no one else ever found the treasures they buried. And no one'll ever come and steal these treasures from me 'cause I'm gifted, you see, and anyone who steals 'em will be cursed.'

There was no doubt the villagers considered Millicent to be gifted. Each day someone would visit her asking for help. Some were sick or had lost something, while others wanted their lands blessed or wished to know what would happen in the future. Young girls often wanted to know who they were to marry.

During these visits, Millicent asked Elizabeth to sit at the side of the room with her dog, Talbot, and remain quiet, which she was happy to do. Visitors always eyed her suspiciously when Millicent introduced her as Gwendolyn, claiming she was her sister's granddaughter.

Elizabeth admired the wealth of knowledge Millicent had. Along with herbs and the medicines she made with them, she knew countless written charms by heart and chanted many others. She would scatter a pile of small bones on the floor, swing a key on a piece of string or stare at the surface of a bowl of water and garner profound meaning from each of these routines. Millicent could also read. She told Elizabeth her mother had taught her, and that she had several books her mother had made using rough parchment. Elizabeth looked inside at the instructions and drawings for the remedies Millicent carried out, all written in dark brown ink in the language of the old people.

There was a knock at Millicent's door in the middle of the night on one occasion. Through her heavy eyelids, Elizabeth could see someone with a lantern. She could just about make out the silhouette of Millicent as she put on her cloak and followed the visitor outside. Elizabeth lay awake, wondering how often Millicent left her home at night. She suddenly realised she could hear crying, and the woman's cry soon turned into a scream. *Was there trouble?*

Elizabeth sat up, listening to the cries, and wondered if

she should go to Millicent's aid. *Was she all right?* The woman's cries stopped after a while and were replaced by the high, thin wail of an infant. Elizabeth smiled to herself as she realised that Millicent was helping the local women have their babies when the time came.

A regular visitor at Millicent's was Auriol Swynford. Elizabeth learnt she was the wife of the village reeve and considered herself to be extremely important. Auriol was thin with high cheekbones and a pinched mouth. She walked with her head held high and wore clothes that were more colourful and of better quality than those worn by most of the other villagers.

Auriol was worried about the crops. There had been a bad harvest the previous year and everyone was short of food now that it was late winter. Millicent was helping by blessing the fields and carrying out ploughing and sowing ceremonies. She told Elizabeth she did this every year but that Auriol wanted her to do it a few extra times as spring approached.

'How long will you be staying with Millicent?' she asked Elizabeth during one of her visits.

Elizabeth had been sitting quietly with the dog at the edge of the room.

'As soon as the weather is warmer,' she replied. Her plan was to leave soon, but she decided to keep her answer vague. There was something about Auriol she didn't like.

'Really? You are well enough to travel, are you?'

Elizabeth felt uncomfortable about the way Auriol was looking her up and down. She scrutinised the loose tabard Elizabeth wore over her dress, which she had pulled out a little to cover her stomach.

'Well, I wish you a safe journey,' said Auriol, 'although it is a dangerous journey for a girl on her own. There are bandits on the road over the other side of Winchester. I think you should call at an inn in Winchester to find some travelling companions.'

'Thank you, I will,' replied Elizabeth.

After Auriol left she spoke to Millicent: 'I should continue with my journey; people are starting to ask a lot of questions.'

'Are you surprised?' asked Millicent.

'No, I suppose not.' Elizabeth sighed. She no longer had a place she could call home. She felt she would always be running. There was so much to run away from.

'How about I leave tomorrow? I am quite well enough now.'

'We'll find out tonight,' replied Millicent. 'There'll be a full moon and I'll wake you up for a little walk.'

'Why?'

'You'll find out.'


Millicent kept her word. After Elizabeth had slept for an hour or two, the older woman woke her and they left the hut together. The moon was large and bright, the landscape around them grey. Millicent carried a lantern and led Elizabeth along the road out of the village before turning left down a narrow path that ran alongside a stretch of woodland. The path was littered with stones, but the moonlight was bright enough for Elizabeth to pick her way along without stumbling. Her breath froze in clouds in the air, and in the trees beside her she could hear the occasional rustle and hoot of an owl. The dark no longer scared her; she felt safe there.

The path broadened into a field and Elizabeth saw a small circle of dark stones in the centre of it. Fingers of mist drifted around the stones. There was something alive about the place.

She shivered. 'Why have you brought me here?'

'We ain't there yet. Follow me.'

'What are these stones for?'

'The old people of this land put 'em there. Come on, follow me.'

A distant hillside was bathed in moonlight as they passed the stones and made their way toward the crooked outline of a dead tree. It had lost most of its branches and the remains of its stump appeared jagged against the starry sky. As they reached the tree, Elizabeth saw that it stood beside a small pool of water, which shone silver in the moonlight. Black ripples moved slowly across its surface. Moss-covered stones sat around the edge of the water and the moss felt soft and springy under Elizabeth's feet. Although she had only recently awoken, her mind felt fresh and alive. There was something about this place she liked.

Elizabeth followed Millicent around the pool until the tall tree stump was a dark shard in the water with the full moon behind it. Millicent knelt down by the water's edge and extinguished the lantern.

'Don't worry, it's light enough for us to find our way back without it,' she said.

Elizabeth could see the moon and stars in the water with the black reflection of the tree stump cutting through them. She stood behind Millicent as the old lady quietly chanted a few words. Then there was silence. Even the owl stopped hooting. As Elizabeth looked around her at the moonlit hillsides and the dark outlines of rocks and trees, she felt a shiver run down her spine. *Was there really magic in this place?*

Millicent muttered to herself for a bit and then spoke. 'Help me up, will you? Can't get me knees straight.'

Elizabeth reached down for Millicent's arm and helped her to her feet. 'So what happens now?'

'That's it, we're finished here. I use this pool for scrying.

It's been 'ere since afore the old people. Are you wanting to know what it told me?'

'Yes.'

'It told me there's only one new moon left afore your bairn's born.'

Elizabeth stepped back and stared at Millicent's shadowy form in the darkness. 'What bairn?'

'Don't pretend you don't feel it kicking inside you. I know you'll birth a bairn. You think I 'aven't noticed your belly? And that ain't all. There should be two months o' the moon before your bairn's born and I saw that it'll come sooner. I've helped birth many bairns and I know the ones what come early can be weak and sickly. We 'ave to take care o' you so the bairn's got the best chance.'

Elizabeth didn't know what to say. She thought she had managed to keep her pregnancy secret, although she was certain Auriol had noticed earlier that day. She had done all she could to keep her growing stomach hidden, but it was becoming impossible to fool everyone.

'I shall leave the village tomorrow.' There was no sense in staying now that her secret was out.

'You'll do no such thing.'

'But I have to go otherwise I will bring shame on you.'

'Don't you worry about that. I've brought enough shame on meself over the years.'

'But you don't need me staying with you any longer, and you certainly don't need a baby to look after.'

'I've 'elped most of the mothers in this village birth their bairns. And I've 'ad ten children meself. Believe me, you're with the best person now.'

'But I have sinned.' Elizabeth felt tears on her cheeks. She knew she could not have prevented what had happened to her, but she felt it must have been a punishment for a sin she had committed in her past. *She must have deserved it. Maybe she hadn't mourned her mother long enough or helped her father suffi-ciently after her mother had died. Maybe she hadn't prayed enough.*

Whatever the reason, she was living out her punishment. She was certain her child would also be punished. The bastard child would have no place in her family. She could never face her father again; he would never be able to forgive her.

'I don't want none o' that talk now,' said Millicent. 'Sooner or later you'll tell me what 'appened to you. And you'll tell me your real name and all.'

# Chapter Sixteen

A lice and Jon stood in front of the prior, watching as he poked at his teeth with an ivory toothpick. He had summoned them to his rooms and they were waiting for him to speak. Gilbert was climbing along the mantelpiece, knocking the silver plates into one another, and Alice was nervous that his long tail would dangle into the fire and catch light. On the prior's table was a rolled-up piece of parchment. The wax seal it bore looked familiar to Alice, but she couldn't think why.

'How shall I put this?' the prior said, examining the tip of his toothpick before putting it back in his mouth and sucking on it. 'Mistress Wescott,' he continued, placing the toothpick on the table and steepling his fingers. She shifted from one foot to another and stared into his pale eyes.

'Yes, Father?'

'I would like to take this opportunity to say how grateful I am for all the work you have done at St Hugh's. It is an act of charity I would previously have considered beyond the capabilities of a lay woman. To devote your time and energies to the needs of the children here is a commitment worthy of the Lord God himself.'

Alice had never received praise from the prior before. It suggested that the conversation would have an unfortunate outcome. The prior was going to ask her to stop looking for Constance again, she was sure of it. Whatever he said she vowed she would continue; she would find a way to outwit him.

She glanced at Jon, who was standing next to her, unsure why he had also been summoned. Jon stared straight ahead, his lips pressed tightly together.

'On behalf of the hospital of St Hugh and St John Within the Walls, I would like to thank you,' continued the prior, 'and to acknowledge your impressive dedication, particularly after suffering your own bereavement. You have channelled the energy of your grief into an extremely worthy occupation and there are few who would have committed themselves with as much devotion as you. You are a credit to God and may his blessing be upon you.'

The prior made the sign of the cross and Alice looked down at her feet, impatient for him to finish his idle flattery and get to the point.

The prior afforded John a similar barrage of complimentary words, in response to which Jon simply nodded and remained expressionless. He then went on to talk about the godliness of St Hugh's and the great honour its work had bestowed upon the memory of the founder of the order, Abbot Beroldus. The candles burned lower as he spoke and Alice tried to catch Jon's eye, but he refused to look at her.

*Perhaps he's worried he will start laughing*, she thought.

Eventually, the prior picked up the parchment that was lying on the table. 'There is a piece of documentation that I do not believe you are aware of, Mistress Wescott. In fact, I was not aware of its existence until yesterday, when our esteemed scribe Brother Rufus came across it in a drawer of documentation that had not been opened for many years.'

The prior cleared his throat and unrolled the parchment. 'This was passed to me by the Worshipful Company of Glove Makers, a guild I believe your sadly departed husband was a member of?'

Alice felt puzzled. 'Yes, that is correct.'

The prior busied himself with reading the parchment. 'This is a wordy legal document, of course.' He smiled apologetically, but Alice detected insincerity. 'How I did not come to read it two years ago when you first joined us, I do not know,' he said, laughing at his own apparent shortcoming.

Then his face became solemn. 'I must apologise that I did not read it sooner, for it is a very important document indeed. I shall pass it to you to read in a moment, but, to summarise, this document states that should you, Alice Wescott, widow of Thomas Wescott of the Worshipful Company of Glove Makers, devote your time to St Hugh's for a period of time exceeding one year and one day, the Worshipful Company of Glove Makers decrees that the property and estate of Thomas Wescott be passed to St Hugh and St John Within the Walls, and an annual stipend of ten pounds be paid to you thereafter.'

'Property of Thomas Wescott?' Alice was immediately suspicious. 'That is now my property. My dower.'

The prior nodded.

'So my dower is passed to St Hugh's because I have been working here for more than a year?'

The prior nodded again.

'Give me that manuscript.'

The prior stared at Alice and blanched, offended by her directness. He passed the parchment to her slowly, but Alice snatched at it, desperately trying to read the rows of cramped writing.

The document was written in Latin and she could only make out every third or fourth word, but she clearly saw her name and the name of her husband written upon it. The signature and seal confirmed that the manuscript was from the Worshipful Company of Glove Makers, the guild that regulated the work of glove makers in London. The guilds wielded a great deal of influence and Thomas had worked hard to be accepted. But Alice was struggling to believe that the document was genuine. *Why hadn't she been informed of its existence? What right did the guild have over her dower? She could try to question it in a court of law. But would she have any success?*

'You are taking my home from me,' she said quietly, staring at the wax seal.

'Ten pounds a year is a generous stipend,' said the prior.

'But that is *my* money!' said Alice. 'You are taking my money and house away from me.'

'And giving you ten pounds a year,' replied the prior firmly. 'And that is not all. St Hugh's is offering you accommodation here in the grounds of the hospital in return for the generous donation of your husband's estate.'

'I have to come and live here?'

The prior shrugged. 'It is an offer I thought you would be pleased to accept.'

'You are trying to control her,' said Jon, finally breaking his silence.

The prior laughed and his large body shook all over. He got up from his chair and walked over to Jon. '*Control her*? What a ridiculous suggestion. You think I had anything to do with this? It was drawn up by the guild two years ago! They must have rules for their members and, as Alice chose to work here at the hospital instead of continuing with her husband's profession, the guild decided the dower should be put to good use here. The Church is always in need of these kind donations.'

'No it is not,' Jon snorted.

The prior scowled. 'Remind yourself who you are addressing, Brother Jon de Grey. The contents of this document do not concern you and I call the declaration a fair exchange. Having chosen to spend her days at St Hugh's, Alice Wescott can now live among us. Surely *you*, in particular, should be happy about that?'

The prior leered unpleasantly and snatched the parchment out of Alice's hand. 'I understand you have been talking in the garden together with that soon-to-be-hanged criminal. I cannot see why he should come back here and bother us.'

'He's trying to clear his name,' said Alice.

'Or pretending to. The man is up to no good.'

To Alice's annoyance, Jon nodded in agreement.

'And as for *your* relationship,' the prior said, pointing at them both with a podgy forefinger, 'it has become inappropriate. A monk should not be spending so much time with a widowed woman. With *any* woman.'

'The only time we have spent together has been used to search for Constance,' said Jon. 'We have never sought out each other's company for any other reason. I can assure you there is nothing inappropriate about our relationship, Father.'

'You should both know better,' replied the prior. 'Alice, as a widow you are only too familiar with how a relationship between a man and a woman grows. I cannot permit you to spend any more time in each other's company. Besides, it is no longer necessary.'

'Who is looking for Constance now?' asked Alice.

'I have already told you. The bailiff is in charge,' replied the prior, his jowls wobbling with irritation. 'There is nothing more you can do now other than return to your work and serve God and the needs of the patients within these walls.'

Alice was not convinced by his reply. 'How do we know they are actually looking for her?'

'Because they said they would! It is not your job to be searching the streets of London for her. Your time is better spent here, looking after the children.'

'I can still look for Constance,' said Jon.

'Brother Jon, need I remind you of the sadly futile search you carried out for your own sister?'

Alice saw Jon's face stiffen.

'You also have an important role here at St Hugh's, tending the gardens. I think in both these tragic cases we simply have to accept that the girls may have gone of their own accord and fallen into trouble.'

The prior affected a regretful face and Alice sensed Jon's body tensing. Looking down at his hand she saw that it was balled into a fist.

'We will never give up looking for them,' said Jon.

'Never give up *hope* is what you mean,' smiled Prior Edmund. 'We shall keep them both in our prayers and let us hope they are safe wherever they are now.'

'You cannot do this!' shouted Alice.

The prior raised his eyebrows.

'You cannot take what is rightfully mine away from me! My husband worked hard for our home and our money. For ten years before we were married he toiled here in London as an apprentice, then a journeyman. To be accepted into the guild was his greatest honour.'

Alice remembered the moment proudly: the grin on her husband's face that evening when he told her he had finally become a member of the guild. Nine months later their son Christopher had been born. 'I wish he could be here now to see what you are doing with his property. He never would have agreed with such a proposition! I will visit the guild myself with this piece of parchment and ensure that they retract it.'

'You would have no hope,' sneered the prior, 'Grateful as I

am for your help here, it would not distress me in the slightest to see you removed from St Hugh's. Sister Emma is capable of caring for the foundlings without your assistance. And with no home, where would you go then?'

'More threats,' said Alice quietly. 'You are taking my home from me. Our home, the home we lived in as a family.' She felt tears pricking the back of her eyes, but she did not want the prior to see them fall.

'Alice,' said Jon calmly, 'Now is not the time to challenge this document.'

She glared at him. *Was he supporting her or the prior?*

'I need to speak to you,' Alice hissed at Jon as they left the prior's rooms. Her body shook with rage.

'We're not allowed to meet, remember?'

'I don't care,' she replied. 'Meet me in the graveyard shortly.'

## Chapter Seventeen

❦

They stood at the dingy end of the graveyard, where Alice hoped they wouldn't be seen. Simple wooden crosses marked the plots of patients and children, while at the other end of the graveyard elaborate stones stood at the heads of the departed great and good of St Hugh's. A brisk wind blew spots of rain into Alice's face.

'Why did you tell me not to challenge that document?' she asked Jon. 'Should I stand there and allow the prior to take my home and money from me?'

'You heard what he said,' replied Jon. 'He has threatened to make you leave St Hugh's. I was concerned you would upset him so much that he would enforce it there and then.'

Alice sighed. 'Why did the guild never explain this legal clause to me? Why would such an important document remain hidden at St Hugh's for so long without me seeing it?'

'It is a convenient coincidence, is it not?' said Jon. 'That was why I told the prior he was trying to control you. He wants you to live here so he can keep an eye on you.'

'How do you know that?' Alice asked, watching a crow land on the lichen-covered tomb of Abbot Jeremias.

'It's obvious. He wants you working here and looking after the children. Walking around asking questions upsets people. I tried to tell you that at the start.'

'So he has conjured up a document that says he can take away my home and house me on the hospital premises?'

'Conjure is almost correct; it is a forgery,' replied Jon with a bitter smile.

'*What?*'

'Brother Rufus is a renowned forger. The prior hires out his services to those who are wealthy enough to buy influence and power.'

'How do you know that?'

'Brother Rufus told me.'

'But that document had a seal from the Worshipful Company of Glove Makers on it. And a signature!'

'He is a *good* forger.'

'So all I need to do is get hold of that parchment and take it to the guild and explain what has happened. Then they will be able to confirm that it has been made up so the prior can steal my home and estate.'

'You could try. But it would not surprise me if the prior has had a word with them already and even paid them a generous sum to be agreeable on the matter. Challenging it could mean taking the case to the courts.'

'So you expect me to do nothing? They take my home and my money, everything my husband and I worked for, and I have to *accept* that?'

'Keep your voice down!' Jon glanced around nervously. 'No, you should not accept it, you must fight them. But only fight them where you know you can win. If you challenge them in a clumsy fashion you will lose, as they have more money and power. They will be expecting you to put up a fight. You will have to go along with this for now.'

'No!'

'And perhaps this is what you wanted in some ways?'

'Now you're making no sense.'

The rain was beginning to fall more heavily.

'Why keep a home you hardly live in? I expect you have forgotten about most of the belongings you keep there. You choose to spend all your time here, so living here makes your daily routine easier, does it not? You could have reopened the shop and continued your trade very successfully but you decided not to do so. You could have remarried...'

'Stop!' Alice flung her hands over her ears and screwed her eyes tight shut. She did not wish to hear any more.

Jon remained silent.

She took a deep breath and reopened her eyes. 'You don't understand, do you? And why would you? You have lived in this place since you were a child. What do you know about the world out there and about working hard for a living? What do you know about marriage and children and loss? And how it is to love someone with such intensity that you would die to spare them. And to pray in vain and watch helplessly as that person fades away before your eyes. Without hope. Without reason. Do you know what it's like to walk the earth for twenty-five years knowing your son only lived here for two? Why did that happen? Why am I here when he is not?' Tears streamed down Alice's cheeks and it felt as though they would never stop.

Jon stepped towards her and she buried her face in his chest as his arms wrapped firmly around her. There they stood as the wind and rain whipped about them. He spoke only after her tears had subsided. She looked up at him and he wiped her cheeks dry with his thumb.

'I do understand,' he said softly, 'more than you think. I am sorry my words upset you.'

'There is no need to be sorry,' she said, struggling to move her eyes away from his. 'These are things I do not wish to dwell upon. You can see the effect they have on me.'

'What the prior has done is an injustice,' said Jon, releasing her from his arms. His face remained close to hers. 'He is making you live here and he is trying to stop you looking for Constance. He is trying to take control, and for now you must let him. Keep quiet for now, do what he expects of you and he will think he has won. When he relaxes, that will be your opportunity to fight for what is yours. Take some time to think about your next step and don't do anything hasty, otherwise you will make things worse for yourself.'

It hadn't occurred to Alice to think this way before. There was something about Jon she was sure she could trust.

'He sees you as a threat,' said Jon. 'Pretend you are one of his quiet little obedient nuns and soon his attention will be diverted elsewhere.'

She looked up at him and was reminded of her husband once again. Jon's eyes moved down to her lips and then back to her eyes. She felt a tingle run down her spine.

'Alice!'

The shrill voice was like a kick in the chest. Alice leapt away from Jon and saw Sister Katherine striding across the graveyard towards them.

'What are you two doing out here in the rain?' she scolded. 'Brother Jon, do you not have some work to be getting on with?'

Jon nodded and walked away. Alice watched him leave, a mixture of frustration and excitement simmering inside her.

'You are needed in the children's dormitory,' said Sister Katherine.

'I shall go there now.'

They walked back to the hospital building together. 'People are talking,' said Sister Katherine.

'And what are they saying?' asked Alice, irritated that she had to answer to a woman for whom she had little respect.

'At St Hugh's we serve the Lord, not ourselves.' Sister Katherine's lips were pressed firmly together in an expression of superiority. 'There is no place for affairs of the heart here.'

'I don't know what you mean.'

'Oh, I am sure you do.' Sister Katherine stopped and fixed Alice with her grey eyes. 'You may not be a sister or even a lay sister, but by choosing to live here you choose a life of chastity.'

'How do you know I am to live here?' Alice was angry that the news had travelled so quickly. Or had Sister Katherine known about it before the prior had spoken to her?

Sister Katherine ignored her question. 'Brother Jon has sworn a vow. He is a brother at St Hugh's and has lived here since the age of seven. He serves us well and does not need the distractions of a worldly woman.'

'Brother Jon's sister Elizabeth and my friend Constance are both missing. We have been searching for them because we want to bring them both home safely.' Alice almost spat the words at Sister Katherine. 'Our only care is for the people we love, and through our shared concern we have been searching for them together. My heart still belongs to my husband and son. They are lost to me, and that is why I want to do all I can to bring Constance back. If people are talking about me and Jon, they are the ones who should be devoting their energies to serving God rather than engaging in sinful gossip.'

Sister Katherine's lips tightened. 'As Prior Edmund has asked you to stop looking for Constance, there is no further need to converse with Brother Jon, is there?' She smirked.

Alice breathed deeply and remembered Jon's advice to fight back only when the time was right.

Once she was back in the children's dormitory, Alice felt guilty for staying away so long. Having recovered his health for a few days, Nicholas was suffering a relapse. His face was pale but his skin was hot and clammy once again. He lay in bed and stared at the ceiling as his chest rose and fell rapidly. Alice held his small, hot hand in hers and prayed he would pull through as he had done before. She lifted his tunic so she could check his breathing, the muscles under his ribs sucking in deeply with each breath. Brother Ralph had recommended a tincture of angelica every hour. Alice dipped a cloth into a bowl of water, wrung it out and bathed Nicholas' face.

He turned to look at her. 'Am I dying?' he asked, his voice barely audible.

'No, Nicholas, you are not dying,' replied Alice. 'You will get better very soon.'

The door swung open and Prior Edmund entered, his brow furrowed. He exchanged a glance with Alice but said nothing. Alice decided to leave him alone with Nicholas and moved away to busy herself with the other children. Rain lashed at the windows and Alice watched the children, grateful to see that they were noisy, happy and healthy, as children should be. She hoped they would stay that way and that their lives would not be cut cruelly short.

Matilda toddled over to her, banging two wooden animals together and smiling with the only two teeth she had. Alice kissed her warm, chubby cheek and looked over at Nicholas' bed. His little body barely created a lump in the blankets.

The prior sat carefully on the edge of the bed, resting his hand on the boy's cheek. Alice stood, picked Matilda up and walked over to the prior.

'I've summoned the physician,' he said, still looking at the boy.

'I have tried everything Brother Ralph suggested,' said Alice.

'I know. And thank you.' His eyes remained on Nicholas, whose eyelids were becoming heavier and heavier.

Alice gave Matilda a squeeze and realised the anger that had possessed her just a few hours earlier was gone. All she saw in the prior was a bereft father.

'Nicholas probably wants to sleep now. I'll watch him for you and let you know if there is any change,' said Alice.

'Thank you.' Prior Edmund stood up and struggled to meet her gaze. His face was sunken and he seemed smaller than usual. 'Time to prepare for prayers.' He spoke brightly, as if trying to cheer himself up, and left the room.


Alice walked around each room of her house that evening, struggling to comprehend that her home was about to be taken away from her. *Why would the prior forge a document so he could take control of her husband's estate? Was Jon right in saying that he wanted to control her?* As a widow she had more independence than an unmarried girl or a wife. *Did that make the prior uncomfortable?*

She decided this would not do anything to stop her. Nothing would stop her searching for Constance. She and Jon had committed themselves to finding out what had happened to the girls.

Then she thought about the prior visiting his son and how he had worn the lost expression of a parent who fears the worst for his child. Alice's anger subsided. She stopped next to her dresser to pick up a baluster-shaped jug and, tracing her finger over its glassy green glaze, recalled how it had once belonged to her parents. It had been a gift from them on her wedding day. Since then it had sat idly on the shelf, an object from what felt like a previous life.

Alice had kept it out of her son's way, worrying he would break it, and then she had simply forgotten about it. She felt a sudden sadness that it would no longer sit on the shelf and would be packed away somewhere when she moved out of her home. She held it with both hands and remembered the people who had handled it; the people who were now departed. The ceramic jug remained cold in her hands and a heavy sensation descended upon her as she realised it could bring her no closer to those she had lost. There was no use in clinging to an object in the hope that it would somehow fill the hole in her heart.

Alice got ready for bed and picked up Constance's embroidered blue songbird. Three days after Constance had disappeared, Alice had embroidered three small crosses along the edge of the fabric. This had become a habit and every day she embroidered another cross. That evening she found herself stitching the ninth cross. She was unable to bring her family back, but there was a chance she could find Constance if only she knew where to look. It felt as though she was the only person who still cared for the young girl. If she did nothing for Constance, no one would.

A sudden creak of a floorboard startled Alice and disturbed her thoughts. She looked up from the embroidery and listened. All she could hear was the distant noise of the city: drunken singing from an alehouse nearby and a dog barking. Her room was lit only by a candle. She had covered the fire and the rest of the house was shrouded in darkness.

She was just starting to calm herself when she heard the noise again.

'Who's there?' she called, her voice ringing out in the silence. The noise seemed to have come from one of the other bedrooms. For the first time ever she felt scared being alone in her home. She needed someone with her. Jon would have known what to do now. Trembling, she picked up her candle and walked towards the doorway. Shadows lurched onto the walls as she moved.

'Hello?' she called again.

A cold draught flowed around Alice's feet. Ahead of her was a corridor that led to two other bedrooms, both of which were in complete darkness. The back of her neck prickled as she made her way slowly along the corridor, wincing as the floorboards creaked under her feet. Alice's heart pounded and she tried to quieten her breathing so she could listen out for the slightest sound.

She saw no one.

Alice checked the bedrooms slowly and carefully, trying to see as well as she could by the light of her flickering candle. There were many shadows for an intruder to hide in. Having reassured herself that there was no one upstairs, she relaxed slightly and returned to her bedroom. It was then that she heard a third noise, and this time it came from downstairs.

'Hello!' she called again.

Alice held her breath as she climbed down the stairs. The draught was so cold it chilled her arms and legs to the bone. The stone flags in the hallway felt like ice under her feet. Something seemed amiss at the far end of the room. As she walked across the hall her front door looked quite different in the dark.

It was then that she realised it was standing wide open. On the floor of the open doorway were several small, dark shapes. As Alice drew closer, she recognised them.

It was the contents of the small wooden casket she kept in her room: the cotton baby tunic; the little woollen hood; her husband's belt; her mother's brooch; and the six little wooden toys Christopher had loved so much. They were strewn across the floor with the other items from her casket.

She fell to her knees and scrambled across the floor, gathering everything together again. The empty casket lay nearby and, after searching for some time in the darkness, she found its lid, which had been ripped from its hinges.

# Chapter Eighteen

✽

She heard a gasp and a cry and realised both had come from her. Elizabeth sat up, her breath quick and her head spinning. A sense of impending doom washed over her and there was a churning sensation in her bowels. She breathed deeply and slowly as the feeling subsided.

The baby was kicking.

Elizabeth put her hand on her stomach and smiled as she felt the kicks against the wall of her stomach and her hand. *Was this the reason she was feeling so anxious? The baby?* She wanted to understand the reason for each bout of anxiety, but so much had happened that her emotions crashed over her like stormy waves on a beach until she was no longer in control of them. She lay on her side and focused on the faintly glowing embers of the fire as the early greyness of morning crept into the room. Talbot lay across her feet and she was grateful for the warmth.

The arrival of her baby would announce to the world that she had sinned. *Would she be asked to leave the village?* Elizabeth wondered what the future held for her bastard child.

*Perhaps she could take it to the father. He would probably deny it*

*was his. She was unable to prove anything and few people would
believe her, no matter what story she told.*

*She was just a girl and she was supposed to have been married by
now. What if something went wrong when the baby was born? How
would she look after the baby by herself? Where would she live?*

She got up, pulled on her dress and tabard, and stirred the
fire back to life. Then she went out to the well with a bucket
to fetch water. The sky glowed orange on the far horizon as
the frost crunched under her feet. Millicent was getting out
of bed when she returned to the hut.

'I will resume my journey today,' said Elizabeth, decanting
water into a pot to be warmed over the fire. She knew Millicent would disagree, but it was worth another try.

'And where would yer go if I said yes?' asked the old
woman.

'My aunt in Southampton.'

'You told me she lived in Winchester.'

'Oh, I meant Southampton.' Elizabeth cringed at how
stupid her ever-changing story must have sounded.

'There's no aunt, is there?' asked Millicent. 'And what's
yer name?'

She stood in the centre of the room glaring at Elizabeth,
her arms folded. She looked small and thin in the short,
ragged tunic she slept in.

'Elizabeth,' she said quietly.

'That's a pretty name,' Millicent said with a smile. 'And
while we're being honest, can you tell me why you're runnin'
away from the bairn's father? Does 'e know?'

Elizabeth sat down on a stool. 'I cannot talk about the
father. He has no knowledge of the child. Please don't make
me talk about him.'

Millicent nodded. 'You shouldn't have went travelling on
your own, but I can tell you got your reasons. I know you've
come up with a story 'cause summat bad 'appened to you and

you're trying to escape it. But you've got to be honest from now on. You've got to think about 'ow you can give this bairn a proper start in life. And you need to stay 'ere until the bairn's born.'

'But I cannot stay here with you. You have already done so much for me and all the villagers will find out who I am. Even worse, they will know of my shame.'

'There's enough people around here with shame o' their own,' said Millicent. 'Don't you worry about them; you've got to think about yoursen. Stay 'ere with me and you'll 'ave someone with you who knows all about babies and birthing 'em.'

'But you are...'

'Too old? Is that what you was about to say?' laughed Millicent.

'No... Well, yes, I suppose I was.'

'You stay here until that bairn is born. And you can carry on 'elpin' me with all the jobs, like sowing the crops and looking after the pigs and the chickens, and spinning. No, on second thoughts, p'r'aps not the spinning.'


Elizabeth was feeding the pigs when she noticed two well-dressed women walking towards Millicent's hut. She paused to watch and one of them waved. Elizabeth recognised her as Auriol, the reeve's wife. The other lady wore a deep blue cloak lined with fur. As they drew nearer, Elizabeth caught a glimpse of a fashionably high-waisted red dress under the woman's cloak.

'Here's Gwendolyn!' said Auriol.

Elizabeth greeted them both.

'Millicent is at home. I shall tell her you're here.'

'There is no need,' replied the lady, 'it is you I would like to talk to.'

Elizabeth's mouth felt dry.

'This is Lady Margery,' said Auriol, 'the wife of Lord Marlston.'

'Who is your father?' asked Lady Margery. She had a pretty, fair-skinned face with blue eyes set far apart.

'I would rather not say,' replied Elizabeth, looking down at her tabard and hoping it was loose enough to cover her growing stomach. She was in trouble now; she would be sent back to London if Lady Margery found out who she was.

'Why is that?'

'We had a disagreement and I am now unable to return to him.' Elizabeth looked her in the eye and hoped Lady Margery would notice her pleading expression.

But Lady Margery remained frosty. 'Unable to or do not want to?'

'I cannot.'

'I hear you are with child,' said Lady Margery.

Elizabeth glanced at both women and then down at the ground, feeling her face flush a hot red.

'Is this the reason you do not wish to return to your family?' asked Lady Margery.

Elizabeth nodded.

'I understand you are unmarried.'

'That is true,' Elizabeth said. Then, in an attempt to change the subject, she added in a flustered voice, 'Millicent has been very kind.'

Margery smiled. 'We are fortunate to have Millicent here in the village. There is no better person to have by your side when your baby is born. You must realise, however, that Lord Marlston has a duty to inform your father you are here. As an unmarried girl you are your father's property. I am certain he must be worried about you and will be relieved to hear you are safe. Your mother as well.'

'My mother is dead.'

'I am sorry to hear that.'

'If you inform my father I will have to return to London.'

'And that is where you belong,' replied Lady Margery. 'Would it not be a better life for you than the life you have here, farming the lord's land? I do not think this is what you were brought up to do. I can tell you come from a good family.'

Millicent stepped out of her hut and joined them. She had obviously been listening. 'Excuse me, my lady.'

'Hello, Millicent.'

'If Gwendolyn's to return to 'er family, it would be best if she made the journey after the bairn's born,' said Millicent. 'The day is close now and it ain't safe for her to travel. The bairn could be born on the road.'

Lady Margery considered this for a moment. Elizabeth was sure she would not agree.

'Very well. We can wait until your baby is born and then inform your father. I understand your embarrassment, but it is your duty to inform me who your father is, just as it is my duty to ensure that you are returned safely to him.'

'Tell Lady Margery who yer father is, Gwendolyn,' said Millicent. 'You don't want to find yoursen in any more trouble, believe me.'

Elizabeth bit her lip as she considered what to do. 'Sir Robyn de Grey,' she said eventually.

Both Lady Margery and Auriol raised their eyebrows in response. Elizabeth guessed they were impressed with her pedigree.

She decided there was little use in lying any more. 'And my name isn't Gwendolyn, it's Elizabeth. But please can I remain as Gwendolyn while I'm here? I don't want word spreading about where I am.'

'What are you frightened of, Elizabeth?' asked Lady Margery. 'Who are you running away from?'

There was silence as Elizabeth gathered her thoughts. 'I am running away from shame.'

Elizabeth stirred the bowl of pottage that hung over the fire. They had run out of oats, so the pottage contained only dried peas and leeks, which Millicent had harvested earlier that day. Despite the lack of ingredients, it smelt delicious.

'They took me while I was at the market,' Elizabeth said as she continued to stir. She wondered whether she had thought the words or actually said them. For some reason she felt ready to talk about what had happened to her. Perhaps it was the relief of having finally admitted who she was and the knowledge that Lady Margery was allowing her to stay away from London until the baby arrived.

Millicent was spinning wool and didn't reply.

Elizabeth took her silence as encouragement to keep talking. 'I was with Eloise, one of our servant girls. I wanted to buy some new cooking pots and it was very busy that day. I almost lost sight of Eloise a few times. There was a lot of shouting and jostling, and I paused next to a fruit stall to let a group of soldiers pass by. Then I felt a hand on my arm, pulling me.' She stopped stirring and sat on her stool by the fire, watching Millicent spin.

'I turned to see who it was, but a hood covered his face. Then my other arm was held by another man. I shouted at them to let go and a few people looked at me, but no one intervened. They dragged me quickly through the crowd and I screamed for Eloise, but it felt like my voice was lost among the noise. Eloise didn't hear me; I don't know where she was by then. They held my arms so tightly it hurt. I asked who they were and what they wanted but they didn't reply. I told them they had the wrong person, but still they did not speak.'

Elizabeth could feel herself shaking as the memory flooded back into her mind.

'Then I was pulled into a narrow passageway; the one that runs behind St Martin's. They put a sack over my head and told me to stay quiet or they would hurt me. I could hardly see where I was going. I was pushed into a carriage and I remember thinking at the time that it must have belonged to a wealthy person. By this point they had tied my hands behind my back. I stopped shouting because I was frightened; I didn't know what they would do to me. If I had known then what I know now I would have kicked and screamed and shouted as much as possible. I was so surprised I didn't have time to decide how to react.'

'That ain't your fault,' said Millicent. 'No one expects to be snatched from a busy street in full view, do they? I can't believe no one came to 'elp you. That's London for you. Down 'ere an 'undred people would've tried saving you.'

'I remember sitting in the carriage, squeezed between these two men. The sack was still over my head and it stank. I could hardly bring myself to breathe.'

Elizabeth suddenly felt nauseous, as she had done at the time. Talbot walked over to her and nuzzled his nose in her lap.

'We didn't travel for long and then they pulled me out of the carriage and in through a small door. I remember it had a stone step and inside the building was a stone corridor. I thought I was in the courthouse at first, but then I decided it was either a church or a palace. I could tell by the echo of our footsteps that it was a big place. I asked them where I was and what they wanted, but still they refused to speak to me. I was taken to the foot of a flight of steps and I remember them dragging me up them. My feet slipped and I bruised my ankle. Then they stopped and pulled the sack off my head, and that was when I saw him.'

'Saw who?' asked Millicent.

'Sir Walter Rokeby.'

'Never 'eard of 'im.'

'He is well known in London. I knew him because the man I was betrothed to was his vintner. I had been introduced to him a few times and had always thought he was a decent man because he helps the poor and sick. Everyone thinks he is a kind man, and I was of the same opinion. I smiled at him, thinking it was a joke he had arranged with my husband. I waited for my hands to be untied, but they were not. And then I started to realise something was seriously wrong. His face looked different; he had a strange look about him. He was smiling, but not in a friendly way. He looked like a wolf that had caught a sheep. I started to worry that he would hurt me, and I was right.'

'Ugh!' Millicent exclaimed, spitting on the floor. She stopped spinning, 'What did 'e do to yer?'

Elizabeth noticed her hands were shaking and her voice faltered as she continued. 'He walked around me, looking at me like I was a piece of livestock he was planning to buy. And then he laughed and said he wondered what Geoffrey Edington, the man who was to have been my husband, would think.

Something started to feel very wrong then; it was difficult to believe he was the same man. I had always respected him, lots of people did. And I couldn't understand why I was standing in his room or why he was looking at me like that. I asked him what he wanted, and he laughed and told me I was his prize. He said it was unfair that Geoffrey should have me to himself. None of it made sense, but I didn't have much time to think about it because he started to undo my dress.'

'Evil man! May his soul rot in 'ell!' Millicent got up and put an arm around Elizabeth's shoulders.

Elizabeth felt the need to keep talking. 'I tried to push him off, and I kept expecting someone from his household to come in and stop him, but no one did. He told me if I made a noise he would have me killed. That frightened me into silence. I knew he was a strong, powerful man and that he could do whatever he wanted with me. Nothing I did made any difference; he seemed to enjoy it more when I tried to fight back. So I chose to stay still and...'

Elizabeth stopped again. There was a sharp constriction in her throat and tears welled in her eyes. 'I allowed it to happen. That's what I did wrong. I let him do those things to me.'

'No you didn't! You was forced. You said yourself you was frightened. There ain't nothing you could've done.'

'I could have fought him off.'

'No, you couldn't 'ave. He was much stronger than you, and he'd threatened you. You mustn't ever blame yoursen. He's an evil man and I'm set on cursin' 'im. What did 'e do with you next?'

'He put me in a small room and locked the door. It had two beds in it, a bowl for washing and a bucket. I don't know how long I was there, but there were other girls too.'

'More of them? It weren't just you?'

'No, there were many of us. We saw each other at his parties, when he invited his friends to come and do whatever they wanted with us. He made us wear nice dresses and told us to leave our hair uncovered and loose. They gave us wine and I drank a lot of it because it made the parties easier to cope with. It didn't hurt so much when I had drunk a few glasses of wine.' Elizabeth choked at the memory and wiped the tears from her face.

Millicent left her side and stood by the fire. 'Did yer talk to the other girls?'

'A bit. They were frightened, like me. And talking wasn't allowed. There also women there from the brothels. Some of them laughed at us but others were kind. They seemed to enjoy the parties just as much as the men, but I know they were paid to attend. We were forced to sit and watch. I hated it and I wanted to see someone I knew who could take a message to Geoffrey or my father, but I was also ashamed to be there. A lot of the men ignored us, because we didn't make any advances and tried to hide away. But Sir Walter always wanted us, and if one of his men was interested he would make us stand in a line so the guest could choose which girl he wanted. Usually they wanted the youngest ones. I was grateful that I wasn't chosen as often, but I felt so bad for those girls. And then one evening I saw Geoffrey at a party.'

'He knew you'd been taken?'

Elizabeth nodded.

'And he *didn't do nothin*?' Millicent's eyes burned like flame.

'He must have been too frightened. Sir Walter is a powerful man and has a host of guards. I tried to signal to him from across the room. I wanted him to tell my father and brothers where I was so they could rescue me, but he pretended not to know me and looked away. I suppose if he had been seen talking to me his life would have been in danger. I never saw him again.'

'And how did you escape this tyrant?'

'They tried to kill me.'

'*What*? Oh my poor Lizzie. It just gets worse.' Millicent walked back to her and put an arm around her again.

'There was another girl who started to fight the guards. She and I were alone in a corridor. They couldn't subdue her, and then she screamed and they couldn't keep her quiet. One of them put his hand around her neck and she choked and fell to the floor. I watched her lying there, and then they decided they would have to get rid of me as well because I had seen what had happened and might tell someone. The guard put his hand around my neck really hard.'

She reached up and touched her throat. 'Sometimes it still feels sore now. The next thing I knew I was surrounded by blackness. I woke up in the cart and realised they were taking us down to the river. I didn't want them to know I was alive, so I pretended to be dead. They threw us both into the river, but somehow I managed to get out again. I don't know how. I think the Lord saved me. He knew I had suffered enough.'

'He did the right thing.'

Elizabeth felt tired all of a sudden. She was unable to remember the last time she had talked so much. Sharing her story with Millicent had relieved some of the heaviness in her chest. She was still shaking, but she already felt better for talking about it. She felt encouraged that Millicent had not judged her.

'I will have to tell you the rest of the story tomorrow, I'm tired out now. But I've got something to show you.'

Elizabeth reached under the neck of her dress and pulled out a chain of rosary beads. She showed them to Millicent.

'I noticed you wearing them beads, they're pretty,' said Millicent. She felt some of them with her gnarled fingers. 'Looks like silver, and is that there glass? I think they're glass beads. And a letter "J".'

'I don't even know what her name was.'

'These belonged to the lass they killed?'

Elizabeth nodded. 'I knew she was dead as we lay on the floor of the cart. There was something so undignified about what they were doing to us I wanted to do something to acknowledge her death and remember her. I swapped our rosary beads over. I hope she was somehow reunited with her family and buried wearing my beads.'

Millicent rested her hand on Elizabeth's and squeezed it. 'I 'ope so too. You did all yer could've.'

There was a long silence as they both stared into the fire. Elizabeth watched the flames dance and looked deep into the embers, where the wood blistered white. She felt an urge to walk into the fire and let the flames burn away all the guilt and sin that swam inside her.

'I've bin around a long time and I still can't understand for the life o' me 'ow people can be so cruel,' said Millicent. 'I saw similar things years ago in my village; what bandits did to our women when they raided one night. I remember the two children found butchered in the forest a few years later. I always prayed it would never 'appen again; that we would all learn to 'ave kind hearts. I even practised new charms to stop it 'appening again, but it didn't make no difference. Evil will always be among us and take the place of some people's hearts, whether they're bandits on the road or the king's own knights.'

# Chapter Nineteen

❦

'God bless you, Sir Walter,' said the dirty, skinny woman with only one tooth. Three equally dirty children clung to her skirts and she held a thin baby in her arms.

'You look like you need a slice of pie as well as the bread,' said Sir Walter. 'Give them pie and some cake as well,' he ordered his men. He smiled kindly at the family.

'Thank you, Sir Walter, thank you,' said the skinny woman. 'Withou' you we would starve.' She moved out of the queue and another bedraggled family took her place.

'Waste of good cake,' muttered Sir Walter quietly to one of his men. 'You deal with the rest of them now, I've had enough.' He grinned at the people still waiting. 'You must excuse me, my attendance is required at court.'

He made a polite bow, left the doorway and strode through a corridor and across his courtyard towards his private rooms. Poor people made him uneasy, although he took great pains never to show it. As an unwanted bastard boy he could have been thrown out onto the street and been one of them scrabbling in the dirt for scraps and begging.

Instead, his mother had sent him to Sir Bertrand de Marren, who took in waifs to serve in his household. Those who showed promise could become pages and then start their training as a knight.

Reflecting on his upbringing, Sir Walter decided Sir Bertrand had recruited boys for the enjoyment of brutalising them more than anything else. Sir Walter had survived the cruelty and risen to the top. He was exceptionally proud of his achievements and the wealth he had accumulated.

Pausing in his courtyard, he frowned at a half-built structure, which should have been serving its purpose as an elaborate stone mews to house his hawks and falcons. He found the falconer in the old timber mews.

'Where are the stonemasons and the builders?' he barked at the man.

'There is a shortage, Sir,' replied his falconer.

'I thought I paid the best wages.'

'You do, Sir.'

'So if I pay the best wages, why are they not working for me? Who are they working for instead?'

'I'm not sure, Sir, I will find out,' replied the falconer.

Sir Walter tutted. It was frustrating having the work half-finished. He strode back to his apartments, his mind restless and irritable as it had been for some time.

He could not understand why there had been no sign of Elizabeth de Grey. Had she returned to her father he would have heard about it as Sir Robyn de Grey would have alerted the authorities. *So why had the stupid wench not returned to him? Where had she gone instead?* He could only hope she was dead, but until her body was found he had to believe she was alive and keep his men out searching for her.

He was still angry that she had managed to escape in the first place. He had spent many years cultivating his image as a well-bred, chivalrous man, and now there was a risk he could be found out. It was a small risk, but the worry was still eating away at him. It had been an experiment to see whether he could make Elizabeth disappear under the noses of her family and future husband. It had worked well for a while, but now he wondered whether he had taken too great a risk. He had to find her.

Theobald and Richard were waiting for Sir Walter in his apartments, and he was pleased to see that they were accompanied by a curly-haired, olive-skinned man. All three men stood to greet him.

'Welcome. You must be Valerian Baladi.'

The man nodded in reply. Sir Walter sat down and the men took their seats again. 'How is the search progressing for the whore who ran away, Richard?'

The look on Richard's face told him all he needed to know. 'Nothing so far, Sir Walter.'

'Where have you looked?'

'Her home, and the streets between here and her home. And down by the river where she climbed out onto the jetty.'

'She could be many miles from London by now, of course.'

'Yes, I understand, Sir Walter. We're trying to ascertain whether the girl has relatives she might have gone to stay with.'

'And her father has not seen her?'

'Not that I know of. I believe he still considers her missing, but we have stopped short of visiting him because that would arouse suspicion.'

'Very good. You do have some sense after all. However, time is running out, Richard.'

'I am aware of that, Sir.'

'It will not be long before the harlot starts talking. Do you think she is likely to stay quiet?'

'I realise that, Sir Walter. It is reassuring that we have not had word of her being found. Perhaps she caught cold and died somewhere on the street.'

'That is wishful thinking, Richard. I think her body would have been found by now if that were the case, do you not agree? I suspect she is hiding and we need to find out where. Get more men looking for her, and any man who breathes a word of this search will be killed. Is that understood, Richard?'

Richard nodded his head and Sir Walter glared at Valerian to ensure that he understood the conversation was confidential.

'I am growing impatient,' said Sir Walter. 'Each day this whore is allowed to run free gives her the chance to appear somewhere or talk. I am forced to employ more and more men for this search and that brings risks with it. Do you expect me to be happy about this?'

'No, Sir.' Richard rubbed his throat as if concerned Sir Walter might choke him again.

Sir Walter turned away from him and addressed Valerian. 'On the other hand, I am indebted to my good friend the Earl of Wykeham for allowing you to work in my household, Mr Baladi.'

He nodded at the two guards by the door, who walked over to stand next to the table. Sir Walter knew a little intimidation would help.

Valerian's face remained expressionless. Sir Walter knew he would have to work on him.

'You may be wondering why I have asked you to join my household.'

Valerian shrugged and said nothing.

Sir Walter sneered in response to his surliness. 'Let me explain how things work in my household.' He stood up and leant on the table so that his face was within spitting distance of Valerian's. 'People work for me for two reasons: money and fear. Often it is a combination of the two.'

Sir Walter chuckled. 'Everyone does what I ask them to do, and if there is any resistance to my instructions or a mishap occurs while they are carrying out their duties for me, it is severely dealt with. I will not say any more on the matter, but when you are next drinking ale with my esteemed adviser Theobald here, why not ask him what happened to Heward Lovell? And before I continue with our conversation, let me also add that nothing discussed here is to be spoken of beyond my private quarters. Is that understood?'

Valerian nodded.

'A word from you would be polite.'

'Yes, Sir Walter.'

Sir Walter sat back in his chair, studying Valerian. It was possible the man was untrustworthy, but Sir Walter needed him. He lightened his demeanour in the hope this would appeal to the man more effectively.

'I have brought you here to help me. I understand you took a wench from St Hugh's hospital?'

'No!' Valerian leapt up from his seat. 'I did not do it! She was taken by someone else!'

'I can see I have stirred a hornet's nest,' said Sir Walter, turning to his guards and smirking. 'She was taken by someone else you say? By whom?'

'I don't know. Three men called at the hospital and took her away. My friend Roger and I tried to stop them, but he was hit and killed. I tried to follow the men but I lost them. The Earl of Wykeham believes me, but the bailiff doesn't and neither does the prior at St Hugh's. If I can prove I am innocent, hopefully everyone will leave me alone.'

'I believe you.'

'Really?'

Sir Walter smiled at how easy it was to bring this man around. 'Yes, I do. You do not know who the men were?'

'I have no idea.'

'I can help you prove your innocence, Valerian.'

'Thank you.' Valerian relaxed back into his chair. 'Can I ask how?'

'I will tell you in good time, but I require your help first.'

'Of course. What would you have me do?'

'Let's talk about St Hugh's again. What are they doing about the missing wench?'

'Her name is Constance.'

'Pretty name.'

'They have asked the bailiff to help them. Unfortunately, he thinks I took Constance.'

'And we all know you didn't. So what happens next?'

Valerian shrugged. 'I don't know. A few people there are still looking for her.'

'And who are they?'

'There is the widow who works there, Alice Wescott. And one of the monks, Brother Jon. The monk who wants to be a knight.'

'A soldier monk?'

'He comes from a family of knights. His father is Sir Robyn de Grey.'

Sir Walter tried not to appear surprised at this news but was unable to suppress a slight smile.

'Do you know him?' asked Valerian.

'Sir Robyn and I have known one another for many years. We fought together in France. The monk is his son, you say?'

'Yes.'

*So the monk was Elizabeth de Grey's brother. That explained why he was assisting in the search for Constance. He was probably hoping to find his sister at the same time.* Sir Walter chuckled to himself.

'What amuses you, Sir Walter?' asked Theobald.

'Nothing of any import. I was just thinking how funny it is that this poor monk is trapped in a monastery when he would rather be out in the real world fighting. He was born too late for the Knights Templar. As Sir Robyn's other sons are all knights, I imagine Brother Jon is the youngest and was sent away to the monastery at a young age. He was the one who had to be a monk; they had enough knights. Better to be sent to the monastery as a boy than to the household of Sir Bertrand. I was nine years old when I saw him kill one of his squires with his bare hands. He was a boy of twelve, and had been a good friend of mine. I forget what his misdemeanour was; it was something small. Sir Bertrand had a dreadful temper.'

An image of the boy's boots kicking up the dirt in the courtyard as Sir Bertrand held his hands around his neck entered Sir Walter's mind. 'Anyway, this conversation is going nowhere,' he continued. 'Let's discuss what I need you to do, Valerian. Let me make it clear, first of all, that Constance does not wish to be found.'

'You know what happened to her? She is alive?'

Sir Walter ignored the question. 'Nobody needs to go looking for her now. The problem we have is that a few people are determined to undermine all authority and search for her. I have done my best to stop them, but there is only so much I can do. Now, if I have someone who is able to report back to me on what those people are planning to do next, I can take control of the situation. Do you understand what I am asking of you, Valerian?'

'You want me to spy for you?'

'Yes, that's right. You catch on quickly. I take it this widow, Alice Wescott, trusts you?'

'I'm not sure. But she believes me that I did not take Constance.'

'Good, well she must like you in that case. Unlike the nuns at St Hugh's, her blood runs warm. She has been married before and I imagine she is drawn to your charm. The problem is that the widow has brains. She needs to be distracted from thought, and concern herself with what's between her legs instead. I think you can encourage her to do that. Seduce her if you like.'

Valerian scratched at the back of his neck awkwardly.

'Pay her regular visits and make her happy to update you on what she plans to do next. Then your only task will be to keep me informed.'

'And what about Constance?'

Sir Walter clenched his jaw. 'As I have told you, you must forget about her.'

'But I'm concerned...'

'You do not need to be!' Sir Walter stood up and slammed his fist into his palm. He glared at Valerian and estimated that he was thirty years older than the young man sitting in front of him. Despite this, he was certain he could fell him easily with one blow. Sir Walter had been one of the strongest knights on the battlefield and he was still powerfully built.

Valerian fell quiet and, once again, Sir Walter wondered if he was taking too much of a risk with the man. Everything he did seemed to be risky now. It had once felt exhilarating, but now it was making him anxious. 'Remember that you are to do whatever I ask,' he said quietly. 'Otherwise you will find yourself hanging for the murder of your friend Roger.'

'I did not kill him.'

'Only you and I are sure of that.' Sir Walter sat down again.

'The Earl of Wykeham will defend me,' said Valerian.

'No he will not, he will take my side. He may be your employer, but the earl is a close friend of mine.' Sir Walter stared into Valerian's dark eyes. 'Now, you do as I ask and not a word to anyone about what you hear and see in my household. Do you comply?' He continued to stare, and Valerian glared back.

'Yes, Sir,' replied Valerian eventually. The sullen expression had returned to his face.

'Good. Now then, Theobald, I received a message from you about our friend Geoffrey Edington.'

'Yes, that is right, Sir Walter. Although I need to speak to you alone about the matter.'

'You can tell me freely in front of Richard and Valerian, who is now a member of my household and can be trusted on pain of death.'

Theobald cleared his throat. 'Geoffrey Edington has been drinking a good deal lately, Sir Walter. He has been at The Crown every evening this week and his tongue has become loose.'

'Sounds like normal behaviour to me,' chuckled Sir Walter. 'What has he been talking about?'

'I'm not sure I can say in the present company.'

Sir Walter pounded the table with his fist. 'I have already said you are free to speak, now get on with it. What has Geoffrey Edington *been talking about*?'

'About how his future wife was snatched from him, and that she has escaped and he is going to look for her.'

Sir Walter felt a heavy thud in his chest. This was a real cause for concern. 'I hope you shut him up.'

'I was not present, Sir. The report came from one of my men.'

'And when did this wild talk begin?'

Sir Walter gave Valerian a sideways glance to gauge his reaction, but his face gave nothing away.

'I'm not sure exactly. The reports were only passed to me this week.'

'And has anyone been taking Geoffrey seriously?'

'I cannot tell. I heard he was also drunk at The Swan last week.'

'And talking about what? To whom?'

'I'm not sure, Sir Walter.'

'It seems you are unsure about many things.' Sir Walter was growing tired of Theobald. 'Do we know if this man has begun looking for the woman he calls his future wife?'

'I... don't know.'

'I see, well thank you for passing me half the information. It's a shame the other half is missing. I will tell Serle and Grimbold to pay him a visit. I was impressed by the manner in which they dealt with Heward Lovell.'

Sir Walter saw Theobald and Richard stiffen at this news and was unable to hide a triumphant smile.

# Chapter Twenty

Alice's new home was a single room in a long, timber building that ran alongside one length of the hospital garden. The building had been divided into living quarters for people connected to St Hugh's. Next to Alice's room lived an elderly widow who was a distant relative of the king. Alice had a sneaking suspicion that Prior Edmund's mistress, Tillie Buckley, lived in the next room along.

Alice's belongings were brought over to the hospital by cart and the brothers helped carry the goods into her new home. Her room was furnished only with a bed, a small fireplace, a table with a bowl for washing, and a couple of stools. The room was too small to house all her furniture and she had just two wooden cases with her: one large one containing her clothes and a smaller one she had previously kept in her bedroom. Most of her sheets, blankets, wall hangings, pottery and silverware had been placed in a storeroom in the main monastery building, along with the cabinets, beds and tables from her former home. On the table in her room sat the casket that had been emptied onto the floor during the break-in. The lid rested on it now, and Alice was no longer able to close it properly or lock it. Nevertheless, she felt fortunate to have her precious things with her.

Alice regularly fought the urge to hammer at the prior's door and demand her home back or to visit Brother Rufus in the cloisters and break his writing desk into pieces. Instead, she tried to remain calm and follow Jon's advice to fight back when the time was right.

She placed one of the stools next to the narrow window and looked out at the rain falling in the garden. Nearby were some rosemary bushes, their thin leaves dancing with the raindrops. Alice had been shaken up by the break-in at her home. Nothing had been taken, so it appeared to have been an attempt to frighten her.

*How did the intruder know the casket and its contents were so precious to her? And who was the intruder? Why had they done something like that? Perhaps she was safer at St Hugh's?*

The walls of the monastery gave her a sense of security, but they were also starting to feel like the walls of a prison. Her life was becoming increasingly like that of a nun. *Perhaps it was God's will? Perhaps she should take her vows after all?* She had chosen a life of seclusion after the deaths of her husband and son, but she was beginning to wonder if that had been the right choice.

Now that she was trapped at St Hugh's she wanted to leave. But if she left she would be making the decision to leave the children, and that was something she simply couldn't face. With her family and Constance gone the foundlings were all she had.

The children loved visiting Alice in her room because it provided a welcome change to their dormitory, and after a while the visit became part of their daily routine. Alice let them play there each afternoon following a game of hide and seek in the garden. Sometimes she got out the toys Christopher had enjoyed playing with, and it made her happy to see little hands playing with them again rather than having them shut away in a chest. Her only regret was that he wasn't there to play with them.

Each day was the same. Alice rose early, helped the children get ready for the day and, while the nuns taught them, helped with other jobs in the hospital: washing and drying clothing and bedding, preparing food and cleaning. In the afternoon there was song time with Sister Emma and then play. After this there was supper to prepare before supervising the children as they washed their hands and faces and got into bed.

There were also regular breaks for prayer. The children did not attend all the services in the chapel, but when they did go Alice accompanied them. She was expected to attend each service, but sometimes while the brothers and sisters attended prayers she was able to continue with any unfinished work.

Nicholas also had to be looked after. His condition was slowly worsening and he needed someone by his bedside day and night. Alice took turns with Sister Emma and some of the lay sisters to ensure that he was properly cared for.

The days passed and Alice felt herself sinking into a routine of daily tasks, which she carried out without question or emotion. The fervour of searching for Constance and the constant worry about what had happened to her had calmed to a strangely numb sensation. Sleep was difficult, colours seemed dull and food was flavourless.

The only joy she found was in looking after the children. While her own life felt as though it was grinding to a halt, their little lives kept developing and changing. They learnt new words and skills; they kept growing and laughing. There were often tears, but the tantrums were always short-lived. Alice loved the way they recovered so quickly from upset. She envied the way they could live without concern for the past or future.

She also missed conversing with Jon. They would nod to each other when she passed him in the garden and occasionally they exchanged a glance at prayer times, but there was no conversation. She was worried about him. She was concerned about how he would cope if he never found out what had happened to his sister. Their search had been brought to an abrupt end and she had to do something about it.

The number of crosses encircling Constance's blue songbird now numbered forty. Counting them reminded Alice of the notches Jon cut each day on the birch tree in Elizabeth's memory. Alice couldn't imagine Constance being missing for that long. *How did Jon not lose his mind with worry?*

Yvette de Beauchamp was a good friend of the prior's, and Alice began to wonder if she could ask Yvette to urge him to reconsider. Perhaps Yvette could persuade him to allow Alice time each week to look for Constance and Elizabeth. She needed to speak to Juliana's family, but she needed permission to leave St Hugh's. If she went without it she would never see the children again.

Alice knew Sister Emma sometimes left the hospital and decided to ask for her help.

'Do your errands ever take you near Westcheap, Sister Emma?'

'Yes, I sometimes pass through there,' she replied. 'Why do you ask?'

'I was wondering if you could call on Yvette de Beauchamp.'

'What would you like me to say to her?'

'Some time ago I discussed her visiting St Hugh's to make a donation to the hospital.' This was the truth, but it had been so long ago Alice was not sure Yvette would even remember. 'The prior will not allow me to leave St Hugh's and I need to speak with her.'

Sister Emma bit her lip. 'I would like to help, but...'

'Please,' begged Alice.

'I think it would go against the prior's orders and I do not wish to disobey him.'

'I realise that and I am sorry that my request is putting you in a difficult position. But if the prior should ever find out I asked you to do this you could explain that it was because Yvette always lifts the spirits of the patients and children when she visits. And she makes generous donations to St Hugh's.'

Alice watched as Sister Emma considered this.

'I will call at her house and ask her.'

'Thank you!'

'But this is only because your mother and I were friends. Otherwise I would not undertake such a risk.'

Alice couldn't help giving Sister Emma a hug. 'Thank you, Sister Emma! Thank you.'


Sister Emma was true to her word, and two weeks later Yvette de Beauchamp swept through the doors of St Hugh's with her lapdog in her arms and two maids in tow. She toured the hospital with the prior at her side, a beacon of colour in her orange and yellow satin dress. Her hat and veil were covered with hundreds of tiny beads, which glittered as she walked. The children were fascinated by her.

After visiting the patients she strolled in the garden with Alice. Her little dog sniffed in the hedges and relieved himself on the onions. The sun was shining, but a breeze whipped around the walls of the building.

'So this is your home now,' Yvette said with a thin smile. 'I warned you against this way of life.'

'I only ever wanted to help,' said Alice, realising as she uttered the words that there was something pathetic about them.

'And now you see where helping has led you. You have martyred yourself,' said Yvette. 'You have no freedom any more. This is the price of your selfless mission; a determination to pay your penance for what sin?'

'I survived.'

'But that is not sin. You were chosen to live. And what did you do with that freedom? You made yourself a prisoner. If only Thomas could see you now.'

Alice sighed at the mention of her husband's name.

'It was foolish not to continue Thomas' trade,' continued Yvette, 'and I think you realise that now. Do you ever think about how your life could have turned out? You could have had another husband by now. And another child.'

'Why do people assume that was what I wanted?' snapped Alice. 'Perhaps I'm happy as I am.'

'Are you happy?'

'I enjoy my work.'

'But that is not the same as being happy.'

Alice refused to let the comment upset her. 'St Hugh's owns my home now.'

'I know!' Yvette shook her head. 'You should never have got involved with the Church. Helping is not far removed from meddling, and now you have upset people and find yourself tied to the life you chose.'

'Not forever,' said Alice. 'I can change this.'

'How?'

'I am hoping you can help me.'

Alice's request was met with silence.

'You know the prior well. I was hoping you could speak to him on my behalf.'

'And ask him to let you walk about freely?'

'Yes.'

'And you think he would do that on my request alone?'

It seemed Yvette would not be easily convinced.

'You are held in high esteem,' said Alice.

'As were you at one time.'

'I think I still am. I may have upset a few people, but only because I wish to uncover the truth. I want to find the missing girl, Constance. She's my friend. Would you not do the same for a friend?'

'It would depend on the friend.'

'Constance is young and she needs me. If I can do nothing to find her, who will? I never intended to insult or undermine anyone. If it has been taken that way it is their problem, not mine.'

'But at the moment it *is* your problem, is it not?' said Yvette. She stopped walking and turned towards Alice. Her eyes were a cold, icy blue.

'You are the one suffering because you have had your liberty taken away as a result of a choice you made. For some reason you ran away to this place to escape the pain in your life. Instead of facing your tragic circumstances, you chose to hide from them. Continuing with your former life would have been the stronger, worthier choice. You cannot run away from the pain of your past; you have to face it. If you don't it will eventually catch up with you. '

Alice looked across the garden at Yvette's dog, who was digging a hole next to a row of leeks. She knew there was an element of truth in what Yvette was saying.

'Remember that I come from that very same place,' continued Yvette. 'My husband also died during the plague, as did two of my children. We both understand how hard it is to continue when life brings such suffering, but I made the choice to fight and prove what I could do on my own. I did not seclude myself with the nuns and monks. I put on my finest dress and continued on from where Simon had left off. I cannot tell you how difficult that was, but it became slightly easier each day. Death may have taken my family from me, but it never diminished my strength. I will not let it. Like me, you are a survivor and you need to start behaving as one.'

Yvette's eyes were as hard and bright as sapphire. Alice knew she would never be as strong as her friend.

'Perhaps I made a mistake,' Alice said. 'I only did what I thought was right. I can see how I have been backed into a corner as a result of my actions, but I look after those children every day. What would their lives be like if I were to leave?'

'I am sure you have done a great deal for those foundlings.'

'And chastising me for my mistakes is of no benefit now, is it?'

'No.'

'I need to think about what I can do now.'

'You do.'

'So will you help?'

'Your problem, Alice, is that you are confrontational and disobedient, and although those qualities can be useful, they need to be used appropriately. I heard how you interrupted the prior's prayers and challenged him in front of everyone. That raised his hackles from the outset. It is not the way to succeed.'

'I was just so upset; that was why I spoke out. I was angry and frustrated. I still feel that way now.'

'Alice,' Yvette's face softened, 'you are driven by your heart and not your head. In the eyes of the Lord you are a good person and you would probably be a better nun than any of the sisters here,' she smiled. 'But if you want to influence others you need to be wiser in your actions. If you stop to think before you act you will find those around you more receptive.'

'So will you speak to the prior for me?'

'I will. I am not convinced it will make any difference, but I will try.'

Alice had grown too impatient to wait for Yvette. Once the children were tucked up in bed that evening and the nuns and monks were at prayers, Alice went up to the nuns' dormitory. Checking no one else was around, she opened wardrobes and looked for a habit that wouldn't be missed for a day or two. Having found one she hoped was spare, she rolled it as tightly as she could under her arm and made her way back to her room to change.

There was a little-used doorway in the precinct of St Hugh's. Alice chose to walk to it after sundown, past the room belonging to Tillie Buckley and the storeroom that housed Jon's gardening tools. The door was close to the birch tree where Jon cut the notches for his sister.

Alice hid her lantern under her cloak until she reached the door. Its latch was rusty but unlocked. She had never been through this door before, but she guessed it opened into an alleyway than ran from Gracechurch Street. Once she was through it, she found herself giggling under her breath. She was free. The lantern didn't throw much light into the darkness of the alleyway, but Alice felt confident about the route she would take.

Few people paid attention to the nun who walked through the blustery streets of London that evening. Her habit was a little long and dragged in the mud, but she walked with a quick stride and was curt with the men at the gate when they told her it was closed for the night. She had to get to The Strand, which lay beyond London's walls.

'My sisters have requested that I join them in prayer.'

'Can't it wait 'til tomorrow?'

'We are praying for the soul of a dying man. The Lord will have taken him by then.'

'You should 'ave been 'ere afore curfew.'

'Sir, please take pity on a nun who has walked across London this evening and seeks only to do the work God has commanded of her. Death does not adhere to curfews.'

The guard tutted and unlocked the small door in the gates.

'God bless you and your family, Sir.'

Alice knew she was taking a great risk and she wasn't entirely sure why she was doing this. Perhaps it was the desperation to feel free, and perhaps she had been encouraged by Yvette's words earlier that day: *You are a survivor and you need to start behaving as one.*

Alice had never looked at her situation that way before. Until now she had felt guilty that she had survived. Maybe she had undertaken this night-time adventure as a challenge to herself. Perhaps she could prove she was capable of more than she imagined.

The Strand was lined with the high walls and large palaces of nobles and bishops. The Swan sat just beyond the church of St Clement Dane. Its sign – depicting a white swan swimming – creaked as it swung in the wind above the door.

The Swan was a tall, narrow tavern. The heavily timbered upper storey overhung the street and its beams bowed in the middle, as if it were about to fold in on itself. The lower storey was in darkness, while upstairs a dim orange light glowed from a window. If Jon was right, this was where the girl in the river had lived.

Alice guessed Juliana's family were preparing for bed. She

held her lantern up to the dark window and tried to peer in. There was no sign of anyone in the tavern now and there was no use knocking on the door at this hour. The family would not thank her for it. She would have to find another time to come, but she felt pleased that she now knew where the family lived.

She looked across the road at a large stone building, its tall chimneys silhouetted against the night sky. It looked like the home of a nobleman and she recalled Sir Walter saying during the dinner at Yvette's home that he lived on The Strand.

In the gloom she could see something at the foot of the wall that surrounded the palace. She crossed the street and saw what looked like a bundle of clothes. Then she realised she was looking at four or five people. They were sleeping outside in the cold, unsheltered from the wind, next to a door in the wall. They were the poor, waiting for daylight to come and food to be handed out to them. *Was this Sir Walter's home they were waiting outside?* It seemed unjust that one man should have such a large palace for himself while a group of people with nothing slept outside its walls.

Alice turned and began the long walk back to St Hugh's.

# Chapter Twenty-One

꧁꧂

Jon had never spoken to Geoffrey Edington about his
sister's disappearance. His father had met with Geoffrey after Elizabeth went missing and Jon understood
that Geoffrey had been as upset and confused as
everyone else.

He had never suspected that Geoffrey could have had a
hand in Elizabeth's disappearance. On the few occasions the
men had met Geoffrey had seemed very keen on marrying his
sister. Dour and serious, he was twelve years older than her
and had lanky, thinning hair. He didn't have much to offer her
in Jon's opinion. Geoffrey Edington may have come from a
wealthy family, but Jon could see no benefit for his sister in
marrying him. However, Geoffrey had been Sir Robyn de
Grey's choice for his daughter and Jon had to respect that.

The discovery of Elizabeth's rosary beads had led to a
number of sleepless nights for Jon. *Could Geoffrey provide a link
between Juliana the taverner's daughter and Elizabeth?* It was
unlikely, but the more Jon thought about it the more he
realised he had to ask him. If Geoffrey couldn't help with

that, perhaps he might know something else that could provide Jon with a clue about what had happened to her.

After repairing the holes in the garden that had been dug by Yvette de Beauchamp's dog, Jon set out to Geoffrey's home early that evening. He took one of the horses from the monastery stables and rode to Carter Lane near St Paul's, where the Edington family had lived for many years. Jon had heard that Geoffrey now lived alone in the house he would have shared with Elizabeth.

It was dark by the time Jon arrived in the street of smart, timbered homes and there was no light shining from Geoffrey's place. Jon tethered his horse and stood in the street wondering where Geoffrey could be at this hour. *Was there a tavern he liked to frequent?*

A brisk wind blew and Jon was alerted to the sound of a door banging. Holding his lantern up, he saw that Geoffrey's door was open and swinging in the wind. Jon felt uneasy but knew he had to investigate further. He approached the open door.

'Hello?'

There was no answer. He knocked on the door and called out again, but still there was no reply. Jon felt his heart thumping slow and steady. But there was no need to panic; he was sure there must be a sensible explanation. *Perhaps Geoffrey was elsewhere for the evening and had not shut his door properly. The wind had probably knocked it off its latch. But he was sure Geoffrey had at least one servant, so was the servant not at home either?*

Holding out his lantern, Jon stepped into the hall. There were well-trodden rushes on the floor and a tapestry on the wall. The fireplace was empty and cold. Jon shivered and continued through the hall to a smaller room, where there was a desk and a cushioned chair.

Something glowed in the lamplight at the far corner of the room. Jon stepped forward towards it and took a moment to fully understand what he was looking at. It was the face of a young man who was lying on the floor. His eyes were open and there was a dark, wide gash across his neck.

The boy was dead.

His limbs appeared to be tangled up in something and Jon realised the boy was lying on top of another person. He didn't want to look closer but knew he had to. He held the lantern above the boys' legs and saw another man's face. This man was older and streaks of blood could be seen on one cheek.

Geoffrey Edington.

There was also a large gash across Geoffrey's throat. Jon recoiled and his feet felt sticky on the floor. Looking down he saw he was standing in a pool of blood, a smell that reminded him of animal offal hitting the back of this throat.

He leapt back and stared once again at the gruesome tableau in the corner of the room. Geoffrey must have been attacked first and then the young man, who Jon assumed was his servant. Their bodies had been tossed to the side of the room and there was little sign of a struggle. The killer must have been quick and powerful.

*Perhaps Geoffrey had disturbed intruders*, he wondered. The question that played on Jon's mind was why anyone would want to kill Geoffrey Edington. He remembered him as a mild mannered man; he was no threat to anyone. He had been wealthy, but Jon could see that the items on Geoffrey's desk were undisturbed. *If robbery had been the motive, surely the house would have been left in disarray?*

Jon left the scene and ran outside. He knocked loudly at the doors of the houses either side of Geoffrey's home, raising the hue and cry. Within minutes a group of people were swarming into Geoffrey's house to witness the awful scene.

Jon got back onto his horse and helped a handful of men search for the murderer in the nearby streets. He must have struck recently and still be close by. But there were many shadows to hide in, and once people in the nearby taverns and alehouses had been alerted there was so much noise and commotion that the murderer could easily have slipped away unnoticed.

After helping with what appeared to be a futile search, Jon set off back to St Hugh's later that evening. He had never held a great deal of affection for Geoffrey Edington, but he was shocked and saddened by the man's death. *Was his murder connected to Elizabeth's disappearance?* It was difficult to see how, but with poor Juliana found wearing her rosary beads and her future husband senselessly slaughtered, Jon wondered whether people who knew Elizabeth were being targeted. *Could someone in his family be next?*

Jon didn't feel afraid, but he could feel his hands trembling as he gripped the reins. He felt the need for some strong wine when he returned to St Hugh's. Perhaps just this once he would join the drinkers in the refectory.

Groups of men were still out on the street looking for Geoffrey's killer, but as Jon rode up Old Fish Street he saw a lantern ahead of him that seemed to belong to a person who was walking alone. As he drew nearer he could see the person was concealed in a large cloak and was bent over as if trying to hide his or her identity.

He got his horse to a trot in a bid to catch up. *Could this be the murderer subtly trying to escape?* Jon could see that the person was small and did not look strong enough to cut the throats of two men. As he drew alongside the solitary walker, he realised he was looking at a woman. A nun. Her wimple shone white in the lamplight.

'Is it not rather late to be on the street, Sister?'

She looked up at him and he realised he knew her from St Hugh's. And she was not a nun.

'*Alice?*'

'Sshh!' she replied. 'Call me by another name. Sister Joan will do.'

'What are you *doing?*'

Seeing Alice in a nun's habit was alarming. Jon prayed she would not decide to become a nun.

'I went to see Juliana's family.'

'Dressed like *that?*'

'They didn't see me. The hour was too late to speak to them, but I have found out where The Swan is now so we can return there and find out more about Juliana.'

'Have you thought about what the prior will say when he discovers you left St Hugh's? And whose habit are you wearing?'

'He does not need to know. He will be drunk by now and I shouldn't think anyone else will notice me gone.'

Alice looked down at the long baggy tunic. 'I don't know who this belongs to. I hope no one is missing it.'

'We need to get back. Let me help you up.'

Jon held out his hand but Alice didn't move.

'Come on, we need to get back to St Hugh's before anyone notices we're not there. It must be past midnight now.'

'I am not good with horses.'

'All you have to do is sit up here, I will do the rest.' Jon dismounted and held out his hand again to help Alice up into the saddle.

To his frustration, she still refused to move.

'You haven't told me what *you* are doing out here at this hour,' she said.

'I will tell you once you are sitting up on my horse.'

Although Jon liked Alice's independent spirit, her stubbornness could be infuriating.

Eventually, Alice agreed to travel on the horse.

'Can you sit astride the saddle?' asked Jon, 'If you are not used to riding you will be more likely to stay on that way than if you ride side saddle.'

'This tunic is large enough to allow me to do it without ruining my modesty,' replied Alice.

She sat in the saddle while Jon climbed up in front of it. She held on to his waist and he nudged the horse to move on.

'Are you holding on tight?' asked Jon.

'Yes.'

Gripping the reins with one hand and holding his lantern with the other, he coaxed the horse into a canter and they made their way quickly through the silent street. Alice's arms were wrapped tightly around Jon's waist and her extinguished lantern knocked against his thigh as they rode.

'You still have not told me what you are doing out here tonight.'

'Geoffrey Edington's dead.'


Once they reached Gracechurch Street, Jon slowed the horse to a walk and described to Alice the scene he had witnessed at Geoffrey Edington's home that evening.

'That's dreadful,' said Alice. 'Who could have done such a thing?'

'The same person who killed Juliana perhaps.'

'You think there is a connection?'

'They both knew Elizabeth.'

'But it doesn't make sense.'

'We need to speak to Juliana's family as soon as we can. They must know something more.'

## Chapter Twenty-Two

The bell rang for eight as Alice stepped out into the garden. She had only slept a few hours before being called to Nicholas' bedside early that morning. His condition was steadily worsening and she was certain the end was in sight.

Sister Emma sat beside Nicholas' bedside while Alice took a short walk to refresh herself. There was some warmth in the sun and a scent of spring in the air, but Alice's head felt leaden and tired. She was relieved that no one appeared to have noticed her disappearance the previous evening. She had already washed the mud off the nun's habit and would dry it by her fire later that day before returning it to the wardrobe she had found it in. The morning air felt rejuvenating. Alice took a deep breath and wondered how she could escape again to visit Juliana's family.

'Valerian, you surprised me!'

He had appeared from around the corner of the building, dressed in a bright, parti-coloured jacket: red on one side and gold on the other. Alice had the uneasy feeling he had been lying in wait for her.

'What are you doing here?'

'I came to see how you are and whether you are any closer to finding out what happened to Constance.'

'No, I have discovered nothing,' she sighed. 'There is more I would like to do, but it is not easy for me to leave St Hugh's at the moment as the prior has forbidden it.'

'What is it you wish to do?'

'When we were looking for Constance a girl's body was pulled from the river. Her name was Juliana and she had not drowned. She had been murdered.'

Valerian grimaced.

'The girl was wearing a set of rosary beads that belonged to Jon's sister Elizabeth.'

'Really?'

'Elizabeth went missing last summer, so how the rosary beads came to be around the girl's neck is a mystery. Jon spoke to the coroner to find out who the girl was and we now have her family's details. We need to speak to them and work out how she could have known Elizabeth.'

'But what does that have to do with Constance?'

'The disappearances could be linked, but as yet we cannot draw any parallels between how Constance and Elizabeth went missing. Maybe we will find out more when we speak to Juliana's family. I am probably pinning my hopes on nothing, but it seems a strange coincidence that three girls appear to have vanished. It is possible the same person is behind all three disappearances. And last night we discovered that the man who Elizabeth was meant to marry, Geoffrey Edington, has been murdered. Something is happening here, but I cannot fathom what it is. Do you have any advice, Valerian?'

He avoided her gaze as she asked the question. 'I don't think I do. That is sad news about Geoffrey Edington. All you can do is remain hopeful, I suppose. You have to believe the girls are still alive.'

'But one was found dead. Poor Juliana. I didn't even know her, but seeing her laid out like that, and so young as well...' Alice trailed off as the memory of the girl's body in the small, dismal room came back to her mind. 'I hope you are right. But tell me what you have been doing. You are still a free man, I see. Does this mean you are now believed to be innocent?'

'Yes, I think so.'

'Well, that is good news! This means you are free to get on with your work for the Earl of Wykeham. He must be happy for you. Where will your travels take you next, do you think?'

'I am not sure yet,' he replied, glancing up at the bell tower and then down at the ground. 'In fact, I must get back to him now. He will be wondering where I have got to.'

Once again, Alice noticed that Valerian did not look directly at her when he spoke. Something about him had changed and it wasn't just the smart clothes.

That night a single candle flickered in the children's dormitory. It sat on the little wooden table Alice had moved next to Nicholas' bed. In hushed tones, she asked the lay sister to wake one of the monks to fetch Prior Edmund.

'He told us to wake him if anything happened.' Alice prayed he had not consumed too much wine to be stirred.

The prior arrived a short while later wearing a voluminous linen nightgown and carrying a lantern. In the dim orange light, Alice could see grey stubble on his chin. She was accustomed to seeing him clean-shaven. He sat on the stool Alice had placed next to Nicholas' bed.

'Has he spoken?' he asked in a whisper.

Alice shook her head.

The boy's breathing was quick and shallow, and his chest rattled with phlegm. The noises in his chest had grown worse over the previous few days. As the physician was leaving earlier that evening he had told Alice he was running out of treatments for the boy. Alice had partly felt relieved by this, as seeing the little boy bled with leeches and purged to make him vomit had been heart-breaking. Although she knew the doctor had been trying his best, it had been a relief to see him go.

Alice knew they were going to lose Nicholas; that was why she had called the prior. The little boy had become less responsive during the day. His breathing had become more laboured and he was no longer able to take any food or drink. Her heart ached to see him suffer. She hoped he was spending most of his time in a deep sleep, unaware of what was happening to him.

The prior held his son's hand and watched him intently. The boy's chest was hardly moving. Nicholas sighed a little, startling the prior, but his eyes remained firmly shut and a cold pallor was settling across his skin.

Alice sat at the foot of the bed, knowing she had done all she could. She watched in the flickering light as the prior rested his hand on the boy's forehead. She could hear the other children in the room breathing. She and the prior had been sitting motionless for some time when the prior held his forefinger beneath the boy's nostrils.

'I can hardly feel his breath,' he said, looking over at her, alarmed. His eyes appeared large in the gloom.

Alice moved closer and placed her hand on Nicholas' narrow chest. She felt a slight occasional fluttering beneath her fingers.

He was slipping away.

The prior held the crucifix that hung around his neck and began to say the last rites, his voice breaking at intervals. He had brought a small phial of oil with him, which he used to anoint Nicholas on his forehead, eyelids and lips. Then he stopped praying and held onto his son's hand while Nicholas, almost imperceptibly, sank lower into his pillow. Alice held her breath for what seemed like an eternity.

Finally, the prior spoke. 'He has left us.'

Alice felt empty. Numb.

Another child taken.

'I am sorry.' Her eyes filled with tears.

There was a loud gasp as the prior gathered his son into his arms and sobbed. His large form shook with grief.


Nicholas was buried in a small plot under the yew tree. The prior had found money for a coffin and, as Alice watched the earth being shovelled onto it, a deep sense of loss burrowed deep inside her.

She felt hollow.

*Why did children die? How could it be God's will?*

Looking around her she noticed a woman she had never seen before among the small group of mourners at the graveside. The woman had hidden herself under a cloak and hood to escape the rain, but Alice also guessed she was trying to obscure her identity. She had to be Nicholas' mother, Tillie Buckley. She exchanged no words or glances with the prior, but once Brother Ralph had finished his prayers and the mourners had dispersed Alice noticed that the two figures remained by the graveside.

She made a detour through the garden on her way back to the children's dormitory, hoping to see Brother Jon. She needed someone to talk to after the sadness and there was something comforting about the way Jon listened to her. She was rewarded when she saw him at the far end of the garden, digging over a patch of soil.

'Hello,' she said softly.

Jon turned and smiled when he saw her. 'How are you?' he asked.

'We have just buried Nicholas.' She wiped her eyes.

'Oh, I'm sorry.' Jon's shoulders slumped. 'I heard he had died. Is the prior very upset?'

'Yes, although we are not supposed to know that he is. It seems strange seeing a man like that grieving. When I look at him I feel anger because of what he has done to me, but I feel sadness too when I think about him losing his son.'

'I would not waste time considering him,' replied Jon turning over a large clod of earth with his shovel. 'We need to decide how we are going to continue our search for Constance and Elizabeth.'

'I agree. When shall we visit Juliana's family?'

'I think we should go very soon. Did anyone notice you were missing the other evening?'

'No. You?'

'No one. Some were still drinking in the refectory, so I joined them.'

Alice tutted.

'I needed wine after discovering my sister's intended husband with his throat slit!'

'Valerian was here yesterday morning, did you see him?'

Jon's face clouded. 'No. What did he want?'

'He was wondering if we had found out anything. I told him we hadn't. It seems he is no longer a suspect. I don't know why he was here; I suppose he is keen to clear his name.'

Brother Ralph emerged from a doorway and started walking towards them.

'You don't want to be seen talking to me,' said Jon. 'Ralph won't mind but you never know who is watching. I will get word to you about visiting Juliana's family.'

Alice nodded. 'I am sorry I interrupted you.'

'I was glad of the interruption.'

Alice felt heat rising in her cheeks. 'I should also return to work.'

A knock at Alice's door that evening surprised her as she was getting ready for bed. She picked up her candle, walked over to the door and unlatched it. She did not expect to see Prior Edmund standing there. He had never visited her in her room before. His shoulders stooped, he was unshaven and his eyes were rimmed with red. He stank of wine. Alice recoiled instinctively.

Prior Edmund stared at her without speaking, one hand clasped shut as if he were holding something. Slowly, he reached his other hand out and gently touched her cheek with his forefinger. She stood frozen, staring into his eyes, which looked sunken and wretched with grief. She did not feel afraid, but she had no idea what he wanted. The candle in her hand spluttered hot tallow onto her fingers. She flinched, but refused to move her eyes away from the prior's face. She was unable to fathom what his intentions were. *Was he drunk?*

'What do you want?' she asked, unused to the prior being so quiet. His frame was twice the size of hers and completely blocked the doorway. She would be unable to get past him if she needed to, but he could easily push her back into her room if that was his aim. The situation was beginning to make her nervous. If she called for help the prior might do something drastic.

He moved his hand away from her cheek and spoke. 'I wanted to say thank you.'

He opened out the hand he had held shut and she saw that there was a small, intricately decorated cross in his palm. It looked like a pendant of some sort.

'There is no need.' She didn't want his gifts.

'Please.' He thrust the pendant into her hand and then grasped it with both of his, closing her fingers over it. 'Thank you for looking after Nicholas.'

'I was only doing my duty.'

The prior stepped forward as if he wanted to come into her room. Slowly, Alice stood back and allowed him in. 'He needed someone like you,' continued the prior. 'I couldn't be a proper father to him and that is a regret I will live with for the rest of my life.'

Alice didn't know how to reply. She rested her candle on the table next to Christopher's wooden toys, which the children had been playing with that afternoon.

'I suppose it is my punishment. I have not served God as respectably as I could. I have erred and sinned and begged the Lord's forgiveness, but he has seen fit to ensure that I suffer for my wrongdoings.' The prior picked up one of the toys and examined it. 'You looked after Nicholas so well because you knew what it was like to have a sick child, didn't you?'

'Yes.' Alice wasn't going to open up to him. She felt uneasy with him in her room. *Would this remain a friendly conversation, or was he planning to deliver some unpleasant news?*

'Suffer little children, and forbid them not, to come to me: for of such is the kingdom of heaven.' The prior raised his hands and eyes to the ceiling as he uttered these words, then he looked at Alice. 'They are at peace now.'

She nodded in reply.

'I hope the relic I have given you brings you much health and prosperity. It is the least I can do in return for your kindness.' He smiled and made his way towards the doorway.

'Thank you, Father,' said Alice. 'I wonder if there is something I may request of you before you leave.'

The prior raised an eyebrow and waited for her to speak.

'My home. I would like my home returned to me.'

There was a long pause and the prior sighed. 'It is out of my power to grant you that wish.'

He stepped out of the door and closed it behind him.

Alice cursed and sat down at her table. She placed the prior's relic next to Christopher's toys and looked at it while she thought about her inability to get her house back. The relic was shaped like a cross, brightly coloured and studded around the edge with little gold rosebuds. In the centre of the cross was an engraved image of Christ, and at each point was an engraving of a saint. The pendant had some depth to it.

She picked up the cross and realised it was hinged. Prising it open, she found a small piece of wood inside. *A piece of the true cross?* Alice knew this relic had been important to Prior Edmund. He had talked about it often, but she had never seen it. Presumably he had worn it as a pendant under his robes.

It was difficult to appreciate the gift; Alice felt both honoured and embarrassed. But she also felt angry that St Hugh's owned her home but that it was somehow out of the prior's control. *Was he lying or was there something else at work she was unaware of?*

# Chapter Twenty-Three

'We'll 'ave to cut some branches down soon, there's 'ardly any wood left on the ground,' said Millicent as she picked up some sorry-looking twigs from a bed of dead leaves. 'These won't keep a fire burning,' she said as she examined them. She looked up at the fresh, green leaves dancing in the sunlight in the canopy above their heads. 'They'll be full o' the sap o' spring now and will spit rather than burn.'

Elizabeth's belly was so large she was unable to bend over and pick up firewood, so she held on to the twigs and small sticks Millicent collected and handed to her. Between the trees a short distance away she could see two other women in brown cloaks collecting firewood. She recognised them from the village.

'Ain't much left, is there?' one called over to her.

Elizabeth shook her head.

The other woman stood up and stared at her, then said something to the first and they both looked over. It seemed they were talking about her. Elizabeth looked away and watched Millicent.

'Lettin' the old lady do all the work, are ya?' called the second woman.

'Who said that?' Millicent stood up as straight as she could and winced as her back cracked.

Elizabeth looked over at the women again. They had moved closer.

'Who is it, Lizzie?' asked Millicent. 'My eyes ain't as good as they once was.'

'Two women from the village,' replied Elizabeth quietly. She could sense a confrontation. 'We should go.'

'*What*? We ain't got nowhere near enough firewood yet. We'll 'ave to go deeper into the woods. What do they want?'

The women were only a few steps away from them now and Elizabeth could feel their eyes on her.

'Didn't you 'ear me?' asked the larger of the two women. Her cloak was worn and the veil over her head was a grubby cream colour.

Elizabeth said nothing. She felt vulnerable in her heavily pregnant state and she was also worried about Millicent's frailty.

'She's acting deaf, ain't she?' said the other woman.

The larger one stepped up to Elizabeth and pushed her round, pimpled face up close. 'I said, are you letting the old lady do all the work?'

'Leave her alone!' said Millicent. 'Of course she ain't. And I'm quite capable of work, you know. I'll thank you to stop calling me old.'

The woman ignored her and Elizabeth stayed where she was, not moving a muscle. She stared back into the woman's large, close-set eyes.

'She's dumb and all, this one. You don't speak, do ya?'

'I said leave 'er!' snarled Millicent.

The woman turned to her. 'What are you doin' keepin' this woman as a guest in yer 'ouse, Millie? I thought better of yer. 'Ere she is, some highborn living among us and takin' all our firewood when her family proberly owns a forest of their own. Only she ain't with them, is she? 'Cause she's ashamed. She's a whore and she's got herself with child. Your family ain't gonna help you now, are they?'

A large globule of saliva shot out of the woman's mouth and into Elizabeth's face. Some landed in her eye, while the rest slid slowly down her cheek. The women laughed as she wiped her face with her sleeve.

'I shall be leaving as soon as the baby is born,' she said meekly. She didn't want to antagonise the women any further.

'Good.' The woman spat at her feet this time.

'You should be ashamed of yerself, Rosa Nash!' shouted Millicent, 'What would yer mother think if she saw you be'aving like this? And as for you, Meriel Taylor,' she jabbed a bony finger at the other woman, 'I thought you was the clever one. You should know better than to get involved with the likes o' this one.'

'I'm lettin' this highborn whore know she ain't welcome 'ere,' said Rosa. 'Eatin' our food, usin' up our firewood. It's been an 'ard winter and a whore carrying a bastard bairn could curse our crops and cattle.'

'No she won't! Now run off and get back to your work afore I go tellin' your families what you've been doing out 'ere.'

The two women shrugged and walked away.

'Are you all right, Lizzie?' Millicent asked.

She nodded in reply, too upset to talk.

'Now you ignore them two, they don't mean nothing by it. It's been a tough winter, as they say, and people are easily riled this time o' year. They've not had much to eat and we're all waiting on the fresh crops to feed us proper again. Just forget about 'em.'

But Elizabeth couldn't forget about the women they had encountered in the woods. She struggled to sleep that night. As Millicent snored loudly at the other end of the room, Elizabeth was sure she could hear footsteps beating the path on the other side of the thin walls. She told herself she was imagining it and took comfort from Talbot, who was sleeping next to her. Then a new sense of worry flooded over her. The baby seemed quieter than usual. She had become accustomed to the regular nudges and kicks from within, but as she felt her stomach there was no movement. *Was the baby all right?*

Elizabeth heard a thud against the side of the hut. She gasped and Talbot awoke, his ears pricked up. Another thud came, followed by footsteps and laughter. There was someone outside.

Elizabeth sat up.

'Whore!' came a shout. It sounded like a child's voice. There were more thuds against the wall and then a chant rose up. 'Whore, whore!'

Talbot barked and then whimpered, nuzzling his nose into her side for reassurance.

'Whore, whore!'

Millicent stopped snoring and Elizabeth saw her stirring. 'What's this?' she croaked.

'Some people outside, I think it's only children. They will go away shortly.'

A heavier thud shook one of the walls, knocking several jars and bowls to the floor.

'Are they throwing stones at *my house?*' shouted Millicent. She scrambled out of bed and put on her cloak.

'Don't go out there, Millicent.' Elizabeth got up as quickly as she could and went over to her, 'You might get hurt. They'll go away soon.'

'It's just kids out there,' replied Millicent. 'They can't do nothin', I'll find their mothers.'

She went to open the door.

'But they're throwing stones. You might get hit!'

'No one throws stones at my 'ouse and gets away with it. I'll threaten to curse 'em, that'll put a stop ter it.'

It was then that they saw smoke seeping in through the cracks in the walls. There was more laughter from outside and a strong smell of burning.

'Well, we'll have to get out of 'ere now!' shouted Millicent.

Elizabeth pulled on her cloak and grabbed the bucket of water they kept for washing. Millicent opened the door to reveal a group of laughing faces bathed in orange. Stepping outside, Elizabeth turned to see the bright flames soaring from one side of the hut. She threw the bucket of water at the fire but her attempt to extinguish it was futile.

'There they are!' cried someone from the crowd.

More stones were pelted in their direction. Talbot had headed outside with them but soon ran off in the direction of the fields in fright.

'Follow me!' said Millicent. She grabbed Elizabeth's hand and together they ran as fast as they could down the lane away from the crowd. But the mob followed and several stones hit Elizabeth's back, followed by a sharp rock on the side of her head. For a moment she felt dizzy, but then she became aware that Millicent had fallen. Elizabeth tried to pick her up, but it was impossible with her large stomach in the way.

'Millicent? Are you all right?' she yelled.

The crowd surrounded them. They chanted 'Whore!' over and over again and hurled more stones.

Millicent got to her feet again. 'I'm fine. We 'ave got to keep movin'. We can't stay 'ere, they'll stone us to death.'

In the glowing orange of the fire, Elizabeth could see a dark streak of blood running down one side of Millicent's face. She was leaning heavily on Elizabeth for support and Elizabeth felt sick every time she heard a stone thud against the old lady's body.

'Let's go!' said Millicent. But there was nowhere to go. The crowd encircled them. Elizabeth tried to cover Millicent's head with her arms, fearful that one more blow would kill her. The shouting continued and she could feel the heat of the fire on her back. She and Millicent crouched on the ground and shielded themselves with their cloaks, the stones raining down on them. An image of the man who had choked her flashed into Elizabeth's mind, followed by a memory of the inky black river. It felt like she was being thrown into the water again and sinking fast.

There was a moment of waiting.

*Would she sink or float?*

The shouting was accompanied by a sudden thundering noise, and then the shouting stopped. No more stones were thrown and Elizabeth realised the thundering sound had been hooves on the ground. She heard shrieks and the barking of dogs. *What new madness had joined them?*

'Get away!' shouted a man's voice.

As Elizabeth looked up she could see the silhouettes of people running.

A lantern was thrust into her face. 'Are you all right?' asked the voice.

Elizabeth saw a man's face in the lantern light. He had a neat brown beard and friendly eyes. 'Who are you? Are you hurt?'

'Yes, Millicent is hurt!'

'No I ain't, I'm fine.' The old lady got up from the ground and started stumbling towards her hut, which was fully ablaze. Sparks crackled and flames flickered tall into the night sky. There was a crowd nearby. Some were watching, while others hurled buckets of water at the flames. Elizabeth thought of all the precious items in Millicent's hut: her amulets, charms, books, herbs and treasures.

'Millicent, come back!' called Elizabeth, alarmed to see how close she was to the flames as she staggered towards her home.

Elizabeth leapt forward to grab her but was stopped by a sudden sharp twinge in her abdomen. She couldn't help yelping.

'You are hurt,' said the man.

'No, it is my baby.'

'*Baby*? We need to take you up to the house.'

'Stop Millicent first. She mustn't go back in there. *Millicent*!' she screamed, her throat becoming sore from the exertion.

But the old lady refused to turn back. Instead, she moved closer to the doorway of her flame-covered home. Elizabeth scrambled after her. The pain in her stomach had subsided a little and she had to do all she could to stop Millicent endangering herself in the flames.

'Millicent!' she shouted again. 'Stop!'

She was gaining on the old lady now and the heat of the fire was so strong she couldn't understand how Millicent could stand so close to it. She reached out an arm to grab Millicent but then another sharp pain crippled her, it was so strong she was unable to think about anything else.

She must have let out a loud cry because Millicent turned and looked at her bent over on the ground. In an instant, Millicent was back by her side.

'That bairn's comin' ain't it?'

Elizabeth nodded, her teeth clenched hard as her muscles tensed up around her chest and stomach.

There was a crack followed by a crumbling noise and the timbers of Millicent's home fell to the ground.

A lifetime's work was gone.

One of the men caught up with them. 'We're trying to get her up to the house,' he said.

'Get 'er there now!' ordered Millicent. 'And take me, too. I'm the midwife!'

# Chapter Twenty-Four

I t was warm enough for the children to play out in the garden without Alice worrying about them catching cold. They played with a ball on a patch of grass beyond the vegetable garden while Sister Emma and Alice watched.

'No one has seen Prior Edmund since the day of his son's funeral,' said Sister Emma. 'Brother Ralph has been leading prayers and Sister Eleanor says the prior has been consumed by a grief so passionate he is unable to speak.'

'How does anyone know he cannot speak if no one has seen him?' asked Alice.

'Are you paying any attention to what the children are doing?' asked Jon, suddenly appearing. He was slightly breathless and held a leather ball in his hand. 'This just landed on my carrot seedlings. It will take me hours to resow them. And I had only just finished repairing the damage done by Yvette de Beauchamp's dog.'

'I am sorry,' said Alice. The sight of his muscled forearms, which were visible below the rolled-up sleeves of his habit, stirred a flutter in her chest.

'I don't mind really,' continued Jon. 'I would rather

resow carrot seedlings than sit through plainchant.' He threw the ball back to the children and one of the boys caught it.

'I will go and make sure they keep the ball away from the plants,' said Sister Emma, with a knowing look that suggested Alice and Jon might prefer to be left alone. It was a look that irritated Alice. She resented people's insinuations that she and Jon wanted to be together.

'Now is our chance,' said Jon.

'What do you mean?'

'With the prior shut away in his apartments I think we can go and see Juliana's family without him noticing.'

'Is the prior all right?'

'Why should you care?' said Jon, 'He is hardly a friend of yours. I know that Brother Ralph is keeping him supplied with milk of the poppy, but other than that I cannot say. The door to his apartments remains locked.'

'Oh dear. I am worried about the prior.'

'There is no need to be worried.'

'But his son has died.'

'A son he should never have fathered in the first place! That shows you how seriously he takes his vows.'

'You never recover from the loss of a child.'

'I understand, and the prior has my sympathies. But we can make the most of this opportunity and resume our work. Who can stop us?'

'Sister Katherine?'

'And what can she do? Turn you to stone with her Medusa stare?'

Alice laughed. 'You are right; we finally have a chance to do something. Hopefully we'll be able to find out more from Juliana's family. It will not be easy for them, but we have to try. When shall we go?'

'How about now?' suggested Jon.

'But I'm looking after the children and you have carrot seedlings to resow.'

'The carrots can wait and I think Sister Emma will be happy looking after the children for a few hours.'

They looked over to see her playing ball with the children, her face red and puffy against the whiteness of her wimple.

'I should let her know where I'm going.'

'No, leave her for now.' Jon rested his hand on her arm. 'We can walk off quietly.'

'We ought not to.' She pulled her arm away, but the look of mischief in his eye was tempting.

'Come on,' he took her arm again. 'We won't be long. We know where we're going.'


Alice felt a bubble of excitement in her stomach. It was exhilarating to snatch some freedom with Jon at her side, but the excitement was mixed with foreboding. They were going to visit a grieving family. *How would they be received?*

Alice had walked the main streets when she had visited The Swan on her own. This time they took some short cuts through various alleyways Jon knew. They walked along a narrow passageway and reached a flight of slippery wooden steps, which they began to climb.

Jon stopped halfway up. 'I think we should wait here a moment,' he said.

'Why?'

'I think we need to stay quiet for a short while.'

Alice shuffled impatiently and leant against the timber wall, watching her companion. Jon was staring back at the route they had just taken. *What was he doing? Was he checking there was no one around so he could seduce her?* She felt her scalp tingle at the thought and coughed awkwardly as she tried to dismiss the idea from her mind.

'Quiet!' hissed Jon.

The tingling sensation stopped. He seemed to be searching for someone.

'What is it?' whispered Alice.

All she could hear was their breathing. An old man lumbered along the passageway towards them.

'Let's go,' said Jon.

They climbed the remaining steps.

'Can you tell me what's going on?'

'I had the feeling we were being followed.'

'Who did you see?'

'No one. It was a sensation. It is probably nothing.'

They stepped out into Ludgate, from where they would pass through the gate, continue over the River Fleet and along The Strand.

'Have you heard anything more about Geoffrey Edington's murder?' asked Alice. She was convinced there was a connection with Elizabeth's disappearance, but she couldn't work out what it was.

'Only that it has shocked many people. The killer has not been found.'

'I wonder what his employer, Sir Walter, must be making of it.'

'I hear he is very aggrieved and has asked for the man responsible to be found. That was the first time I have ever raised the hue and cry, I am still worried about it because sometimes when the killer isn't found the person who discovered the body – in this instance two bodies – becomes the suspect.'

'No one would believe a harmless monk would do such a thing!'

Jon scowled. 'True, but I am not completely harmless!'

Alice laughed again. 'I am certain no one will suspect you of Geoffrey's murder, Jon.'

When they reached The Strand, they found a group of minstrels playing. A small crowd had gathered to listen. The sound of the harp and flute carried on the breeze long after the pair had walked past them. The tune made Alice think back to her wedding day. The musicians had played throughout the wedding feast and most of the night. That day belonged to a different lifetime now.

The spire of St Clement Danes became visible and soon they reached The Swan. Jon pushed open the door and Alice followed. They were greeted by a smell of wine and wood smoke mixed with the scent of fresh rushes, which lined the floor. A handful of customers sat at tables covered with white linen.

A young, slender girl with red hair stood behind the bar polishing a pewter jug. Alice was struck by the similarity she bore to the girl who had been pulled out of the river. There was no doubt this was Juliana's sister.

'Can I help?' she asked.

Alice introduced herself and Jon. Her knees felt weak as she worried about the girl's reaction when she mentioned her dead sister's name.

'We would like to speak to someone about Juliana.'

The girl stopped polishing and stared at Alice.

'My friend Constance is missing and has not been found yet. I was wondering if her disappearance had anything to do with what happened to Juliana.'

'Juliana is dead.' The girl's face was frosty.

'I know. I am sorry.'

'Why do you need to talk to us about her?'

'Because of my friend, and also because Brother Jon here's sister is missing and we think she may have been connected to Juliana in some way.'

The girl remained sullen. 'I think it would be best if you speak to my mother and father.' She disappeared through a narrow doorway behind the bar.

A black dog sauntered over and sniffed at Alice's skirts.

The girl reappeared. 'You can come through,' she said.


The doorway led to a room in which a fire burned brightly in the hearth and a middle-aged woman sat at a table sorting coins into leather purses. A candle flickered close to her. A heavy-set man sat on a stool by the fire, silhouetted against the flames. He was polishing a small sword. The woman stood as Alice entered. Her lips were thin, her cheeks hollow and her eyes a deep blue. She wore a dark brown dress and several strands of red hair had escaped from the veil she wore on her head.

'My daughter says you want to talk to me about Juliana.' She appeared tense, like the string of a drawn bow.

The man glanced in Alice's direction, listening to the conversation but not taking part.

Alice introduced herself and Jon, and learnt that Juliana's parents were called Beatrix and Frederick. Alice explained what had happened to Constance and Elizabeth, and once she had finished talking Beatrix dropped her guard a little and asked them to sit at the table. Alice sat on one of the stools and felt she should tell Juliana's parents they had seen her body. Perhaps it was wrong to admit they had seen their daughter in death, but Alice felt they had a right to know. She wanted them to understand that she shared their pain.

'We saw Juliana,' she blurted. 'After she was pulled from the river.'

Beatrix put her hands up to her face and Frederick stopped what he was doing to glare at Alice.

She felt the need to explain quickly. 'We asked them to let

us know if they found a girl in the river and when they found Juliana they had no idea who she was and wondered if she was Constance. Or Elizabeth.'

There was silence and the air in the room felt still and heavy. Alice looked nervously at Frederick, expecting him to banish them immediately.

'We think Juliana might have known my sister,' said Jon.

Alice felt grateful to him for keeping the conversation going.

'Juliana was wearing a set of rosary beads when she was found. The rosary beads belonged to my sister Elizabeth. Look, I have an identical set of beads.' He pulled them out from under his tunic and walked over to Beatrix to show them to her.

'They are very fine,' she said, 'and just like the ones Juliana was wearing when she was found. We wondered how she came by them.'

The rosary beads had shattered the tension; they were tangible proof of Alice and Jon's story. Alice relaxed slightly as she watched Frederick stand and walk over to the table, his sword now sheathed at his belt.

'Have some wine with us,' he said. He took some goblets down from a shelf, placed them on the table and poured out the wine from a pottery jug. Alice took a large sip, enjoying the warmth in her throat.

They talked about the three girls and tried to understand how Juliana and Elizabeth might have known each other. Juliana had always lived at The Swan and had worked there with her sister as soon as she was old enough. Elizabeth had lived at her family home within the city walls, so it was difficult to see how their paths could ever have crossed. The only answer was that they had been taken by the same person.

'I know it cannot be easy for you to think about it,'

ventured Alice, 'but can you tell us where Juliana was when you last saw her?'

'It was a busy day, we had lots of people in,' said Beatrix, staring into her goblet of wine. 'I remember a group of merchants trying to sort out some business in one corner and a rowdy crowd from Sir Walter's household in another. We get a lot of his men in here as his palace is nearby.'

Alice felt her stomach flip, but she kept her lips shut tight as she waited to hear the rest of their story.

'And a few ladies, too. I refuse to let the whores in, though. It was a job to get everyone to leave at the end of the night. Juliana spent most of the evening serving drinks behind the bar. At closing time I asked her to remind everyone to finish up their drinks and leave. I often asked her to do that and she was never intimidated by it. She was a tavern owner's daughter, you see. She had done it many times and was used to the customers' ribaldry.'

Beatrix paused to drink. 'Once everyone had left we assumed Juliana was in this room here, out the back. When we realised she was not here I thought she might be upstairs. I went looking but did not find her there either. It took me a while to realise she was missing. That time between me seeing her for the last time and noticing she was gone was long enough for someone to whisk her away.'

'How much time do you think had ensued?'

'It could have been an hour. It's busy at closing time and I was getting on with the jobs I usually do: clearing the tables and cleaning everything ready for the morning. I didn't notice she had vanished and that is what I feel bad about. If only I had realised straight away. We could have run out the door and caught up with whoever had her.' Beatrix's voice cracked.

'You cannot blame yourself,' said Alice. 'She was working and old enough to look after herself. She wasn't a young child who needed watching all the time. Someone took advantage of an opportunity to steal her away and there is nothing you could have done.'

'We raised the hue and cry, and search parties were sent out,' said Frederick. 'The bailiff started investigating, but there was no sign of her.'

'Did you speak to any of the people who were here that evening?'

'I went over to Sir Walter's household and spoke to some of his men, but none of them had seen anything, as you would expect,' said Frederick. 'Some of the merchants have been in since and I have asked them. The night she went missing I searched the streets until dawn. Then Beatrix and our three daughters searched before I went looking again. Friends and neighbours also joined the search. Between us we covered most of the city, but there was no sign.'

'And then the coroner came to tell us about the girl in the river,' said Beatrix, her eyes filling with tears. 'We went to see her, but it didn't seem real at all. I didn't want to believe it was her.'

She broke down and Frederick put his arms around his wife's shoulders. Alice and Jon exchanged a solemn glance and Alice wiped away the tears that flooded into her eyes. She watched Beatrix sobbing and wished she could take away her pain, but it was impossible. Nothing could bring Juliana back and anger seethed in her stomach as she thought about the person responsible for taking Juliana, Constance and Elizabeth. The two girls had to be found and those guilty of abducting them needed to be stopped.

Alice was developing an idea of who might be behind it all.

Slowly, Beatrix recovered herself. 'I must apologise. It still doesn't seem real. I am certain I will wake up one day and discover this has all been a terrible dream. In fact, I hope I will. Life can feel unbearable at times. I look at our lives and wonder why God has chosen to punish us in this way. My husband and I have only ever done the right things, as have our daughters. We work hard, we respect the Lord and this is how our prayers are answered.' Her voice choked with emotion again.

Alice reached out and laid a hand on Beatrix's shoulder. 'No one brings these things upon themselves. Tragedy can strike whether you pray every day or sin without care.'

Alice took in a deep breath of air as they stepped out of The Swan. The smell of the street was unpleasant, but she was relieved to be outside again.

'That was difficult.'

'It was to be expected, I suppose,' replied Jon. 'Those poor people.'

'A name came up that I keep hearing,' said Alice.

'Oh, look who it is!' interrupted Jon. 'I knew we were being followed!'

Across the street stood Valerian. He grinned and sauntered over to them. 'Good afternoon,' he said.

Once again, he was well-dressed and wore a fine black felt hat, but the colour of his clothes was more sombre on this occasion.

'You have been following us!' said Jon.

'Jon, that is nonsense,' said Alice. 'Why would he do that?'

'Well, what is he doing here?' asked Jon with a frown. 'And why are you always defending him?'

Alice did not like the way he had suddenly turned on her. He was short-tempered whenever Valerian was nearby.

'I am not always defending him. I don't understand why you are so distrustful of him.'

Valerian looked at them awkwardly as they bickered. 'I am not worth arguing about,' he said. 'I was just passing by.'

'And where were you going to?' demanded Jon.

Valerian took a step back. 'Is it your business to know? I was passing by. What do you think I was doing?'

'Following us.'

'Why would I do that?' Valerian grew wide-eyed and Alice wondered if he was telling the truth. 'I don't know where you got the idea I was following you from. I thought we were friends.'

Jon snorted in reply.

'I am on my way to the tavern for dinner,' continued Valerian. 'Would you like to join me?'

'No, thank you,' replied Jon curtly, 'but she might.'

He gestured at Alice and she glared at him, angered by his rude manner.

Valerian shrugged at Jon. 'Alice, would you like to join me?'

She wanted to accept because she felt embarrassed about Jon's rudeness, but she was worried about the murderous expression on Jon's face. *Why did he dislike Valerian so much?*

Valerian's dark eyes implored her to join him, but Jon's eyes were like hard emeralds as he glared at Valerian. She felt torn between the two of them.

'Sister Emma will be wondering where you are,' snarled Jon. He was right; she had to get back to work.

'Another time, Valerian. Will you come and visit us again soon?'

She heard Jon mutter something under his breath.

'Of course, Alice.' She liked the way his face relaxed easily into a grin. 'I shall see you very soon.'

Jon strode off as Valerian doffed his hat. Alice followed after Jon, wondering whether she had made the right decision.

# Chapter Twenty-Five

✦

Elizabeth stared down at the baby girl in her arms. She was swaddled in linen and only her tiny creased face was visible. It was angry, red and crying.

'She's an 'ealthy bairn,' said Millicent, standing at Elizabeth's bedside. 'She's only little 'cause she's come early, but she's 'ealthier looking than bairns twice her size.'

Elizabeth smiled at Millicent's words, still unable to take her eyes off the baby. *Could she accept her as her daughter?* She looked at the baby's tiny nose and the creases next to her mouth and eyes, searching for any resemblance to her father. She could see none.

What she had endured during the baby's conception seemed disconnected to this moment. Elizabeth wanted to believe she had created this baby all by herself and she was doing all she could to convince herself she had. This baby was part of her, and as she rocked and shushed her crying daughter she felt as though the cord Millicent had cut was still connected through an invisible bond. Her daughter was as much a part of her as any part of her own body; as much as her heart. And this was how it would always be. For the first time since the birth Elizabeth smiled. The creased, angry face of her daughter looked perfect to her.

There were other women in the room, but it was only now that Elizabeth noticed them. During the labour and birth her world had narrowed down to just the pain in her body and Millicent's voice. She had unconsciously shut everything else out. Now she was aware of a general bustle around her as women straightened out the bed she lay in, tended the fire, poured water into bowls and scattered fresh rushes on the floor, as if they were preparing the room for visitors. The large bed was hung with drapes, the mattress was soft and filled with feathers, and she finally realised she was at the manor house. Grey daylight filtered through the window. The memory of the fire and the stones flashed back into her mind.

She turned to Millicent. 'Your face,' she said. There was an open gash on Millicent's swollen forehead.

'It's nothin',' replied Millicent. 'A wound salve of goutweed will soon heal it.'

'And your home...' Elizabeth trailed off as the memory of the fire burnt brightly in her mind.

'I know,' Millicent said, looking down at the floor. 'It ain't nothin' I can't replace. You and me's safe and so's yer baby girl.' She looked back at Elizabeth and smiled. 'That's what's important.'

'This is all my fault,' said Elizabeth. 'If I had not been staying with you they would never have attacked your home. It was me they were shouting at. I should have left long ago, and because of me you have nothing left.'

'That's enough!' Elizabeth felt Millicent's hand on her shoulder. 'I won't hear no more. Ain't you listenin' to anything I'm sayin'? The important thing is we're all safe.'

There was movement by the doorway and Lady Margery strode into the room, accompanied by several women.

She walked over to Elizabeth's bedside. 'God bless you and your beautiful baby daughter!' she said.

Lady Margery wore a dress of deep, shimmering blue with a fur-trimmed green surcoat over the top. 'You are both healthy and well, I see. Well done, Millicent. Another baby brought safely into this world. Thank you. Did I tell you Millicent has birthed three of my children? And there is to be a fourth.' She smiled and patted her stomach.

'That is very happy news,' said Elizabeth, feeling a twinge of envy that Lady Margery's children would all be born within wedlock.

Lady Margery asked someone to bring her a stool and she sat next to Elizabeth's bed.

'Hand 'er to me,' said Millicent, gently lifting the baby and walking over to the fire with the tiny bundle in her arms.

'Elizabeth, I know you have only just birthed your baby,' said Lady Margery, 'but you know duty is pressing on me to inform your father that you are here in my home. We agreed to wait until your child was born, and now she is here we can proceed. I understand you and Millicent were attacked last night, and while we will do our best to punish those involved I do not believe it is safe for you to remain in the village any longer.'

Elizabeth looked over at Millicent and watched the bent old lady as she walked up and down the room cuddling her daughter. Millicent was cooing at the baby, and as she rocked her in her arms the little girl's crying subsided. The thought of another journey made her heart sink. *How would she manage it with a baby? How could she face her father again? And what if the men she had escaped from discovered she had returned?*

'You will need your lying-in period, of course, but after that you must return to your home.'

Elizabeth nodded, knowing there was no use arguing.

Another woman joined Lady Margery at her bedside. She

was a young woman dressed in a simple green dress with a rope belt. She had a round face with cheeks that reminded Elizabeth of red apples.

'This is Iohane,' said Lady Margery.

Elizabeth smiled and then looked back at Millicent. She wanted to hold her daughter again. She also needed to learn how to feed her. She hoped Millicent would show her how.

'She recently had her own baby and has more than enough milk for two. She can take your daughter from you now.'

Elizabeth continued to watch Millicent as she repeated Lady Margery's words in her head. *Had she heard her correctly?*

'Take her away?' She looked up at Lady Margery's pale, pretty face.

'Yes, Iohane has six children and lives in a neighbouring village, where no one will know where the little girl came from. You can return to London and your journey home will be easier. I will lend you a carriage.'

'But my baby must stay with me.'

Lady Margery laughed as if Elizabeth had made a foolish mistake. 'A girl of your status cannot return to her father with a baby born out of wedlock. He would disown you! Remember how important you are to him. He must choose a marriage for you that will benefit your family and your husband's. How can your father marry off a daughter who already has a child? No man would be interested in you; you will be tainted with sin and shame and become a spinster. That is no destiny for a girl as highborn and pretty as you. You must return to London and pretend you are pure. Your duty is to marry as your father intends, and once you have done that these troubled few months will become a distant memory. You will likely forget them altogether.'

A cold fear snaked its way through Elizabeth's stomach. 'Millicent!' she called.

The old lady looked up.

'Please can I hold her?'

Millicent started walking back towards the bed.

'That is not a good idea,' said Lady Margery. 'The baby needs to be with her new mother now.'

Millicent paused, her brow furrowed.

'Give the baby to Iohane please, Millicent,' ordered Lady Margery, her tone becoming stricter. 'She is to be the girl's mother and my word on this is final.'

# Chapter Twenty-Six

❧

Alice placed a bright daffodil on Nicholas' grave. Each of the small wooden crosses around her stood in the resting place of a child who had died in the hospital. Despite trying her hardest to keep the children healthy and happy, a few succumbed to an illness that prayers could do nothing to prevent. Alice had seen many people die during the plague, but that didn't mean she was accustomed to it. It was always devastating to see a life cut short.

A rustling noise came from behind her. She spun round but there was no one in sight.

'Hello?' she called.

The only sound she heard came from the rooks cawing on the bell tower.

*Was there someone else in the graveyard?* Alice felt she must have misheard, but her heart beat faster as she bowed her head and said a prayer at Nicholas' grave. She said a prayer here each day, and every evening she saw the bulky silhouette of the prior in that same spot at dusk.

Once she had finished her prayer, Alice thought about the meeting with Juliana's family the previous day. She was sure there was a man she could link to all three disappearances. She had to discuss it with Jon to see if he agreed. *But if he did, what should she do then?*

She heard a shuffle of gravel just before the greasy hand was clamped over her mouth. Alice grabbed hold of it and dug her nails in, trying to pull it away. The hand smelt metallic. She tried to bite it to force the person to let go. But then her head was pulled back and her throat was exposed.

That was when she felt cold steel on her neck.

'Stay still and quiet and I'll let yer go,' rasped a threatening voice. 'But I don't wanna hear a word from you. Do you 'ear me?'

Alice did her best to nod and let go of the hand that held her. She felt the grip on her neck loosen and she pulled herself away. She turned to face a small man in a brown tunic. He had narrow, shifty eyes and puckered skin on one cheek.

'It won't do to go snoopin' around no more,' he hissed.

Alice glanced at the long, shiny blade and lifted her hand to the spot where the blade had been held at her throat. Her heart thudded heavily in her chest.

'How did you get here?' she asked, glancing quickly around her in the hope someone would see him and raise the alarm.

'Never mind that,' replied the man. 'What's important here is my message. Can you remember what it is?'

'Yes.'

'Repeat it back to me so I knows you've understood it.' Light glinted on his blade as he brandished it a little nearer.

'No snooping around, whatever that means. I haven't been snooping; I have just been trying to find out what happened to my friend.'

'Same thing,' growled the man.

'Does that mean you know what happened to her?' Alice's voice wobbled with fear, but she tried to look assertive.

'I don't know nothin' about yer friend. But I knows you shouldn't be askin' no questions.'

'Who do you work for?'

'Nobody.'

'But your message must come from someone?'

The man stepped forward and pushed his hand against her throat. She tried to step back, but he raised the blade with his other hand. She tried to call out for help but her neck was being squeezed between his thumb and forefinger, and she was struggling to breathe. Alice widened her eyes and stared hard at him, trying to somehow signal that she would not speak any more. *Was this the man who had snatched Constance? Would he take her as well?*

'You ask too many questions and it's gettin' you in trouble,' he warned. He stank of stale ale. 'Women 'ave an 'abit of being nosy and I 'ate nosy women like you.'

He let go of her neck and Alice gasped for air, clutching at her throat where he had grabbed her. She decided it was safer to remain silent.

'Stay away from that family at the tavern,' he spat, 'and tell yer monk friend to keep his head down an' all.'

She shivered at his words. *Who was he and how did he know what she had been doing?*

The man backed away and walked along the edge of the graveyard. He stopped by the yew tree and quickly shinned up into its bushy branches. Alice watched the foliage shake as he escaped over the stone wall.

Once she was certain the man had gone, Alice ran to the monastery to find Brother Jon. She knew prayers would be finishing and she dashed to the chapel, where she found him with Brother Henry.

'I need to talk to you,' she said breathlessly. Her throat was sore when she spoke from where the man had grabbed her neck.

The other monks in the room looked at him with amused expressions on their faces. Alice glared at them, angered that their cloistered life afforded them no idea of what was taking place in the world beyond St Hugh's.

'What is it?' Jon looked concerned.

Alice knew he had never seen her so animated before. She pulled his sleeve and led him over to a quiet alcove, ignoring the other monks' chuckles.

'A man just threatened me in the graveyard!'

Jon's eyes widened. 'Are you all right? Did he hurt you?'

'I am fine.'

'Did you recognise him?'

She shook her head.

'What did he look like?'

'Nasty. He was a small man, agile, with narrow eyes. And he was carrying a large sword. He looked like the type of man who does other people's dirty work. He knows we went to see Juliana's family at the tavern.'

'I knew we were being followed!'

'I think I know who he works for. I think his employer is Sir Walter.'

'How do you know that?' Jon asked with a frown.

'I told you, his name keeps coming up. He was here visiting St Hugh's shortly before Constance went missing. And he has visited a number of times to see Brother Rufus, so he knows this place well.'

'But Sir Walter is generous. He donates his money and time to people who are in need.'

'I know! But perhaps that's a cover for what he's really doing!'

Jon snorted doubtfully. 'Elizabeth was to be married to Geoffrey, Sir Walter's vintner. If what you say is true, would Sir Walter be stupid enough to take a girl who was to marry one of his own men?'

'Perhaps he is stupid. Who knows what goes on in his mind? His men regularly drink at the tavern owned by Juliana's parents, so that's another link.'

'But we don't know if Sir Walter has been there himself.'

'I would assume he must have. And suppose he had his man Geoffrey murdered as well? Perhaps Geoffrey knew something about what happened to Elizabeth?'

Jon looked thoughtful as he considered her words.

'Think about the fact that Juliana was wearing Elizabeth's rosary beads. We know from speaking to Juliana's family that it was unlikely Elizabeth and Juliana knew each other; their paths were unlikely to have crossed. So I think they were both taken by the same man. They must have met each other at that point.'

'And if you are right, what can we do about it? It is unlikely anyone will believe us. Sir Walter is one of the *good* men. He is highly thought of and he is powerful. I find it hard enough to believe myself.'

'I know he is considered to be a good man, but I have met him myself and I did not like him at all.'

'You make instant judgements about people. Just because you dislike like Sir Walter, that is not confirmation that he has been snatching girls. We have spent so long trying to work out what has happened to Constance and Elizabeth that I think you are trying to create a perpetrator in the desperate search for answers.'

'I am not making this up! I have given this a lot of thought!' Alice could feel the frustration bubbling inside her. *Why couldn't Jon just agree with her?*

Sister Eleanor hobbled up to them and paused, leaning on her stick.

'You two,' she pointed a bony finger at them. 'Here you are together again in a house of God. Sinners, the pair of you! What would Abbot Beroldus think if he knew what had become of his holy order? He would leave his grave and walk the earth once more to seek out those who bring shame upon his good work. May the devil find you first!'

'Go away!' shouted Alice.

Sister Eleanor recoiled, her gummy mouth agape and her eyes wide.

'Alice!' scolded Jon. 'That was disrespectful.'

He turned to Sister Eleanor. 'I can only apologise, Sister,' he said.

'I have just been threatened by a man with a knife in the graveyard of this hospital and you take sides with *her*?' Alice pointed at the elderly sister, who was muttering a prayer or a curse, Alice was unable to tell which.

'Forget I said anything,' she sniped at Jon. 'I can do this on my own.'

She walked back to the children's dormitory, ignoring Jon as he called after her.

Sister Emma sang to the children, her voice as discordant as ever. Alice hugged Matilda and a little girl called Winifred as they all sat together on the blanket. She rested her cheek on their heads and sang along, although her mind was elsewhere. Her stomach churned with anger and her thoughts were racing. She should never have shouted at Sister Eleanor and Jon, but she had been unable to stop herself. A brew of frustration and fear had simmered within her and there was nothing she could do to stop her emotions boiling over.

Jon didn't seem to care that a man had threatened her with a knife. It demonstrated that she could not rely on anyone to support her. Jon didn't want to believe Sir Walter was responsible for the girls going missing and there had been no word from Yvette de Beauchamp. Alice could tell that even Sister Emma was losing patience with her distracted behaviour.

She wondered if Valerian was her only hope. Having seen Constance taken he would still be interested in finding out what had happened to her. Alice would need to call on the Earl of Wykeham and ask to see Valerian. *But what if someone saw her visiting the earl and the man with the knife came back?* Alice shuddered. She could tell he had been hired to frighten her, but he looked like a man who would think nothing of slitting someone's throat. She hugged the girls closer and tried not to think about what could happen to her. The children would have to grow up without her if she put herself in danger again.

*But what if she had been threatened because she was moving closer to finding Constance? Had visiting Juliana's family brought her a step nearer?* The fact that someone had hired a man to threaten her meant she was also a danger to them. *Was it Sir Walter? Was she close to revealing who he really was?* Sir Walter had the money to pay men like that to do his dirty work. The more she thought about it, the more it made sense.

Sister Emma caught her eye and Alice realised she had been so deep in thought she had stopped singing. She tried to look apologetic as she joined in with the children's happy voices.

Winifred looked up at her with large blue eyes and smiled. The little girl was a foundling who had recently been taken in by the hospital. She had been filthy when she first arrived, with sunken cheeks and dull eyes. Now she was as happy and chubby as Matilda. Alice leant forward and kissed her cool, soft forehead. It was her favourite time of day with the most important people in her life. If only she could be content and enjoy this moment.

After songs with the children Alice walked to the cloisters, where she knew she would find Brother Rufus bent over his desk. The little man sat on a high stool engrossed in his scribe work as Alice approached. Silence was supposed to be observed in the cloisters, but the sight of Brother Rufus angered Alice and she no longer cared who she upset. Rufus looked up at her, his round, meek face devoid of expression.

'Did the prior order you to forge a manuscript to take my home away from me?' she asked.

Brother Rufus blinked slowly and said nothing, as if he had not understood a word she had said.

'The manuscript Prior Edmund claimed had been drawn up by the Worshipful Company of Glove Makers. It was you who created it, wasn't it? You forged it so that St Hugh's could take my home away from me and keep me a prisoner in this building!'

Rufus remained silent and started to climb down from his stool. It was clear that he wanted to get away.

'You are *not* going to walk away from me while I am talking to you!' seethed Alice. The man was obviously a coward. He couldn't even answer for his own actions.

'Trouble?'

The voice came from behind her. Alice spun round to see a man with a long ginger beard and dressed in a green, brocade tabard. She had seen him at St Hugh's before and she remembered him accompanying Sir Walter on his visits.

'You are a member of Sir Walter's household?'

'Yes, I am his assistant, Theobald FitzAlan. And I understand that you are Mistress Wescott. I have heard much about you, but I do not believe I have had the pleasure of meeting you personally.'

Alice scowled at him. 'Members of Sir Walter's household are no longer welcome at St Hugh's.'

Theobald raised his eyebrows at Brother Rufus, who was standing sullenly by his desk.

Theobald laughed. 'That is unfortunate to hear. Sir Walter has long enjoyed a good relationship with the overseers of St Hugh's. And my friend Brother Rufus here has done much valuable work for Sir Walter and, in doing so, has supported Sir Walter's many charitable causes.'

Theobald's long beard irritated Alice. She wanted to tug it and cause him pain.

'And Sir Walter has paid St Hugh's handsomely for this valuable support, has he not?' she said.

'It is only right that the work is paid for. I must admit that I find your hostility confusing, Mistress Wescott,' continued Theobald. 'Is there something I am not aware of that I should be?'

'Possibly,' replied Alice, 'but I think it would be best if I spoke to Sir Walter directly.'

'Probably. Shall I let him know you will be paying him a visit?'

'Please do,' she retorted.

'And I hope that after you have had your conversation with Sir Walter you will be more welcoming to members of his household at St Hugh's.' Theobald gave a patronising bow. 'It would be a shame if your good friend Valerian Baladi was no longer welcome here, would it not?'

'What has this to do with Valerian?'

'Have you not heard? He works for Sir Walter now. I assumed he would have told you.'

Alice remained calm and tried to conceal the fact that this news felt like a kick in the stomach. 'And when did he join Sir Walter's household?'

'Ah, he didn't tell you.' Theobald glanced at Brother Rufus and grinned awkwardly. 'That is something for you to discuss with him. Please excuse me, I must continue my business with Brother Rufus.'

'The forger? Does he forge documents for you too?'

Theobald laughed again. 'I am quite sure I have no idea what you are alluding to, Mistress Wescott. My time is precious, do please excuse me.'

Alice glared at the mole-like monk who continued to stay silent. Then she walked away, still reeling at the news of Valerian's betrayal.

*That was why he had been waiting outside The Swan. Jon had been right after all. Valerian must have told Sir Walter she had spoken to Juliana's family and that was why the small, mean-eyed man with the long sword had threatened her in the graveyard.*

Alice took a deep breath, but her body shook with rage. She had trusted Valerian and had always believed he was innocent of Constance's abduction and Roger's death. But all along he had been playing her for a fool. She felt stupid and ashamed.

She took a few steps towards the wall of the corridor and leant against it. She squeezed her eyes shut to keep the tears away and opened them again to see a bleary form walking towards her. It was Hilda. Alice groaned inwardly. She couldn't cope with speaking to the mad patient now.

'Has they found her?'

'No Hilda, Constance has not been found yet.'

'She was taken.'

'I know she was.'

'They was all taken.'

'Who were?'

'The girls. He takes the girls. I seen him.'

'Seen who?'

Hilda's eyes darted around from wall to ceiling as if she were frantically trying to recollect a memory.

'His men takes them for 'im.' Her milk white eye was fixed on Alice again. 'They took Adeline.'

'Who is Adeline?'

'My Adeline. They took *my Adeline*. I tried to stop them but they put me in the stews.'

Alice knew Hilda meant the brothels. It was difficult to know whether she was making this story up.

'Was Adeline your sister, Hilda? Your daughter?' She put her hand on Hilda's arm.

'My Adeline.' Hilda's lower jaw quivered and she began to fidget with her rosary beads.

'Tell me who did that to you and Adeline, Hilda. We can go and find them.' Hilda pulled away from her hand and walked away.

'Hilda?'

But the old lady broke into a run and Alice knew it would be futile to chase her.

# Chapter Twenty-Seven

The nervous fluttering that had been growing in Elizabeth's stomach as the carriage lurched its way towards London had turned to nausea by the time they passed through the city gates. The buildings closed in around them and people on the street peered in through the window to see who was riding in a nobleman's carriage.

'Stop here,' she said to Rosaline, the heavy-featured woman Lady Margery had sent to accompany her.

'But this is not your father's house,' Rosaline replied. 'We need to get to Broad Street. Although it may be quicker for us to walk in these crowds and this mud.' She leaned out of the window and grimaced. 'We could walk on ahead to your father's house and the carriage could follow with your trunk.'

'I want to stop here,' said Elizabeth. 'I know where we are. We are close to St Hugh's and that is where my brother lives and works. I would like to see him first.'

Rosaline bit her lip. 'My orders are to take you to your father.'

'I know,' Elizabeth said, taking a deep breath. 'Can you

understand how difficult it will be for me to meet my father again?'

Rosaline nodded.

'I would like to see him with my brother present; that will make it easier for me. Let me get out at St Hugh's and the carriage can take my trunk on to my father's house. You can tell him I have returned, that I am at St Hugh's and will be with him in the next day or so. You have my promise I will go back to him. Please tell Lady Margery that.'

Rosaline sighed. Elizabeth could tell she wasn't happy about leaving her at St Hugh's, but the carriage was making little progress in the crowds and Elizabeth was determined to insist until she got her own way.

She paused on the steps of St Hugh's and looked up at the oak door, which rose tall and arched above her. It had been many years since she had visited Jon. *Was he still here?* She glanced around her, worried that the men who had taken her would somehow appear on the street. She hoped she looked different now and that they would be unable to recognise her. She wore the dark red dress Lady Margery had lent her with a matching cloak. Her clothes had kept her warm during the long journey, but she felt hot outdoors on a warm spring day.

'Here we are,' she said. 'Almost home.'

Her knock at the door was answered by a tall, thin nun with a sombre face. She looked Elizabeth up and down with an air of faint recognition, but did not smile.

'I'm looking for Brother Jon,' said Elizabeth.

The door opened wider. 'And you are?' asked the nun.

'His sister. Elizabeth.'

The nun's eyebrows rose. 'You had better come inside,' she replied.

Elizabeth stepped in through the doorway and found

herself in the infirmary hall, where a dozen or so people lay in their beds. A nun was helping one of them wash in a bowl of water. It was peaceful and sunlight streamed in through the stained-glass windows. The clean, pleasant smell of incense hung in the air. From a room at the far end of the hall Elizabeth could hear children's voices. The solemn nun had vanished and Elizabeth waited by the doorway, her stomach jittery with nerves. *What would Jon think of her? Would he disown her?*

She had felt better about coming to St Hugh's before she visited her father. If she could explain things to Jon first he could accompany her when it was time to return home.

She heard footsteps drawing nearer along a stone corridor; then her brother stepped around the corner. He was just as she had remembered. His cheeks were a little thinner and there were a few extra lines around his eyes, but it was unmistakably Jon. Elizabeth grinned.

Jon stopped suddenly and stared at her. Then she watched his face as a smile spread from his eyes down to his mouth.

In two quick steps he was in front of her.

'Elizabeth, I thought you were... I never thought I would see you again. And who is this?'

She looked down at the baby in her arms, who was starting to stir from her sleep. 'This is my daughter Mary.'

Jon stroked the soft hair on the little girl's head.

'You named her after our mother?' His eyes were damp. 'She is beautiful,' he added.

He threw his arms around his sister, taking care not to crush his baby niece.

It was a relief to be held in someone's arms again. A sob escaped from Elizabeth's chest as she pushed her face into the roughness of Jon's tunic. The dampness of her tears made the wool itch her face.

'Where have you been?' his voice wobbled.

'I stayed with an old lady who looked after me.' She wasn't ready to tell Jon much yet; it felt wrong to sour their happy reunion with her story.

He pulled back from her and looked at her face. 'Did you leave because of the baby?'

'No. There is much to tell you, but not now. The important thing is that I came back. I cannot tell you how happy I am to see you again. How is Father?'

The smile on Jon's face faded. 'He is quiet. He does very little these days. He was devastated when you disappeared.'

Elizabeth bit her lip in a bid to stop her tears. 'I cannot wait to see him. I will need you with me when I go home, though. There is so much to explain.'

'I can see that,' smiled Jon. 'Come and sit down, you must be tired.'

He led her over to a large room, which looked like a refectory. Elizabeth sat at one of the benches, still holding her daughter tight. She heard a child's voice chattering nearby and looked up as a petite woman in a brown tunic and cream veil walked into the room with two young children at her side. She stopped suddenly, as if surprised to see them there.

'Alice!' flustered Jon. 'Elizabeth is safe! Here she is!' Jon was grinning wildly and patches of red had appeared high on his cheeks. 'And this is her daughter, Mary.'

Alice's face broke out into a warm smile. 'Really? *How wonderful!*'

She walked over to Elizabeth. 'I cannot believe you are here! Has Jon told you how much time he spent searching for you? It's such a relief to know you are safe and well. Perhaps some prayers are answered after all.'

'Of course they are!' said Jon.

'And you look so alike,' continued Alice. 'You have the same green eyes. There's no doubt you are brother and sister.

Oh Jon, I am *so pleased for you!*' She gave him a hug, which he clearly wasn't expecting, and his face reddened even more.

It was unusual for Elizabeth to see her brother smile so much.

The little boy standing next to Alice prodded Mary gently. 'Baby,' he said.

'Yes, Peter, a baby girl,' said Alice. 'Her name is Mary.'

The little girl at her other side grinned at Elizabeth with her fingers in her mouth.

'Are these your children?' Elizabeth asked Alice.

'No,' said Alice, 'not that I would mind if they were. I work here, I look after them. They are foundlings.'

'Maybe one day you will have your own,' suggested Elizabeth.

As soon as she had spoken she sensed a coolness, but there was no time for Alice to reply because the tall, thin nun had returned, and this time she also had a smile on her face.

While Jon spoke to Sister Katherine, Alice watched Elizabeth with her daughter and wondered where she had been since the previous summer. *She must have left because she was expecting the baby*, she reasoned. *But if so, why had she returned now and why was she wearing such good-quality apparel? And how had her rosary beads ended up around Juliana's neck?*

Alice had so many questions to ask Elizabeth, but now was not the right time. She would have to be patient.

Elizabeth stood up to speak to Sister Katherine, and that was when Alice noticed how tall she was, just like her brother. They both had strong jawlines and well-defined cheekbones. Alice felt round-faced and squat in comparison.

*People would ask who the father of the baby was. Would Elizabeth tell them?*

Despite Elizabeth's calm demeanour and smart appearance, her fingers fidgeted nervously with her daughter's swaddling clothes.

*Had she suffered while she was away?* Alice felt sure she was picking up on some discomfort from Elizabeth.

She watched Jon as he chatted animatedly. She had never seen him talk to Sister Katherine for so long before and she felt happy to see the wide grin on his face. Any residual anger from the argument she had had with him the previous day had passed and she realised their relationship would change now that his sister had returned. There was no longer any need for him to help her find Constance; his work was done.

She would have to continue the search for Constance alone.

'I will find you a bed for tonight,' said Alice to Elizabeth. 'Come on, Peter.' The little boy was still fascinated by the baby. 'Let's go and find a place for Auntie Elizabeth and baby Mary to sleep in.'

# Chapter Twenty-Eight

❧❧❧

The sparrowhawk swept low across the courtyard, sunlight glinting on its back. With a tinkle from the bell on its feet, it landed on the leather gauntlet covering Sir Walter's arm and pulled at the piece of rabbit flesh he held between his fingers.

'He is learning well,' called Sir Walter to the falconer, who was standing at the far side of the courtyard. The falconer nodded in reply and Sir Walter admired the bird as it sat on his arm. Its hood had been removed and he looked into the predator's keen eyes.

Geoffrey Edington's death should have appeased Sir Walter's paranoia. With Geoffrey dead there would be no more careless talk. But even though he was gone, Sir Walter still felt uneasy. Ever since Elizabeth had escaped he had felt his control slipping.

The latest news from Valerian was that the widow and Elizabeth's brother had visited Juliana's family at their tavern. *How had they found out about her? What else did they know?*

Sir Walter hoped his man Serle had done a good job of frightening Alice for the time being, but he had a feeling she was not yet ready to give up her search. He had to take control again and that meant getting rid of the remaining girls, so that by the time Alice and her monk friend came to his door looking for Constance there would be no sign of her.

He kissed the hawk on its head and sent it back to the falconer.

Theobald stepped out into the courtyard, his feet crunching on the gravel as he watched the hawk land on the falconer's arm. He walked over to Sir Walter, who was wearing a blue-and-gold patterned jacket and a red velvet hat.

'You sent for me, Sir Walter?'

'Yes.' His voice sounded heavy and serious. 'The whores we keep in the dungeons need to leave. They hold no interest for me any more, they are haggard and careworn.'

Theobald tried to comprehend what Sir Walter had said. 'Where will they go? Not back to their families, surely?'

'Of course not!' thundered Sir Walter. 'What a ridiculous idea.'

He shouted over to the falconer. 'Get the ducklings ready!'

Theobald glanced across to the man and saw him dragging a small wooden cage into view.

'This is why I sent for you,' Sir Walter said to Theobald quietly. 'Have you any idea what we could do with them?'

Theobald had sensed this day was coming. Sir Walter was looking thinner and more tired than usual. The worry of being found out was clearly getting to him.

'Do you want them kept alive?' he asked.

'No, they need to be eliminated. I cannot risk them talking to anyone. How many do we have?'

'Eight.'

Sir Walter held out his arm and the hawk returned to him.

'That's a lot to get rid of. We cannot kill them here. It would be impossible to dispose of the bodies in this busy place without arousing suspicion. They will have to be taken somewhere.'

'How about Waltham Forest?'

'That's over the other side of the city.'

'But suitably deserted and wild. They are unlikely to be discovered there for a while. They could be taken there in one of the wagons and we can slit their throats when we get there. If we take some shovels with us they can dig their own graves first.'

'Good man,' said Walter, 'I like that plan. But transporting eight wenches through London could be tricky if they mutiny.'

'Then we must put them under fear of death.'

'But they already are. Once they are outside and get a taste of freedom they might forget about being frightened.'

'So we remind them.'

'How?'

'By killing one of them.' Theobald liked the sound of power in his own voice. 'We could do it in front of the others, right here. One body will easy to dispose of.'

Sir Walter nodded.

'Ready?' he called over to the falconer.

Theobald watched as the man bent down and opened the cage. Five fluffy ducklings waddled out onto the gravel. They staggered about in a group, unsure which way to go.

Sir Walter launched the hawk from his hand and it swept across the courtyard, swooping down onto the ducklings. Sir Walter cheered and the hawk returned to him with a small, fluffy duck wriggling in its talons, blood spreading across its soft, downy feathers.

Sir Walter lowered his voice as the hawk on his arm buried its beak into its prey. 'I agree with your plan. Get rid of one of those whores and put the fear of God into the others.'

The girls were lined up in the stone corridor outside their rooms. They were usually gathered together in this way before they were taken to an evening party and Theobald could see them glancing at each other nervously, aware that something out of the ordinary was happening. No one spoke.

Theobald paced slowly along the line, stroking his beard and looking at their thin, worn faces. Even though he liked seeing girls with their hair hanging loose over their shoulders, these girls were no longer attractive to him. There was no plumpness in their cheeks or brightness in their eyes. There was no innocence left. The only good thing about them was their servility. *Sir Walter has made the right decision to get rid of them*, he thought to himself.

'Follow me,' he said brightly, hoping there would be no resistance. He led them along the corridor and down the winding steps. The girls remained silent and walked slowly; he sensed their reluctance to follow him. They weren't stupid. He was taking them down into the bowels of Sir Walter's palace, where screams could not be heard and the walls and floors could be easily sluiced down.

He reached a small room and opened its barred iron door. Inside, Serle was waiting for them. The unfurnished room was lined with stone and two torches blazed in brackets on the wall. Theobald made sure each of the girls entered the room before he moved inside himself.

He shut the door behind them and smelt the unmistake-able scent of fear as the girls huddled together in a corner. Serle's appearance was alarming. He had a mean look about him, with narrow eyes and puckered, burnt skin on one side of his face. Some of the girls seemed to want to speak but fear was holding them back. They could all see the long knife in Serle's hand.

Theobald tried not to show it, but he felt nervous himself.

'Pick one,' he said loudly to Serle.

The wiry man stepped forward and grabbed the wrist of the youngest looking girl, pulling her into the centre of the room. She had wavy blonde hair, thin pale limbs and wore a dirty cream dress. Theobald recognised her as Constance, the girl from St Hugh's. She didn't fight back, but he noticed she was trembling as she looked back at the group of girls behind her.

'No!' shouted one of the older girls, who was tall with dark hair. 'I don't know what you're planning, but take me instead!'

'I don't want yer,' replied Serle huskily. 'Watch yer mouth or I'll cut yer throat.'

Theobald winced. He didn't want more than one death to take place in this room; it would create too much mess.

Serle pulled Constance towards him and held her across the chest facing the girls. He brandished his knife in the other hand.

Serle turned to Theobald. 'Do you wanna say anythin' afore I do it?' he asked.

Theobald's mouth felt dry. He could see the fear on the girls' faces. He looked at Constance, her face contorted in sheer panic.

'Don't hurt her!' yelled another girl.

'Why are you doing this to us?' a third girl pleaded with Theobald, her eyes wide with fear. He tried to swallow, but still his mouth felt dry. He had to show them he was in charge.

He nodded to Serle to show he was ready to speak, and Serle held his long knife up to Constance's throat. Constance closed her eyes and stood still. Theobald knew he would not be nearly so calm if this were happening to him.

'She's only a girl!' shouted the tallest one again.

'Don't!' screeched another, causing Theobald to jump.

Together, the girls edged forward to where Serle held Constance.

'*Please no! Stop him!*'

Their voices had risen to a cacophony of shrieks.

Serle eyed Theobald. 'I'm waiting fer you ter say the word!' he shouted above the noise. Then he glared at the girls around him, as though he would slay them all given the chance.

Theobald's control was slipping.

'Don't!' one of them yelled at him.

A girl with long red hair ran over to Theobald and grabbed his arm. 'If you kill Constance, you might as well kill all of us!' she shouted. 'Just end it here and now!'

Theobald shrugged her off and nervously reached for the hilt of his knife, which was tucked into his belt. *If the girls were hysterical before Constance had been harmed, what would they be like after Serle had cut her throat? There would be chaos and Serle would have to kill them all.*

'Wait!' he called, holding up his hand.

The noise died down and Constance opened her eyes. Serle's knife remained at her throat.

'Let her go,' he said resignedly, looking at the floor.

Serle pushed Constance back towards the girls and they surrounded her, their arms around each other. Theobald listened to their sobs and waited for them to calm down.

Serle glared at him and Theobald knew he had been cowardly. Serle had a thirst for blood and was visibly disappointed to have been stopped.

'You need to come on a journey with us,' said Theobald, calling over to the girls, 'but you need to travel quietly and without any resistance. Because if you do not,' he paused to make sure they were listening, 'then you will die. Without any question. What you saw just then was a test.'

He felt pleased with the lie he was making up to retain his honour. 'It was a test to ensure that you know exactly what will happen if you do not follow orders. We will leave as soon as the arrangements are in place. Do you understand?'

The faces that turned to him remained fearful, but no one spoke. He felt confident that he had made himself understood.

# Chapter Twenty-Nine

Elizabeth brought Mary into the children's dormitory the following morning. There was a cradle for the baby to rest in and Elizabeth looked as though she also needed to lie down. Jon accompanied his sister and fussed over his baby niece, occasionally grabbing the cradle so the children couldn't tip it over in their curiosity to see the new baby. Before long, Mary had acquired a number of toys, some of which had been thrown violently into the cradle by the younger children.

'It will be a miracle if she gets through the day without becoming bruised and battered!' laughed Elizabeth.

Alice busied herself with her work, patiently waiting for the moment when Elizabeth felt ready to talk. She hoped Elizabeth would confirm her suspicions about Sir Walter. Jon would have to believe her if she did. *Surely Constance was being held by Sir Walter.*

Matilda had stayed in bed that morning. Her face was red and her forehead hot. Alice pulled back her bedclothes to help her cool off, but Matilda pulled them back over her, shivering. Alice tried not to get into a battle with the girl as she bathed her face with cold water, but she knew she needed to cool Matilda down as quickly as possible.

'She has a fever,' she told one of the lay sisters. 'Can you please fetch Brother Ralph?'

Alice sat with Matilda for a while. The little girl cried to begin with but soon became quiet and sleepy. Alice preferred the children to make a noise when they were poorly; silence always suggested something was seriously wrong. She told herself not to worry. Fever was common and often the children recovered. *But could this be the start of a sickness for which there was no cure?* Alice wiped the little girl's arms and chest with the cool cloth.

'Please get better soon,' she whispered. Alice wanted to be hopeful. She prayed Matilda would start to feel better before sundown. Sister Emma took the other children out into the garden for a while and while Mary slept her mother explained to Alice and Jon what had happened to her: from being snatched in the marketplace to her life with Millicent, and how Lady Margery had made her return home. Alice felt certain there was a good deal Elizabeth was unable to tell them; her daughter was living proof that she had been attacked by the men who had abducted her.

Alice admired the way Elizabeth spoke so bravely about what had happened to her. She wanted to ask her how she managed to sleep peacefully at night after suffering such torment. *Was Constance suffering in the same way?* Alice feared she was.

As Elizabeth spoke, Alice watched Jon's face, noticing that his jaw was clenched tight. It was hard to imagine how Elizabeth was coping with what she had been through and how Jon could remain calm when his sister had been brutalised. Occasionally his fist would clench or he would exhale loudly; it was obvious that he was battling with his emotions.

The baby girl was beautiful and each time Alice looked at her asleep in the cradle she felt the urge to kiss her forehead or her soft cheek. It was hard to reconcile her beauty and innocence with the brutality of her conception. She could tell Elizabeth loved her little girl and seemed to have no animosity or resentment towards her.

Matilda stirred and Alice bathed her face again and held her hand until she dozed. Brother Ralph arrived and suggested angelica for the fever. Once he had left, the three of them resumed their conversation.

'There was a girl,' said Jon, 'who was thrown into the river. She was wearing your rosary beads.'

Elizabeth sighed. 'They found Juliana. I am pleased.'

'Yes, that was her; a tavern owner's daughter.'

Tears welled in Elizabeth's eyes and she pulled out a chain from under her dress. 'Look, I wear her beads still. I tried to help her; I hoped they hadn't killed her. But they did. I don't think they meant to, but she put up a struggle and they used a lot of force. When we were on the cart being taken down to the river, I pulled off my rosary beads and put them on her. It was just a way of helping her soul to rest in peace. I could see she would not receive a proper burial and the way in which she died was so...' Elizabeth was not able to speak any further.

Jon reached forward and held her hand. 'When you have recovered more, maybe you could visit her parents. They would be glad to hear what you tried to do for her. We went to see them and they are heartbroken. I think you could help them in their grief.'

Elizabeth shook her head. 'Jon, I am in danger. Those men are still about. They will find me if I start walking about London.'

'It's Sir Walter, isn't it?' asked Alice curtly. She had been waiting so long to ask the question that she simply blurted it out.

Elizabeth paused and looked at her, her face pale and her lips quivering. 'I cannot remember his name.'

'Are you sure? You were engaged to Geoffrey Edington, who worked for him. I can understand why you are frightened, Elizabeth. I have listened to what you have endured and I would be frightened too. But we will protect you. We will make sure we are with you all the time. They cannot hurt you now.'

'They can, and no one can stop him,' said Elizabeth, her voice shaking. 'People have no idea that he does this. If he wants to take a girl from someone, he just goes ahead and does it. Everyone thinks he is a kind, generous person. No one would believe he does these things; they would think I was making it up. It is my word against his and I have no chance of being believed. His men could come to this hospital now, and then what would you do? They are armed and we are helpless.

'I only came back here because I had to. Lord Marlston could not harbour a runaway and his wife had to ensure that I was returned to my father. I could not tell them I was in danger. I tried lying to start with, but I wasn't much good at it. I wanted to keep moving and not stay in one place for too long, but this little girl,' she gestured at her daughter in the cradle, 'put a stop to that. I have not told you yet that they tried to take Mary away. Lady Margery thought I would be disgraced if I brought a baby back with me. They even had another woman ready to be her mother; it was horrible. I argued and shouted until they relented. I had no idea I would ever feel so passionate about my child. It is a love I have never experienced before. I would do anything for her and would never part with her, even if it means bringing shame upon myself and destroying my future.'

Elizabeth's face was creased with anguish. She pulled a handkerchief from her purse and wiped her eyes.

'You should never have run away, you should have come here,' said Jon. 'I would have looked after you and Mary could have been born here.'

'If I had come here you would have had to tell Father and word would have spread. It wasn't safe here, I had to run away. I had no other choice.'

'I am overjoyed you are back.' Jon rested his hand on his sister's. 'Can you imagine what life would have been like for Father if you had disappeared forever? Later I will take you home and you will be sheltered and guarded there. After I have dealt with Sir Walter.'

'What do you mean?' asked Alice.

'I will visit him and cut his throat,' replied Jon calmly. 'I will take that sword I hid in the day room. I knew it would come in useful one day.'

Alice's stomach flipped.

'No, you mustn't!' said Elizabeth. 'You would stand no chance against him! Do you have any idea how many guards he has? You would be slaughtered by his men in an instant.'

'He will kill you!' agreed Alice.

'What else do you expect me to do?' asked Jon, leaping to his feet. 'His men left my sister for dead! And he has abused her and forced her to bear his child.'

He turned to his sister. 'Is Mary Sir Walter's daughter?'

Elizabeth nodded and looked at the floor.

Alice felt her pain. Such a question must have brought back memories she would rather forget.

Jon punched the palm of his hand with a tight fist. 'I want to kill him right now! He has ruined you and ruined your daughter's life. She is a bastard and will have to live with that for the rest of her life. He could never be a father to her.'

'No, but I can be twice the mother,' said Elizabeth. 'She

may be a bastard but I will do my best to ensure she is not burdened by that. I still have a future and so does she. I will do everything I can for her and it feels right to do that. Perhaps you do not understand as you will never be a father yourself, shut up here in a monastery.'

Mary whimpered and Elizabeth got up to check on her.

Jon's face was thunderous.

'Jon,' said Alice, 'we need to think about Constance. What if Constance is in Sir Walter's household? We could go and look for her there, but we cannot go there to fight. We must just go there and ask about her.'

Jon's expression darkened further.

'Did you come across a girl called Constance in Sir Walter's household?' Alice asked Elizabeth.

'I do not remember the name.' She picked Mary up and cuddled her.

'She is fourteen years old with long, fair hair. She is small for her age.'

'There were a few young girls there and a number of them were fair. We were kept in separate rooms most of the time, unless we were at one of his parties.' Elizabeth spat the words out bitterly. 'But we were not allowed to talk to each other even then.'

Jon cursed. 'I don't even want to think about what his parties were like. I want to slice the throat of every man who ever went to them.'

'So it's possible Constance is being held by Sir Walter, but you are not certain?' asked Alice.

Elizabeth looked at her with sad eyes and Alice felt guilty for continuing to question her when she had suffered so much.

'It is possible. I cannot say that she is not, but I do not wish to raise your hopes.'

'I can rescue Constance when I go there,' said Jon.

'Jon, if you were one of our brothers I would think it a reasonable idea,' said Elizabeth. 'But you are not a trained knight, you are a monk. And please listen to me when I say that he has many men to help him as well as being a seasoned knight himself. If you go in there armed you will die.'

The door opened and they fell silent. The prior stood there, his eyes shadowed with grey and a scrappy beard covering his chin.

'A word please, Mistress Wescott.'

Alice didn't like the look of the scowl on his face.

'Of course, Father, although I mustn't leave Matilda for long. She has a fever and I am worried about her.'

'Someone else can tend to her.'

The prior gestured for her to leave the room and Alice followed him through the doorway. He led her down the corridor and into a small chapel dedicated to the memory of Abbot Beroldus. He stood by the altar and glared at her, the conciliatory manner she had seen when he gave her the relic long gone.

'It is with great regret that I must ask you to leave St Hugh's,' said the prior, 'I have heard reports of you leaving the monastery when forbidden to do so. I have also been informed of an unpleasant confrontation with Brother Rufus and Sir Walter's man, Theobald FitzAlan. This behaviour can be tolerated no longer. I warned you and you chose to ignore my instructions. Thank you for all your work, and you know I am grateful for the way you cared for Nicholas, but now is the appropriate time for you to leave.'

'Now?'

'Now.'

'But Matilda is ill! I can't leave her.'

'You left her a couple of days ago without a care. Matilda

does not need you; there are plenty of others here who can care for her.'

'Please let me say goodbye to her and the children.'

'There is no need, it will only upset them.'

'This cannot be right, not when I have found out where Constance is!'

'Where?' The prior raised a sceptical eyebrow.

'Sir Walter took her! He took Jon's sister Elizabeth too. And Juliana, the girl who was found dead in the river. He murdered her. He has taken lots of girls, Elizabeth told us. We have to tell the bailiff and the aldermen and the sheriffs and the bishops. The king himself should know about this! Those girls need to be rescued before they come to any more harm.'

The prior smirked. 'It is clear to me now that you have truly lost your mind. It is just as well I have asked you to leave.'

'But this is *true*! Ask Elizabeth!'

'No doubt she is as hysterical as you are. It is a common trait in women and I have no time for such nonsense. If you continue to talk in this way I am certain you will find yourself in the gaol before sundown. Now please gather your things and leave.'

'I won't.'

'You will. And I have some men here to help you.'

Alice looked behind her and saw three monks – Brother Jarvis, Brother Henry and Brother Arnold – standing nearby.

She was to be forcibly removed.

# Chapter Thirty

Alice reluctantly walked into the courtyard of Yvette de Beauchamp's house. She had heard nothing from her friend since she had asked her for help so she was unlikely to help now, but Alice had nowhere else to turn. She had been allowed to fetch a few belongings from her room at St Hugh's before being marched out of the monastery without the chance to say goodbye to a single soul. Tucked under her arm was the casket with the broken lid.

Alice was desperately worried desperately about Matilda and her fever. *Would she be all right? Would she ever see her again?*

She knocked at the door and a stern-faced servant with a piggy nose answered. There was a long pause as Alice waited to see whether Yvette would be willing to admit her. Eventually the servant returned and nodded. Feeling relieved, Alice followed her through the hall into a well-lit day room. Sunlight streamed in through the window and Yvette sat on a cushioned bench wearing a deep blue satin dress, with her little white dog on her lap.

She stood to greet Alice, holding her dog in her arms. Her smile was genuine but not as warm as it had once been.

'What brings you here?' she asked.

'I need your help.'

Yvette's smile remained fixed on her face. Alice sensed that Yvette did not wish to be involved.

'The prior has told me to leave St Hugh's.'

'Is that so? The last time I saw you, you were a prisoner there. What has caused this change of heart?'

'My behaviour is no longer tolerated.'

Yvette rolled her eyes. 'I am not sure what you expect me to do. As I told you the last time we met, you bring these things upon yourself.'

'Can I stay here with you for a day or two while I try to talk sense into the prior?'

Yvette tutted. 'You will never talk sense into him. I tried speaking to him on your behalf but I would have had as much success speaking to one of the gargoyles on the wall of his monastery. Once the prior has made up his mind he will not change it for anyone. I am sorry I could do nothing for you then, but I was warned away.'

'By whom?'

'By the prior of course. He told me not get involved, so I didn't. I apologise that I did not succeed in negotiating your freedom, but you know yourself the prior is a stubborn man. And now it seems you have your freedom. Surely that is preferable to being shut away in a monastery.'

Yvette sat back down and gestured for Alice to take a seat next to her.

'But I do not have a home or any money.'

'Alice, how did you get into this predicament? It is your own doing. You may stay here a day but no longer or I will find myself in trouble.'

'With whom?'

'With Prior Edmund. I also had a visit from Theobald

FitzAlan, who told me I must stay away from you on Sir Walter's orders.'

'That makes sense now that I know what Sir Walter has been doing.'

'What do you mean?'

Alice told Yvette about Elizabeth and how she suspected Sir Walter had also taken Constance. She told her about Juliana's death and the plight of the other girls.

While Yvette listened, the expression on her face flickered between horror and disbelief.

'I don't know what to make of this. It cannot be true,' said Yvette. 'Sir Walter is such a good man. He would have to be a despicable tyrant to use kindness and generosity to cover up sinful actions such as these.'

'He is despicable,' said Alice, 'and we need to tell the authorities. And Constance needs rescuing.'

'But the authorities will not believe you. The prior doesn't believe you and I am not sure I do either. What evidence do you have?'

'Brother Jon's sister, Elizabeth. She has given birth to Sir Walter's child.'

'*His child?*'

'It is true.'

Yvette stood up. 'I am sorry, Alice, but this sounds like a wild story to me. I refuse to believe it. Sir Walter is a friend of mine. He is well respected and well liked. There is no need for him to do these terrible things you are suggesting. Are you sure being shut up in that monastery has not driven you half-mad? These are crazed tales.'

Yvette called her servant, but the stern woman had been busy answering the door.

'A lady with a baby and a monk are here to see you, ma'am,' she said.

Alice smiled. Jon had guessed where she would be.

'Did they give their names?'

'Brother Jon of St Hugh's and Elizabeth de Grey, ma'am.'

'De Grey?' Yvette raised her eyebrows. 'Show them in, Ida.'


By late afternoon Yvette had become convinced of Sir Walter's guilt. She had listened to Elizabeth's story, admired baby Mary and heard from Jon and Alice about Juliana's family, Geoffrey's death, Hilda's story and the suspicions they had that Sir Walter had taken Constance.

'And now,' said Jon, 'is my opportunity to visit Sir Walter, rescue Constance and avenge my sister's degradation.'

'No!' said Elizabeth and Alice in unison.

'He will kill you,' said Elizabeth. 'Let the authorities deal with him.'

'I want the satisfaction of dealing with him myself,' spat Jon.

He reached under his tunic and pulled out a sword. Yvette gasped and Alice guessed it was the sword he had been hiding at St Hugh's. It was dull in colour and unpolished having been hidden for so long, but it was still an impressive sword.

'Jon, I can understand why you are so angry, but you cannot challenge Sir Walter in this way,' said Alice.

'He will have you cut into ribbons,' added Yvette.

'You cannot stop me,' said Jon, eying them all defiantly, 'I have waited my entire life to fight. And now my time has come. My sister's honour is what I am fighting for.'

He turned and left the room, and the women quickly followed.

'Jon! Stop!' cried Alice. 'There is a better way of doing this.'

Jon strode on ahead of her. 'No, there is not. I have to carry out my duty.'

He opened the door and stepped out into the courtyard.

Alice followed and grabbed his arm. 'And what if you die?'

'I would rather die in battle than as a withered old monk in a monastery. This way my death would be for a noble cause.'

He shook her hand off and strode across the courtyard to the street.

'There is nothing noble about death! What about the people you leave behind?'

Alice ran after him and pulled on his tunic.

Jon stopped and looked down at Alice as she clung on to him. She watched him as he considered her words. Then he moved his face closer to hers. 'The people I leave behind will know I fought to my last breath holding them in my heart.'

Alice was reluctant to let go of him; she wanted to shout and scream and do everything she could to stop him. But she knew there was no use. There was a grim determination in his eyes and she knew she had to let him go. She released her grip.

Jon said goodbye to the three of them and stepped out into the street.

But he was to get no further.

A hump-backed official wearing a scarlet jacket and a blue velvet hat blocked his way. Two guards stood either side of the man, whom Alice recognised as the bailiff who had arrested Valerian.

'Jon de Grey, you are a suspect in the murder of Geoffrey Edington. Hand your weapon to my men, who will escort you to the gaol.'

'I found him, but I did not kill him!'

Jon tried to remonstrate further but the men had hold of him and quickly marched him away.

'Leave that man alone, on my orders!' shouted Yvette as the three women ran after him.

'He didn't do it!' cried Alice. 'He didn't kill him!' But she was quickly silenced as she felt her arm twisted up behind her back.

More guards.

And they also had hold of Elizabeth and Yvette.

'Leave us alone!' shouted Elizabeth.

'Do you realise who I am?' asked Yvette.

But no one was listening.

# Chapter Thirty-One

❦

Sir Walter's room was adorned with tapestries and well
polished armoury. Brightly embroidered cushions sat
on finely carved chairs and Alice would have admired
the apartment for its splendour had it belonged to anyone
else. She stood in the centre of the room with her hands tied
behind her back. Elizabeth stood next to her. She had been
spared the tethers so she could hold her baby. She glanced at
Alice, her face pale.

There was no one else in the room apart from the guards.
Alice felt frightened but was reassured to think that
Constance must be nearby. *He wouldn't have killed her, would he?*
She was certain she would know in her heart if Constance
were dead. Despite the situation they had found themselves
in, she still held out hope.

Sir Walter marched into the room. He was as broad and
arrogant as Alice remembered and wore a green brocade
jacket and a red velvet hat. There was a strong perfume about
him that smelt like roses, only slightly sickly. Alice gritted her
teeth and prepared herself.

'Elizabeth!' He held out his arms. 'You have returned to

me! I am overjoyed to see you looking so well. And I must apologise for the rough treatment you received at the hands of my men. But you are a fighter because you carry the de Grey blood. I cannot tell you how happy I am to have you back with me.'

Elizabeth said nothing as Sir Walter looked her up and down and licked his lips. Alice felt her stomach turn.

'What have you done with Constance?' Alice demanded.

'Mistress Wescott, welcome,' replied Sir Walter. 'I remember our meeting at the home of our mutual friend Yvette de Beauchamp. You left quite an impression on me.'

'Where is Yvette?'

'You ask a lot of questions, Mistress Wescott. Questions are the reason you find yourself in trouble now. Poor Prior Edmund, he did his best but you are a struggle to control. This is what happens when a mare does not have a stallion to keep her in her place.' Sir Walter tutted.

'You didn't answer my question about Constance,' said Alice. She tried to pull her hands free but the twine that bound them cut painfully into her wrists.

Sir Walter lowered his eyebrows, puzzled. 'Constance?'

'The girl who was taken from St Hugh's earlier this year. A young girl with long blonde hair. We know you have her.'

Sir Walter shrugged. 'I have no idea who you are talking about.' He strolled over to one of his chairs and relaxed into it. 'My dear, I fear you are succumbing to a form of delirium. Perhaps it is the effect of working for that drunken prior for too long. I have never met a wench called Constance.'

'I have your daughter in my arms, Sir Walter. Her name is Mary,' said Elizabeth.

Alice stopped struggling with the twine around her wrists and stared at Elizabeth. It was brave of her to admit to Sir Walter that the child was his. *But surely he could snatch the baby away.*

Sir Walter gave an unpleasant, throaty laugh. 'My *daughter*, you say? What lunacy! I fancy you are as deluded as your friend here. Now then, ladies, all I planned to do was welcome you into my home. I am a busy man, so I must be on my way.' Sir Walter nodded to his guards.

'Where is Constance?' shouted Alice.

Sir Walter said nothing further as he strode out of the room, leaving a trail of the sickly scent behind him.

The guards walked up to Alice and Elizabeth, grabbing each of them by the arm.

'Get off me!' cried Alice. She struggled to pull free but the guard increased his grip until she felt a sharp pain.


Sir Walter climbed into the carriage that was waiting for him in the courtyard and asked his postilion to drive the horses as quickly as possible. He was relieved to be heading to the home of his friend, Sir Tybalt d'Orval; a quiet man who helped Sir Walter manage his finances. He planned to stay with Sir Tybalt for a few days so that when he returned home the girls would all be gone, and Alice and Elizabeth would have vanished along with them. Alice's accomplice Jon was hopefully locked up by now and Yvette and Prior Edmund would be bribed to keep quiet. Sir Walter sank back into his cushioned seat and breathed a large sigh. He was pleased with his work. Soon this would be over and he could concentrate on repairing any holes in his reputation.

He had been surprised to see his daughter in Elizabeth's arms. Had he known Elizabeth was with child he would have sent her off to the brothel. Fortunately, few people would believe her story, and soon she and Alice would be silenced forever.

He had wanted to ask Elizabeth where she had been and with whom she had spoken. *How many people knew about her plight?* He hoped very few people knew what had happened to her. Elizabeth's shame and the birth of her bastard child would presumably have discouraged her from telling many people.

He thought she looked well after her ordeal, and she had also been well-dressed. *She was a brave girl with a lot of spirit. It was a shame she had to die, but he couldn't take any more risks.*

He had resisted the temptation to look at the baby girl's face. Taking an interest in her would have been an admission of guilt. But he had to admit that he had wanted to find out whether she bore any resemblance to him. It was possible that he had other children, but there were none that he knew about.

Sir Walter pulled back the carriage window curtain and peered out at the crowds. Up ahead was the steeple of St Mary's, a church he visited often and which was, coincidentally, named after the same saint as his daughter. He asked his postilion to stop there.

The interior of the church was cool and calm, and the air was heavily laden with incense. Father Adam was walking towards the altar, dressed in a violet silk robe.

He turned at the sound of footsteps. 'Sir Walter Rokeby, how pleasant to see you. How can I help?'

'I would like you to pray with me.'

# Chapter Thirty-Two

❦

Jon didn't have to wait long for a visitor. His small dank room was flooded with light from a guard's lantern and in walked a tall, stooped man dressed in black with white hair and a neat white beard.

'Give me that lantern,' said the man to the guard. 'You may wait outside while we speak.'

The guard left the room.

'Father!' exclaimed Jon as he got to his feet.

Sir Robyn de Grey stood and stared at his son.

'You have to help me get out of here,' said Jon, 'I am innocent of Geoffrey's murder. I found him and raised the hue and cry, but they haven't found the killer so now they think it was me who killed him!'

'So that is what happened, is it?' replied Sir Robyn. 'What were you doing at his home in the first place? Your mother and I sent you to St Hugh's to keep you out of trouble. You always were the tempestuous one. I thought the monk's life had calmed your mind, but sadly I have been proven wrong.'

'It has, Father. This is all a mistake. Elizabeth returned yesterday.'

'So I have been told, but I scarce believe it. Her trunk has been delivered to my home but it is locked. I was trying to work out this puzzle and make enquiries when I heard you had been arrested. I didn't think she was still... Have you seen her?'

'Yes! She came to St Hugh's, I was going to bring her to you but I was captured and now she has also been captured.'

'*Captured?*' Sir Robyn took a handkerchief from his purse and wiped his brow. 'Where has she been until now?'

'Sir Walter took her. And I fear he is behind this. He must have taken her again, along with Alice.'

Sir Robyn's forehead was deeply furrowed. 'Who is Alice?'

Jon explained everything that had happened over the past few months, omitting only the fact that Elizabeth had given birth to Sir Walter's child. He felt his father needed to be better prepared for that news. Sir Robyn listened intently, raising his eyebrows as Jon described Sir Walter's duplicitous lifestyle.

'You have never liked Sir Walter. Did you not suspect that his charitable work was a cover for his lascivious behaviour?'

'I suspected that it was not genuine, but I had no idea he was carrying out such depravity within the walls of his palace. Can *anyone* imagine such a thing? Sir Walter always did imbue a saint-like quality in the gullible. And to think his men colluded with him. We must find them all and bring them to justice.'

'After I have slain him.'

Sir Robyn shook his head. 'Tempting though that is, it does not solve the problem in the correct manner. The man must stand trial along with his accomplices. After he has been found guilty we can watch him swing from the gallows.'

'But I have to take my revenge for what he did to Elizabeth.'

'You are not alone. I cannot think too much about how he

has made my daughter suffer. I too would grab the nearest sword and happily slice off his head. However, a knight does not act out of fury, despite what his heart tells him. He must act in the manner in which God intends. Justice will come to Sir Walter.'

'And how can I get out of here? How can I prove that I didn't kill Geoffrey?'

'I will speak to the bailiff. I hear a bag of gold coins usually buys his ear.'

Alice was gasping for air when she came round. It was dark and her head throbbed with pain. She remembered being flung into a room and hitting her head against the wall. *How long had she been lying on the cold floor?* There was a foul smell, which she realised must be coming from a latrine bucket. Her hands were still tied, but she managed to pull her feet over them so she could hold her hands in front of her. Shakily, she got to her feet, her head reeling. Putting her hands up to the side of her head she could feel dampness under her veil.

It had to be blood.

She staggered forward in the dark with her hands outstretched and soon they met a damp wall. Moving along the wall in the darkness she made her way round to a cold metal door.

'Elizabeth?' she called out weakly. 'Can you hear me? Constance? Are you there?' The only sound that greeted her was the echo of her own voice. She felt her way around her cell and came across a narrow wooden bench. She would have sat there, but the stench suggested she was close to the latrine bucket, so she walked back toward the barred door. If anyone appeared with a torch she would see the light there first.

Alice removed her veil and touched the wound on her

head. Her hair was matted with blood just above her right ear. Thankfully, the bleeding seemed to have stopped; the worst of it had probably soaked into her veil. Beneath her hair she could feel that the wound was swollen. She winced as she accidentally prodded it too hard and replaced her veil as if it could somehow bandage the injury.

She leaned against the door and tried to keep herself calm. *But what about Matilda? Would she be feeling better or becoming increasingly sick?*

There was nothing Alice could do for her now. She imagined Matilda lying in her little bed, calling for her and crying because she wasn't there to comfort her.

Alice's heart ached. She sank to the floor in the corner of her cell closest to the door. She should have listened to the prior so that she could have stayed at St Hugh's with the children who needed her. Constance also needed her, but it had been too much of a risk to look for her. The warnings had been there and Alice had ignored them.

Her head throbbed and she closed her eyes. All she could do now was wait.

# Chapter Thirty-Three

T he screech of the door opening was deafening. Alice shielded her eyes from the blinding light of the lantern and saw two men standing there looking at her.

'What are you going to do with me? Where are Elizabeth and her baby?'

'You'll find out soon enough.'

She recognised the smug voice of Theobald FitzAlan.

'Get up.'

Alice staggered to her feet, her legs aching from resting on the hard floor. She felt dizzy. The guard cut her hands free with his knife and she followed Theobald along a dark stone corridor with the guard following behind her.

'Where are you taking me?' There were grooves in her wrists from where the twine had bound them.

'Enough of the questions now, Mistress Wescott.'

They reached a corridor lit with torches, allowing Alice to see Theobald more clearly with his ginger collar-length hair and unkempt beard.

'You may be wishing now that you had made me feel more

welcome at St Hugh's,' smirked Theobald, glancing at her over his shoulder. 'It costs nothing to be polite, but rudeness comes at a price.'

Alice clenched her teeth. 'Where is Elizabeth? And where is Constance?'

Theobald chuckled, and ahead in the corridor she saw a figure she recognised as Valerian. He was wearing a red jacket made in the latest style. They drew nearer to him and Alice's jaw ached as she gritted her teeth even harder. Something in her chest flipped.

Valerian saw her but didn't smile. 'Hello, Alice. How are...'

His words were cut short as Alice's fist smashed into his right cheek. She winced as soon as she hit him, feeling his hard cheekbone crunch against her knuckles, but she smiled as she watched him buckle, swear and clasp his hands to the side of his face. Bellows of laughter came from Theobald and the guard.

Valerian straightened himself and held his cheek with his hand. There was something in his dark eyes that made her look away again: sympathy or sadness, she wasn't sure which.

But she felt good about hitting him. She wanted to stay and tell him what she thought of him, but a shove in the back pushed her forward.

Cradling her sore hand and walking on she could see more people ahead of her and then a doorway that opened into daylight. She must have spent an entire night in the cell. There were two women wearing cloaks and hoods by the door along with two or three guards. Questions ran through her mind. *Who were these women? Were they being taken somewhere? Would she be going with them?*

Alice continued to follow Theobald to the open doorway. She wasn't sure whether to be pleased or worried.

The doorway opened out into a large, gravelled courtyard. Here they were surrounded by the wings of Sir Walter's palace and she could see an archway, which appeared to lead out onto the street.

A large, covered wagon stood on one side of the courtyard with three horses in front of it. Alice could see the women ahead being led towards it with Theobald in pursuit. The other women had to be Elizabeth and Constance. She wanted to call out to them but it looked as though she would find out soon enough. *Were the three of them being taken back to St Hugh's? Perhaps Sir Walter was dead.* Alice's mind span with possibilities, but she tried not to become too hopeful in case she was met with disappointment.

'Where are we going?' she asked Theobald again.

He hushed her and told her to get into the wagon. She climbed the wooden steps and was surprised to see how many girls and women were inside. They sat on the two long benches that ran along either side of the carriage. Most of them had their heads covered and it was difficult to see their faces. Alice paused on the steps, looking at each of them, and was struck by how thin and sad they all looked. A sense of dread curled in her stomach. She could tell that whatever was happening here was not a good thing.

One of the women stood out from the others with her bright clothing. She was biting her lip and holding a bundle close to her chest. Alice smiled at her; Elizabeth was there after all.

'Get in!' growled a guard behind her. 'You're the last one!'

He pushed her and she stumbled into the wagon. As she picked herself up and tried to find a space on the bench, a face at the far end of the wagon caught her eye.

Small, pale and young.

And then there was a smile.

'*Constance!*' yelled Alice.

The women sitting nearest her flinched and Alice could see there was no room between everyone's knees to make her way down the wagon towards her friend. She apologised for raising her voice as the cart moved with a lurch, and she managed to squeeze onto one of the benches just in time. The lack of space didn't stop Constance, however. Amid much tutting and shuffling, Constance made her way along the carriage to Alice. In an instant, her arms were around Alice's neck and Alice felt a huge sob erupt from her chest.

The relief that Constance was with her again was overwhelming.

Constance felt even smaller and thinner to Alice than before. The girl next to her moved a little so Constance could sit next to her on the bench. There were lines in Constance's hollow cheeks and dark shadows under her eyes. It was difficult to look at her face and not feel worried. *She had probably been through an ordeal, but at least she was alive.*

*Constance was alive.*

Alice couldn't wipe the grin from her face. The glances from the girls sitting near them were as cold as stone. Alice couldn't blame them. They had suffered and they didn't know who she was.

'Does anyone know where we are being taken?' asked Alice in a soft voice, which she hoped would appeal to them.

They shook their heads without making a sound. The only noise came from the street outside.


Jon and his brother Moris sat on their horses as they watched the wagon leave Chilham Palace and turn into The Strand. It was accompanied by a handful of men and guards on horseback and was heading slowly towards the city gates.

'And you are certain the girls are being held here?' asked Moris.

'I can't be completely certain. But there is something about that wagon that doesn't seem right,' replied Jon. 'It's completely covered so we cannot see inside. I think we should follow it.'

'But not all of us,' replied Moris, 'I will ask some of the men to call at the palace while a few of us follow at a distance. We do not want to be seen. Although it seems we may already have been.'

One of the men riding next to the wagon glanced over at them. He turned his horse away from the cart and began to ride in their direction. He was conspicuous in his red jacket.

'I know that man,' said Jon, 'it's Valerian Baladi. Stay calm and we'll see what he has to say.'

Before long, Alice heard the patter of rain on the canvas above their heads. All the passengers remained sullen, their faces miserable and grey. The silence was something Alice was struggling to get used to. *Had these girls been so badly treated that all they knew was how to be quiet and subservient? Were they too frightened to talk?*

Presumably the girls she was travelling with had been kept prisoner at Sir Walter's palace along with Constance and Elizabeth. Alice wondered who they were and how long they had been at Sir Walter's home. *Would any of them see their families again?*

'How are you?' whispered Alice to Constance. 'How are you feeling?'

Constance shrugged and Alice wished she could take her pain away.

'I was so worried about you. I never stopped looking for you. From the moment you went missing I said I would find you. And now I have.'

Alice gave her a warm motherly hug and she heard Constance sniff.

'I missed you so much,' she said in a weak voice. 'I can't tell you what...' She was unable to finish her sentence.

'You don't have to,' said Alice giving her a squeeze, 'You don't have to tell me anything. The important thing is that you're safe.'

But as she said the words, Alice wasn't sure that they were safe. *Where were they being taken?*

Baby Mary started to fuss and everyone in the wagon watched her impassively.

Alice wondered where they were going and what had happened to Jon. *Presumably he was now imprisoned for something he didn't do. Could anyone help him?*

To her right, the canvas had been pulled back across the wagon steps. The gap in the canvas had been laced together, but Alice was able to part a small space with her fingers and peer out. Rain fell on the busy street and riding behind the wagon on a large black horse was Theobald. Beside him walked a small, wiry man with puckered skin on one side of his face. It was the man who had threatened her in the graveyard. Alice shuddered.

Theobald caught Alice's eye and she pulled back from the gap, embarrassed that she had been seen. She still felt angry about Valerian. *What had she done to deserve his betrayal? Had his story about Constance being snatched been a lie after all? Had he killed his friend Roger and taken her to Sir Walter? It seemed fairly likely now.*

Alice took off her veil and saw that it was half-covered in dried blood. She looked at Constance, who had her eyes closed. Elizabeth was feeding her baby. *What would these men do to them? What would they do with the baby?* Alice tried to suppress the panic that was rising in her chest.

The rain fell more heavily and thundered onto the canvas. Water dripped through onto the wooden floor and started to travel in rivulets towards the steps at the back of the wagon.

Alice felt drops on her head and at the back of her neck. They made her shiver.

There was a shout from a voice she recognised as Valerian's and the wagon stopped. Alice looked through the gap again and saw Valerian on a horse at the rear of the wagon. He rode up past it and she heard his voice again; he was talking to the postilion. The rain fell, the baby grumbled and the red-haired girl sitting opposite caught Alice's eye.

'Hello, my name is Alice,' she said, deciding to make the most of the opportunity to talk.

'I am Cecily,' whispered the girl. Her long, red hair was loose and hung down beneath her hood. She had red freckles across her cheeks and nose, and held a string of rosary beads in her lap.

'What happened to you?' asked Alice. 'How long have you been at Sir Walter's palace?'

'I don't know how long. They took me during a saint's day celebration. St Nicholas. I think that was some time ago.'

'Sssh!' scolded another girl. 'They told us not to speak.'

Cecily looked down at her rosary beads and Alice peered outside again. There was a guard on his horse behind them now, but there was no sign of Theobald or Valerian and the wagon remained still as they talked. Alice thought she could hear raised voices. *Had there been a disagreement about where they were heading?*

Without warning, there was a lurch to the left and Alice sensed they were turning a sharp corner. The noise from the street grew quieter and Alice looked out again to discover that they were in a street so narrow the wagon was only just compact enough to pass through.

# Chapter Thirty-Four

❧❦❧

The wagon ground to a halt again and Alice sighed with impatience. She looked out through the gap.

'This street must be too narrow,' she said, 'we're probably stuck now.'

Her mutterings were interrupted by loud shouts hailing from the front of the wagon. The guard riding behind them managed to squeeze his horse between the wagon and the wall, taking him to the front of the convoy. Now there was no one behind the wagon apart from an elderly man who was looking out of a doorway.

The shouting grew louder and then came the unmistakeable clash of steel. Some of the girls shrieked and glanced around at each other, their eyes wide with fear.

Alice's first thought was that they should get out of the wagon. She fumbled with the string that laced the canvas together and with a few impatient pulls she managed to yank the canvas open.

'Look, we can escape!' she hissed to the other girls.

A long, narrow street lay behind them. They could scurry

down it and be back on the main street before Theobald, Valerian or Sir Walter's guards caught up with them.

Alice looked at the faces around her but they stared back without emotion.

'Let's go!' she said.

As if she had suddenly been prodded with a spike, Cecily sprang up and leapt down from the cart into the mud. Alice moved her knees as a few of the other girls followed Cecily. She wanted to wait until Elizabeth could get out of the wagon; she wasn't going anywhere without her or Constance. The girls in the street didn't move, they simply waited where they stood.

'Run!' Alice urged them. 'Run down that way!'

But still they refused to move, as if they were waiting until everyone was out of the cart. The shouting intensified and Alice could hear shrieks as men and horses were injured. She had no idea what was happening, but she knew they had an opportunity to make their escape. She waited until Elizabeth and Constance were out of the wagon and leapt out after them.

'Quick! We can get away!' she said with a grin.

Alice noticed Cecily was edging along the side of the cart to see what was taking place at the front.

'Cecily, come with us!' she called.

'I want to see what is happening,' replied Cecily. 'It looks as though they are under attack from a group of knights and a monk.'

'Jon,' said Alice. 'But how has he escaped?'

'Jon?' queried Elizabeth, spinning round. Alice wished she hadn't mentioned his name. Elizabeth had been walking away from the fight, and that was what she needed to keep doing for the sake of her baby.

'Who is Jon?' asked Constance.

'Brother Jon, from St Hugh's,' replied Alice. 'Do you

remember him? He must have come to help us. Come on, we need to go. He knows how to fight; he has rescued us.'

But Alice realised she had spoken too soon when one of the guards ran down the side of the wagon towards Cecily. His robes were covered in blood.

'Get back in!' he yelled, brandishing a blood-stained sword.

'Run!' yelled Alice.

Half of the girls started to move but the others hung back, including Elizabeth, who was clearly worried about her brother.

Cecily ran off and the guard strode towards Alice.

'Run now!' she yelled again at Elizabeth and Constance. She didn't care if the man killed her; her work was complete now. She had found Constance. The children at St Hugh's would be overjoyed to have her back and she could continue the work Alice had been doing. Constance could look after Matilda in her place. Matilda had always been fond of Constance.

'Get back in that wagon!' the guard growled at Alice, his sword raised.

Alice took a step back. Out of the corner of her eye she saw Cecily pull off her cloak and hood and kick over a bucket of fetid water. She ran back up the street with the bucket in her hands, and Alice realised she could distract the guard to help Cecily execute her plan.

'I am not getting back in,' she snarled. 'You'll have to make me.'

The guard grabbed her arm, and at the same time Cecily ran up behind him and smashed the wood-and-iron bucket over the back of his head. He fell to the ground. The blow wasn't enough to injure him badly, but he was temporarily disorientated. Cecily stamped on his arm and pulled the sword from his hand.

'Woah!' cried Alice, astonished at the transformation she saw in Cecily.

'What's happening?' came a cry. Valerian appeared at the side of the wagon with a sword in his hand. He looked at the guard, who was trying to pick himself up out of the mud, and then at Alice and Cecily as they tried to wield the guard's sword.

Alice glared at him. This was her chance to take revenge on the man who had betrayed her.

'Give me the sword, Cecily!' she shouted.

Cecily handed it to her and Alice was surprised by its weight. She held it in both hands and realised she would struggle to do any real damage with it.

Valerian stepped back. 'Careful!' he shouted at her, his dark eyes flashing with danger, his finger pointing behind her.

The guard was back on his feet. As he lunged at Alice she tried to swing the sword in his direction, but it was too heavy. The guard grabbed the hilt and spun the blade towards her. It caught the light as it turned and Alice prepared herself for the sharp pain of cold steel.

But, to her surprise, the guard fell to the ground and his hand slipped off the sword.

Thrust into his back was Valerian's sword. Valerian yanked the sword out of the guard's back and wiped the blood on the man's cloak.

'Hand that to me,' he said.

Alice gave him the sword, unable to believe what she had just seen. At her feet lay a dead man, his blood mixing with the mud. And Valerian, the man who had betrayed her, had just saved her life.

'You need to go,' he ordered. 'You will all be safe if you leave now.'

'Thank you,' said Alice. 'I'm sorry I hit you.'

'I am sorry, too,' said Valerian. 'Now please go.'

'Where is Jon?' asked Elizabeth.

'He is here and I will help him. We will soon deal with these men. Please go, or do I have to threaten you?' He raised the guard's sword.

Alice grabbed Elizabeth's arm and put her arm around Constance, who had shuffled back to join her. 'Come on!' she said.

Cecily accompanied them and Alice looked back, catching a flash of Valerian's red jacket as he ran back past the wagon to continue the fight. When all this was over she would speak to him and hopefully discover exactly what had happened. She and the other women continued to run until they joined the rest of the group at the end of the passageway.

The sorrowful group of women stepped out onto the main street, where people were dashing between the shop canopies to escape the rain. A few stared at the large group of girls; especially at Cecily, with her long, red hair flowing free; and at Alice, who had a large bloodstain on her veil. The girls stood about in the rain looking lost. They should have been happy they were free, but Alice sensed they were too wary to celebrate and were well aware that they had not reached a place of safety quite yet.

'Come with us to St Hugh's,' Alice said. 'We can all get some rest there and it is safe.'

'I know where we are,' said Elizabeth, looking around her. 'Trinity Street. It will not take us long to walk to St Hugh's from here. We need to walk up this way.'

Alice and the others followed her.

'I hope Jon is all right,' Elizabeth said to Alice.

'I am sure he is. It looked like he had the upper hand, and with Valerian's help they should soon be rid of Sir Walter's guards. They will return to St Hugh's as soon as they are done.'

Exhaustion set in as they walked through the rain, which blew against their faces and soaked their cloaks and dresses, making them heavier and more cumbersome. The thick mud slowed their progress.

Alice wanted to ask Constance dozens of questions, but both were too tired to speak. Instead, Alice smiled warmly at her friend and took her arm. It was like being reunited with a lost daughter. She couldn't wait to get Constance back to the safety of St Hugh's.

# Chapter Thirty-Five

❦

Elizabeth sat at the end of Alice's bed with Mary sleeping in her arms. 'How are you feeling?' she asked.

'I feel well,' replied Alice. 'It's not a big wound. There is no need for me to be lying in this bed.' Alice was dressed in a hospital tunic with a strip of linen wrapped around her head.

'The nun who came to clean and dress it thought it looked nasty.' Elizabeth doubted the wound was as superficial as Alice was claiming.

'Where is Constance?' asked Alice.

'In the refectory with some of the other girls. They have been given bread and pottage.'

'And have you eaten?'

'Not yet. I don't feel very hungry at the moment.' Elizabeth kept glancing over at the main door, willing her brother to return. Until she heard news of Jon's plight, she felt unable to eat.

'I understand,' said Alice, also looking over at the door.

'Maybe I could go and look for them,' suggested Elizabeth.

'You are to do nothing of the sort!' replied Alice. 'We are not letting you out of our sight again. I am sure the men will return very soon; they can look after themselves. Has Matilda awoken yet?'

'I don't know.'

Alice had checked on Matilda as soon as they had returned. The little girl had looked very poorly and Alice was increasingly concerned that she would not recover.

'I must go and see her,' Alice said. She started to climb out of bed.

'No!' said Elizabeth, worried that Matilda might have taken a turn for the worse and that Alice was not well enough to look after her. 'She is in good hands. I am sure you will be well enough to see her later, but you need to rest, remember? You have a bad head wound and you will not be able to look after Matilda properly if you are not well yourself.'

The bell rang for Compline, signalling the end of the day. Alice sighed.

Elizabeth counted the hours since their escape. *Why was Jon taking so long to return?* She looked down at her sleeping daughter, who breathed noisily through her nose, her mouth pushed into a little pout as she slept. Elizabeth smiled and stroked Mary's cheek. She looked up to see Alice looking at her, her eyes watery.

'What is it?' asked Elizabeth.

'Watching you with her brings back memories,' said Alice with a sad smile.

Elizabeth was about to ask what she meant when they were startled by a bang at the door.

'That will be them!' said Alice.

Sister Katherine rushed over to the door and opened it. A group of men stumbled in, covered in so much blood and dirt they were unrecognisable. Three of the men were being carried.

'Here, let them have my bed!' cried Alice, leaping out from under her blankets.

Elizabeth stood up to make way for them. Hilda was asked to move from her bed and a spare bed was found at the far end of the infirmary hall. The wounded were laid down and Sister Katherine called for help from every sister and brother at St Hugh's. Elizabeth watched the flurry around her as fresh water and clean linen was fetched and the clothes of the wounded were ripped open to reveal bleeding wounds.

*Where was Jon?*

Then Elizabeth saw someone she recognised. It was her brother Moris, who had been away in Anatolia when she was snatched from the marketplace the previous summer. He was wearing his chainmail and a blue and gold tunic, and he had much less hair than he had the last time she had seen him.

Moris strode up to Elizabeth and embraced her. He smelt of sweat mixed with the metallic odour of blood. His nose was bloody and swollen, and he had cuts on his right cheek.

'Moris!' It didn't seem real that he was there. 'It must be three years since I saw you last.'

'Yes, it is. You look in fine health considering what has happened to you. Jon told me everything.'

She looked down to avoid his gaze, the feeling of shame reddening her cheeks.

'We will find that man,' said Moris. 'We will make him pay.'

'Where is Jon?'

Moris nodded in the direction of a nearby bed and Elizabeth let out a small cry. She had failed to recognise her brother, who was lying motionless, his face swollen with cuts and bruises. One of the sisters bathed his face and another was cleaning a large wound on his upper arm.

Alice stood by the side of his bed, holding the hand of his uninjured arm.

'Will he be all right?' asked Elizabeth.

'I don't know,' replied Alice, her eyes red.

A commotion at the far end of the hall provided a distraction.

'Fetch Brother Ralph!' called someone. 'This man needs to be read his last rites!'

Alice and Elizabeth exchanged glances and ran to the bedside of the dying man. The blankets on his bed were soaked with blood and there were bowls of watery blood and blood-stained rags lying on the floor.

'Valerian!' shouted Alice.

'We have done all we can,' said Sister Isabella, her face solemn.

Valerian's eyes hovered between wake and sleep, his face pale. Blood was flowing from a gaping wound in his chest and bubbling out of his mouth. Sister Isabella and Brother Wilmot tried to wrap linen around his chest to stem the flow of blood, but the expressions on their faces suggested it was futile.

'Can you hear me, Valerian?' Alice put her hand on his cheek, but there was no response.

Elizabeth watched a tear drip from Alice's cheek onto the shoulder of Valerian's red jacket.

'Is Brother Ralph here?' asked Sister Isabella.

'He is tending to one of the other patients,' said a voice behind Elizabeth. 'I will read the last rites to this man.'

Elizabeth stepped aside, allowing a large, bald man with a rough beard to step past her. Everyone fell quiet and Alice's red eyes opened wide with surprise.

'It's Valerian, Prior Edmund. He saved my life today.'

The prior nodded solemnly and asked everyone to leave Valerian's bedside so he could confess in private. Elizabeth suspected Valerian was too ill to make any sort of confession. Everyone stepped away and bowed their heads as the prior spoke the last rites quietly in Latin and anointed the dying man with oil.

Once the prior had finished, Alice returned to Valerian's bedside. 'I did not have the chance to thank him for what he did.' Tears streamed down her face.

Constance joined Alice. 'He tried to help me the night they took me,' she said in a quiet voice. 'And after that I saw him at Sir Walter's palace. I couldn't understand why he had tried to help me if he was one of Sir Walter's men.'

'I think he was another captive of Sir Walter's,' said Elizabeth.

'And now we will never know exactly what happened,' said Alice, stroking Valerian's forehead. 'But I think he was trying to do the best he could.'

Elizabeth felt a cold sensation, as if a cloud had passed across the sun. She looked at Valerian's face and knew he was gone. Alice and Constance hugged each other and cried, and Mary began to stir. Elizabeth kissed her baby daughter on the top of her head and wiped away her own tears.


Jon was well enough to eat some bread and pottage later that evening. He had received some knocks to his head and his arm had been bandaged, but Elizabeth was relieved to see him recovering so well. She also noticed the way he and Alice looked at each other, their eyes holding each other's gaze slightly longer than was necessary. Alice was visibly relieved that Jon was safe and she kept hugging Constance as if she needed to reassure herself that her friend was actually there.

Mary was fretful and Elizabeth paced up and down the infirmary hall rocking her. Alice sat by Jon's bedside with the linen bandage still strapped around her head and two of the children on her lap. Elizabeth strained to hear what Jon was saying above her daughter's grumbling.

'We saw the wagon leave Chilham Palace and I thought it looked suspicious. We started to follow but then Valerian saw us. I thought we were in trouble then; I did not suspect that Valerian was on our side. As you know, I never trusted him. However, he explained that Sir Walter had forced him to work in his household. Sir Walter had threatened to tell the authorities that he was guilty of murdering his friend and abducting Constance if he refused. He had been placed in an impossible position, but he told me he had always planned to find a way out. He then told me Sir Walter was planning to take the girls to a forest and have them killed.'

Elizabeth heard Alice gasp.

'Sir Walter was worried he was about to be found out, so he wanted to be rid of them all. Valerian correctly guessed that you, Elizabeth and Mary would be dispatched with them. That was when he came up with the plan to ambush the wagon. Valerian said he would persuade Theobald to take a detour.'

'And what has become of Theobald and Sir Walter?' asked Alice.

'Theobald ran away,' replied Jon, 'and Sir Walter left the palace long before you were put into the wagon. We have no idea where he has gone.'

Elizabeth's heart sank down to her feet. She could hear the disappointment in Jon's voice.

'I will look for him,' said Jon. 'I will hunt him down and kill him, and Moris is to help me.'

'But we should inform the authorities about him,' said Alice. 'Something has to be done to stop him.' She was clearly worried about Jon putting himself in danger again.

'Yes, we should, but don't forget that most people still

think he is a kindly, charitable man. It will be difficult to convince them otherwise.'

Elizabeth took her baby for a walk along the cloisters, hoping the fresh air would soothe her little girl. It was dark and the ornate arches flickered orange in the light from the torches on the wall. By the time Elizabeth had walked twice around the square, Mary had started to settle. She paused and stepped out into the darkness of the courtyard. Above them the night sky twinkled. Elizabeth looked up at the stars and thought back to the night of the full moon when she had walked with Millicent to the pond and Millicent had told her the baby would arrive early.

*Did Millicent have a new home now?* It had been hard to say goodbye to her, but she knew she had made life difficult for the old lady. It had been right to leave her.

Elizabeth also felt she had put her brother in danger and felt responsible for Valerian losing his life. People would tell her there was nothing she could have done, but that did nothing to stop the intense feeling of guilt.

Nothing stopped the guilt.

She turned as she heard footsteps behind her. It was Moris.

'Are you ready to come home now?'

'And see father?' Elizabeth could hear the tremble in her own voice.

'He knows what has happened to you.'

'I am so afraid of what he will say.' She looked down at her daughter's face.

'Come on,' said Moris, 'I will be with you and Jon can join us tomorrow after he's had some rest.'

Theobald dragged himself up the stone steps of Sir Tybalt d'Orval's home and knocked at the door. A well-dressed male servant answered, visibly annoyed that someone was calling at the house after dark.

'I wish to speak to Sir Walter Rokeby,' said Theobald through clenched teeth. The pain in his leg was unbearable after walking several miles. 'My name is Theobald FitzAlan, I am his assistant.'

'Sir Walter is not here,' replied the servant.

Theobald was surprised to hear this news. 'Sir Walter told me he was coming here today and would be staying for a day or two. I have an urgent message for him.'

'Sir Walter was here but he told Sir Tybalt that pressing business was causing him to depart earlier than planned. I can only assume he is back home at Chilham Palace.'

'He is not there, I have just been there.' Theobald slumped down on the top step, groaning with pain. He had managed to survive the fight with the monk and his men, but he was unable to walk any further. His leg was bleeding steadily and he was beginning to feel weak. All of Sir Walter's guards had been slain and Theobald had not been surprised to see Valerian fighting against them. It had always been a risk to invite him into Sir Walter's household.

It was a tragedy that the girls had escaped along with Alice and Elizabeth. This was the news he needed to tell Sir Walter, but as he sat on the step looking up at the bright stars he thought about Sir Walter's probable reaction. Perhaps it was best that he didn't know the girls had got away.

'That is a nasty looking wound,' said the servant. 'I can ask the maid to look at it for you. Let me help you inside.'

# Chapter Thirty-Six

## FOUR MONTHS LATER

The bell rang nine as the brothers and sisters of St Hugh's gathered on the steps of the monastery on a bright autumn morning. Alice, Constance and Sister Emma stood with the children. Matilda, fully recovered from her illness, clung to Alice's hand. Constance carried Winifred and Sister Emma held her favourite rabbit, Baynard. The knights on horseback would soon arrive. They were making a detour to St Hugh's to say goodbye before they set sail for France.

Alice had been nervous about this moment for some time. She knew she could never stop Jon pursuing his dream to be a knight and after he had reneged on his vows it had been inevitable. There was still a lot of training for him to do, but his father had decided he was skilled enough to help his brothers.

*When would she see him again?* The question sounded foolish in her mind. *How could she hope to see him again?* Ever since leaving St Hugh's he had been focused on his training. She had been a regular guest at the de Grey family home and she got on well with his family. There had been a time when she thought the invitations to dinner might lead to something more between them, but she realised now that she had been mistaken. Jon had chosen his path and she would have to wait patiently for his return.

'Here they come!' someone shouted.

Alice lifted Matilda up so she could see the men in blue and gold on their fine, tall horses. Sunlight glinted on armour, and fluttering in the breeze were the blue and gold flags of the de Greys, displaying the family symbol of the bull.

Alice scanned the riders' faces until she saw Jon, the second rider from the left, looking broader and taller than ever. Everyone cheered and waved, including several bystanders on the street, and Alice felt tears in her eyes as she watched the smiling faces of the men who were going away to fight. She hugged Matilda tightly, fervently hoping that each of them would return safely.

The monks approached Jon and made fun of him on his horse. A chant started up: 'Brother Jon! Brother Jon!'

There was more laughter and Alice watched the happy faces around her. Among them she saw the prior. Rarely seen these days, he was clean-shaven again and thinner. His face looked sad and sunken. Hilda stood next to him, clapping her hands wildly and cheering. Alice had tried to ask her more about Adeline but hadn't learnt much yet. She would never give up.

Some of the horses champed at their bits and pawed the ground impatiently. It was time for the men to go. Alice watched Jon's face. He had not caught sight of her yet among the crowd. This could be the last time she ever saw him. She watched intently as he smiled and waved, and prayed that he would return safely.

'Go on, he's about to leave.' There was a shove in Alice's back. She turned around to see Sister Emma with her rabbit urging her forward.

'No, I will delay him.' She stayed where she was on the steps.

'Go on!' said Sister Emma. 'This is your only chance!' She gave Alice such a hefty shove she slipped off the step and onto the street. People stood aside, assuming she was trying to push through the crowd.

Alice stood in front of the horses with Matilda on her hip. Jon saw her and grinned, climbing off his horse as she walked up to him. He looked much more comfortable in his chain-mail and tunic than he ever had in a monk's habit.

'There is no need to dismount.' Alice felt her cheeks flushing hot.

Jon gave Matilda a kiss. 'Goodbye, Matilda. You will be quite grown up when I see you next.'

'Will you be gone that long?' Alice asked.

Jon's eyes met hers. 'I do not know.'

'You will come and see us as soon as you return?'

'Yes, I will. You will be the first person I visit as soon as I return to London. You have my promise.'

They held each other's gaze. Alice knew there was something else Jon wanted to do in France, and that was why he was unable to tell her how long he would be. No one had seen Sir Walter Rokeby since the day the girls had escaped, but there were rumours he had fled over the Channel. Jon was travelling there not only to assist the king's army but to find out where Sir Walter was hiding.

Alice could not be sure who made the first move; perhaps it was something they had both done at the same time. But in a moment they were in each other's arms.

'Please come back safely. I will pray for you every day.' She wanted to say more, but knew that if she spoke the tears would come.

Jon's face was close to hers and they kissed. A warmth

flooded through her, and there was more laughter from the monks.

Alice stepped back. She was shocked and surprised, but her heart felt like it was dancing.

'I will miss you,' said Jon, his eyes still fixed on hers. Then he turned and walked back to his horse and took something from the saddle bag.

'Here,' he walked back to her, 'I would like you to have this.'

Alice held out her hand and he placed something small and metal in her palm. It was a gold brooch shaped as a heart: decorated with leaf fronds and with a sword shaped clasp.

'It was my mother's,' he said, 'I was going to take it with me but I would prefer it to stay with you.'

'Are you sure?'

'I am sure.'

Jon climbed back onto his horse and Alice held the brooch firmly in her hand.

'Say goodbye, Matilda,' was all she could say as a tear rolled down her cheek.

'Bye bye,' waved the little girl.

Alice walked back to the steps, looking at the ground. She was too embarrassed to meet anyone's eye.

There was a shout and a cheer as the men and their horses rode away.


The day had to continue as normal. Alice consoled herself by giving Constance a long hug. Together they cleaned and tidied the children's dormitory while the children sat for their lessons with the nuns in the day room. At moments during the day, Alice took the gold brooch from the purse which hung at her belt and held it until it was warm in her hand. It was something to remember Jon by while he was gone.

Constance was not the same girl who had been taken from St Hugh's. There was a shade of darkness in her eyes and she no longer laughed as often as she had before. But she had gained some weight since returning to St Hugh's and no longer looked so thin and haunted. Alice knew it would take time for her to recover fully.

Piece by piece, Constance had told her what had happened at Sir Walter's home, but Alice knew she found it difficult to talk about her experience. Alice encouraged her to talk, but never pressured her. Constance would tell her the full story when she was ready.

Shortly after the girls were rescued from Chilham Palace, Alice and Jon had been honoured at a special service held in the chapel. Even the prior had sung her praises. She had been allowed to return to work at St Hugh's and her home was returned to her. She was living there once again and had plans for a big change in her life.

Sister Eleanor had changed her opinion of the woman she had once called 'the meddlesome widow' and now told everyone Alice was a saver of lives. Alice was uneasy about the reputation she was gaining but this did not deter occasional callers at St Hugh's who asked to see her. Her story seemed to become more exaggerated with each telling and the rumour went that she could wield a sword as expertly as a knight.

Alice felt the need to do more with her life now. She could continue to help the children but she also wanted to do something for herself. She had decided to become a leather merchant again and Constance would be her apprentice. Constance was to share her home, as were Matilda, Peter and Winifred. Her former servant Griselda was to return along with one of her hardest-working apprentices, Louis. Alice needed to find a nurse to help with the children and then her household would be complete. Her shop was to open again and her customers would undoubtedly return. If she needed any advice, her friend Yvette would be able to help.

Yvette had persuaded Sir Walter's men to let her go, convincing them that she was on Sir Walter's side. She told Alice shortly after Sir Walter's disappearance that she had received a barrel of coins, which had presumably been sent to buy her silence. But Yvette was as keen as Alice, Jon and Sir Robyn de Grey to see Sir Walter brought to justice and was using her influence to persuade the authorities in London that everything possible must be done to find him in France and bring him back to face trial.

'There is something I forgot to show you,' said Alice to Constance as they tidied the children's toys. She walked over to a table by the window. 'These are the gloves I used to make and together we can make more of them to sell in our shop.' Alice picked them up and handed them to Constance.

'They're beautiful.' The gloves were made from soft white goatskin and the gauntlets were brightly embroidered with songbirds and edged with coloured beading.

'It will not take you long to learn how to do this. I can show you,' said Alice. 'I am really looking forward to it.'

Constance smiled. 'Me too.'

The door flung open, releasing the sound of voices, and Sister Emma brought the children into the room.

'And as you have all been so well behaved in your lessons, we can sing an extra song today!' said Sister Emma, clapping her hands together in glee.

Alice fetched the woollen blanket and she and Constance laid it out on the floor for the children to sit on.

## The End

❦

Read on for the Historical Note and an excerpt of the second story in this series *Forgotten Child*.

# Historical Note - Runaway Girl

⚜

Alice Wescott loses her family in England's first plague outbreak of 1348 - 1350. No community or family would have been left unscathed during those years and many of the religious orders lost their members. It seemed fitting to place a widow of the plague into a monastery which had lost nuns in the plague. When Alice arrives at St Hugh's, the monastery needs her help as much as she needs its sanctuary.

In medieval England hospitals were run by the religious orders. Hospitals in those days not only treated the sick but also provided shelter for the poor and vulnerable too. Travellers could request to stay at a hospital and some foundlings spent their formative years in hospitals, raised by nuns.

Wealthy widows could live in the precinct of a religious house in return for payment. Margaret Beauchamp, widow of the Earl of Warwick, took up residence at the Minoresses without Aldgate in the late fourteenth century. Other medieval widows chose to work in the houses of religious orders and some of these subsequently took the veil themselves.

Double monasteries – those which housed nuns and monks – were declining in popularity by the middle ages. However the English Gilbertine Order lasted until the reformation. Founded by Gilbert of Sempringham in the twelfth century, the order housed both nuns and canons. Scandal ensued at Watton Priory in Yorkshire when a nun, known afterwards as the Nun of Watton, apparently became pregnant by one of the lay brothers. It is related that the nuns castrated him and the nun's pregnancy subsequently ended. Depending on which account you read, the nuns meted out a more gruesome punishment than that which you can google if you're feeling brave enough. Alice and Jon's flirtations are genteel in comparison.

'Medieval women were classified according to their sexual status... virgins, wives or widows,' writes Henrietta Leyser in her book *Medieval Women*. As a widow, Alice Wescott would have had more freedom than many women of her time, and because she trained in her husband's trade of glove making she had the option to continue with this work after his death. Her husband had been a free man and as his widow she is a free woman: this freedom is significant in the fourteenth century. Had Alice been a peasant (known then as a villein), married, or living with her parents then her lord, husband or family would have had the authority to control her.

It is difficult to know what medieval women thought about the male-dominated society they lived in, many may have accepted it was the way life was supposed to be - as God decreed. But even if most women did accept the misogyny in society at that time, it does not mean they didn't feel frustrated at it or disadvantaged by it.

I have included the Jane Austen quote from *Persuasion* on the title page of this book because it reminds us that history has been mainly documented by men:- '...the pen has been in their hands.' I wanted to write about strong female characters in the middle ages because they must have existed, we just don't know their stories. While writing this book I wanted to imagine what their stories may have been.

Sexual offences were treated as serious crimes in the middle ages but conviction rates were low because it proved difficult to produce evidence of rape or find witnesses. A high-profile individual with influence could escape conviction easily when it was his word against his victim's. Sadly this resonates with events today and when writing about Sir Walter I was mindful of the high profile sexual predators we are now familiar with and who, for many years, got away with their crimes while hiding in plain sight.

While researching this book I used a number of sources too numerous to list here. However the following books have been of particular help: *The Time Traveller's Guide to Medieval England* by Ian Mortimer, *Medieval Women* by Henrietta Leyser, *Medieval London* by Timothy Baker, *Growing up in Medieval London* by Barbara A Hanawalt and *The Great Mortality* by John Kelly.

# Please enjoy an excerpt from Forgotten Child

London, 1353

She had not invited the monk into the house. He had simply pushed open the door and walked in. And because he was brandishing a knife, she had thought it wise not to argue.

Her first thought was of the children upstairs. She prayed they would remain up there and stay quiet. The monk stood in the hall, a silver cross hanging from his neck and raindrops dripping from his black cloak onto the floor. His eyes were hidden under the shadow of his hood, but she could see from his face that he was young. He had a thin, mean mouth and a square jaw. His shoulders were broad and he looked strong. From the open door behind him came the hiss of heavy rain.

She wiped her sweating palms on her apron and did her best to appear calm.

'I can assure you there is no need for a knife.' She was annoyed that her voice wobbled when she spoke. She didn't want him to sense her fear.

'Just let me know how I can help you, Brother...'

She waited for him to tell her his name, but he said nothing.

The knife remained poised.

'I have come to see Alice Wescott.' His voice was quiet and he had a foreign accent.

'Are you from St Hugh's?'

'Is she here?'

'No, she is not. Please tell me your name and why you are here so I can tell her you called when she returns.'

His lips pressed together tightly; he seemed disappointed.

'Where is she?'

'She's out on an errand, but I can't tell you exactly where she is because I don't know.' Her heart thudded in her chest as she focused on the knife in his hand.

'Where's the casket?'

'Not here. Some men came and took it.'

'When?'

'Three or four years ago.' She thought back to the visit of the two foreign men shortly after Thomas Wescott's death. They had taken a casket Thomas had hidden under the floor-boards of the bedchamber he and Alice had shared. Alice had known nothing about the casket and had learned little about it since then.

'I don't believe you.'

'Well it's the truth. You can search if you want to, but the men took it, as I say.'

As soon as she suggested the search she regretted it. The children were upstairs and she didn't want them to see the monk or his knife. She didn't want him to see them, either. There was no telling what he might do, especially if he was angry about the missing casket.

She heard a rumble of thunder outside as the monk strode over to a cupboard next to the fireplace. He yanked open the doors and began pulling out its contents. A ceramic jug fell onto the stone floor and shattered into pieces.

'Stop it!' she shouted. 'You are breaking our things. There is no need to look for the casket, it's not here!'

The monk left the hall and she followed him into the parlour, desperate to stop him causing further damage.

She grabbed his arm. 'You must leave this house! Mistress Wescott is not here and neither is the casket!'

He shook her off and cleared the shelves and cupboards in the parlour. She winced as countless items scattered and broke.

*How could she stop him?*

'I want every chest in this house unlocked so I can search through it,' he ordered.

'I asked you to leave!' she shouted.

He turned and grabbed her by the throat. She gasped in pain and tried to pull his hand away.

'Unlock the chests,' he growled. 'Now.'

He let go and she headed into the kitchen, coughing, to fetch the bunch of keys that hung from a nail on the wall.

*Perhaps it was best to do what he said; she had nothing to hide. The casket wasn't in the house, so hopefully he would soon see that the chests were of no interest to him.*

A noise came from upstairs. She froze and listened, but all remained quiet.

*He mustn't see the children.*

She began to unlock the chests.

He followed her as she unlocked each one, searching through the contents and throwing them to the floor. Clothes, pottery, plates, blankets and leather gloves were strewn around the room.

'Open that one,' he said, pointing at a chest carved with acorns and oak leaves.

'It only contains gloves.'

'Open it!' He held the knife close to her face once again and she obliged.

Everything she and Alice had spent days sorting into neat piles was being thrown about the place. He hurled the gloves across the floor and marched into the workshop. She knew there were some heavy tools in there that she could grab and smash over his head, but hopefully there would be no need for violence.

A clattering noise on the floorboards above their heads caught his attention. He turned to face her and then looked up at the ceiling. She held her breath and watched him.

His eyes moved over to the wooden staircase. 'Who's that upstairs?' he asked. 'Is it Alice?'

'No, it's just the children's nursemaid. She doesn't know anything about the casket. You must leave her alone!'

He made his way towards the stairs. As he turned away from her she looked around to see what she could use to stop him. There was a wooden stool by the fireplace.

'You mustn't go up there!' she yelled, but one of his feet was already on the bottom step.

She seized the stool, ran over to him, lifted it and crashed it down over his head. The monk slumped to the floor.

*She had to get the children out of there.*

She grabbed his cloak and tried to pull him away from the stairs.

'Beatrice! Get out!' she screamed. 'You need to get out of here! As quick as you can!'

She dragged the monk by his cloak. He was dazed, but the knife was still in his hand and he was beginning to stir. She didn't know what would happen once he got to his feet again.

There were tentative footsteps at the top of the stairs and she saw Beatrice peering down, a look of horror on her face. The front door was still open following the monk's forced entry and the doorstep was wet with rain.

He tried to get to his feet, but she brought the stool down on his shoulder a second time and he fell again.

'Get out and raise the alarm!' she yelled to Beatrice. 'And get the children out!'

Beatrice nodded and slowly descended the stairs with the children behind her. Their frightened eyes were fixed on the monk who lay on the floor. She hadn't wanted them to see him.

He tried to get up again but she wrapped her arm around his neck and throat, hoping she could hold him still. He began to flail around with the knife in his hand.

'I've got him!' she screamed at Beatrice. 'Get out now!' Her arm was tight around his throat, but she knew she could only hold him for so long.

The children and their nursemaid were at the foot of the stairs. Beatrice told the children to run towards the door, but they hesitated. Matilda climbed back up a step.

Beatrice grabbed her. 'Run!' she yelled.

Fear was etched on their faces, but they saw the open door and ran.

With a roar, the monk freed himself from her arm and lunged across the floor at the children. He grabbed Peter's ankle and the little boy fell over. The children screamed and she prayed someone would hear the disturbance from the street and come to their aid.

Beatrice stepped forward and jabbed her fingers into the monk's eyes. His head ricocheted back and he let go of the boy's leg. She got to her feet and breathed a huge sigh of relief as Beatrice and the children escaped through the door.

She needed to get herself out of there, but the monk stood in her way.

He got up, spun round and glared at her. She knew he was angry as he paced towards her. She tried to run to her right and dodge round him, but he grabbed her arm.

There was no escape.

Another rumble of thunder sounded.

*The children would get soaking wet.*

'Please don't hurt me,' she begged. 'The casket isn't here, I assure you. Leave now and I promise not to tell anyone you ever came here, as God is my witness.'

But there was a look of determination on his face that chilled her to the bone. He wasn't listening to a word she said.

He pushed her into one corner of the room and lunged at her with the knife.

ॐ

Alice's journey continues in *Forgotten Child*, find the purchase links on my website.

emilyorgan.co.uk/forgotten-child

# Thank you

Want to know when I release new books? Here are some ways to stay updated:

1. Join my mailing list and receive a free short story prequel to *Runaway Girl: The Visitors:*

emilyorgan.co.uk/the-visitors.

2. Like my Facebook page:

facebook.com/emilyorganwriter

3. You can see all my books on my website:

emilyorgan.co.uk/books

And if you have a moment, I would be very grateful if you would leave a quick review of *Runaway Girl* online. Honest reviews of my books help other readers discover them too!

Printed in Poland
by Amazon Fulfillment
Poland Sp. z o.o., Wrocław

65869340R00190